LAST CALL ON DECATUR STREET

Also by Iris Martin Cohen
The Little Clan

LAST CALL ON DECATUR STREET

IRIS MARTIN COHEN

PARK
ROW
BOOKS

PARK
ROW™
BOOKS™

ISBN-13: 978-0-7783-0816-4

Last Call on Decatur Street

Park Row Books
22 Adelaide St. West, 40th Floor
Toronto, Ontario M5H 4E3, Canada
ParkRowBooks.com
BookClubbish.com

Printed in U.S.A.

For anyone who has ever seen the sun rise over lower Decatur Street

LAST CALL
ON
DECATUR
STREET

1

"Just wait, wait a second. This is my song." Gaby leaned over, squinting at the radio and then turned the wrong dial, filling the car with static. "Fuck, fuck. Rosemary, how did you get me so damn drunk?"

"Me? It's not my fault. You were the one taking your two drinks to go." I pointed at the two cups in the holders, the melting remains of seven and seven and ice cubes. I was reclined in the passenger seat, watching my dirty sneakers tap time on the glove box. I considered sitting up, but she would figure it out in a minute without my help. It was her car anyway. "That is such a weird drink, who orders seven and sevens?"

"Plenty of people." She thought for a moment. "I got it from my mom, I think." Then she laughed. "It's good, you should try it."

"It's like what I imagine old ladies drink on cruises or something." Whenever I teased Gaby, she would put me off with a bunch of dismissive little sounds that I always felt in my body like pats on the head or quick little hugs. Her tolerance made me feel special, a quick affirmation of intimacy. She was doing it now.

She twisted the dial and found the station again and Brandy's and Monica's voices fluttered into the car. We were obsessed with this song, and Gaby sang along, eyes closed, cigarette and beer in the hand that she raised toward the sagging cloth of the roof's interior. The tan velour already had quite a few cigarette holes above her seat from the same gesture. She had turned it up so loud, I could feel the music in my ribs and since our windows were cracked, I worried just for a second about attracting the neighborhood watch. We were parked and the engine and lights were off, but people were touchy in this fancy part of Old Metairie after dark. I guessed no one living here was a huge fan of R and B, but then the music caught me up and I joined Gaby, singing with her off-key but with great enthusiasm. She shook her head at me, still dancing in her seat, the car swaying a little from the movement of her body. Our voices rose higher and louder with the music, acting out someone else's rage, two other girls' animosity.

There was nothing in the whole world I loved more than being this dumbly, blindly, exuberantly drunk with my best friend. She had moved on to beer and stopped singing to take a sip. It had turned foamy and that reminded me that I was almost done with mine, so I half crawled into the backseat and dug around in the plastic bag from the 7-Eleven that had our supplies: a case of Bud Light, a box of Lemonheads and a large bottle of lighter fluid. The voices on the radio devolving behind me into an epic crescendo seemed to echo the surging in my chest, an escalation of triumph and excitement. I had been getting just a little into punk lately and I wanted to share this new, liberating feeling of badness with my best friend, the straightest, most polite person I knew. She got it coming and going from everyone at the fancy Catholic high school we were both at. I was poor, and that made me pretty unpopular, but she was black. People there treated her like shit. I wanted her to know what it felt like to give a big fuck-you to all the assholes at school, to stand up for herself, to cause some trouble. She deserved that much at least.

Gaby had spilled beer on her cigarette and was waving it around, trying to dry it off with drunk concentration. I slid back into the front seat with my beer and the lighter fluid and cracked it open and toasted her. "To us. To us being fucking awesome."

The song had ended and without noticing she had sunk into a low kind of bobbing dance to the new song that was now playing, but she stopped to point at the lighter fluid. "Rosemary, this doesn't even make any sense."

"I know, but doesn't it sound awesome? Just the idea of it? Setting that mean bitch's bushes on fire?"

"But what if we kill someone?"

"We won't. Look—" I had to stop because the familiar, irrepressible chorus of the new song came on and I had to join her in dancing for a minute. It was hard to dance with your butt while sitting in a car, but we both tried anyway. The obscene suggestions we were singing along to simply required it. "We will just do these little bushes by the road," I said when the verses whose words I didn't know started up again. "Just to prove a point and then we take off. Imagine that nasty-ass Ms. Mancuso getting out of bed all confused, like what the fuck, she probably wears rollers or something, and then she'll just see fire. Like divine justice."

Gaby looked me up and down. "Oh, so we are doing the Lord's work here?"

"We are. She's an asshole. She's been so unfair to you."

"Just so we're clear, you know I sleep in rollers sometimes."

"Well, whatever. You know what I mean. It's only fair. All those detentions."

She got quieter then and rubbed the faded leather around the steering wheel thoughtfully. "It's true she hasn't been the most understanding with me." She was weighing her words carefully, that same equivocating way she voiced everyone else's point of view that drove me crazy. Sometimes you were just right and that's all there was to it, no equivocations.

I wanted her to be mad. I was already mad at everyone all the time and I was frustrated for her, on her behalf. "Dude, last week she gave you detention for being late to lunch. That's not even a thing."

"Girl, I know," she said, forgetting to be judicious for a second. "Only person in the history of that school who has gotten in trouble for being late to fucking lunch. Why does she care so much whether I am on time? It's like an obsession. I'm starting to think she just likes spending Saturdays with me."

"Maybe she's in love with you."

She looked sideways at me and then the silliness of it made her start to giggle. "Can you imagine having sex with that woman? She probably still makes that bitchy face the whole time."

This was the kind of thing that was especially funny when drunk, and I started to laugh too. As we both tried to outdo each other with impressions of our hated principal doing it, we giggled harder, helpless in waves of hilarity. At some point we both stopped making any noise, our laughter totally silent except for a gasping wheeze every now and then as Juvenile rumbled on and we struggled for breath. "Oh no." Gaby held a hand to her chest like an old lady. "No, no, no, you are going to kill me here."

I was crying by now and so was she and I saw that little tilt to her head as she wiped her eyes that meant she was giving in. This was the wonderful thing about Gaby. Sober, she was Little Miss Perfect, but drunk, she could be wonderfully, explosively, delightfully game for whatever dumb ideas I came up with. She was going to do it with me. "Woo-hoo," I said, banging the roof of the car.

"This is because you're hanging out in the Quarter with those Quarter rats all the time, isn't it?" she said. "You're getting crazy ideas from them. You know those guys are losers, right? None of them are going to college, because they all run around huffing glue and doing dumb shit like this." We were going to be seniors next year and talked a lot about going to college. We were definitely both going out of state, out of this fucking place.

"*Brilliant* shit like this, you mean. Fuck Ms. Mancuso."

"All right." She opened her door and the light popped on for a minute and seeing her face all lit up like that made me so glad to see her. Like we had been sitting in the dark for hours and I had forgotten what she looked like. I suddenly leaned over to give her a hug. "I love you," I said.

She patted my arm. "Love you too, you lunatic. For better or worse. Now you've talked me into it, let's go set some shit on fire."

I stepped out of my side of the car and the soft humid night fell across my shoulders. Everything smelled like roots and grass and dirt, the kind of wet jungle night of the suburbs with old-growth oak trees overhead and big sprays of palmetto bushes, and lawns, and a funny smell that I had only ever associated with the one football game I ever went to, which

I now realized was just the smell of this rich, quiet neighbor-hood at night. There was a floodlight somewhere on an-other block, but its sharp beam was turned away from us and everything here was dark and quiet.

Until Gaby hiccuped. "Oh shit," she whispered. "Sorry." Then she did it again, louder. "Beer," she whispered again. "You know beer always does this to me." She tried to hold the next one in and made a strained croaking sound instead and I could see in her eyes that she was about to start laughing again, and if she started I wouldn't be able to stop either, so I ran around to her side of the car, prying open the lighter fluid.

"Wait," she said suddenly. "I gotta pee."

"What?" I had the bottle of lighter fluid open and ready. "Now?"

"Girl, you know my bladder can't wait. Hold up." She still had a beer in her hand. She transferred it to her mouth and clamped the thin metal ridge in between her teeth as she undid her jeans and squatted next to the car.

"Gaby, we are going to get caught. This is not the best time for this."

"If we are going to start all this delinquent nonsense, the least you can do is wait two seconds until I've emptied my bladder. I felt like I was going to burst." The beer can fell when she started talking and she grabbed it before it could spill.

I stood there feeling ridiculous, trying not to listen to the sound of her pee hitting the ground which was kind of mak-ing me have to go too.

"How do they get the grass so soft out here?" She had reached out a hand to stroke the lawn next to her. "Ours is always so spiky."

"Gaby, hurry up." She drank some of her beer, still in

a deep squat and still peeing. "Why are you drinking right now, just finish."

"It takes a while. We've had a lot of drinks tonight." Finally, she stood up and pulled up her pants. "Okay, now I'm ready." Then she opened the mailbox near us and put her empty can inside and raised the little red flag on it with a chuckle. "Go on."

For a second, I almost lost my nerve. I almost told her to get back in the car, that I couldn't do it, and have her drive us to the next shitty bar that would accept our fake IDs and we could laugh about the insane thing we almost did. Another story about Rosemary and her dumb ideas. But I couldn't let her down.

It was important that we do this. That we do this for her. We had grown a little apart since I had been spending more time downtown, hanging out in punk bars and shows. And before too long, we would be hearing back from colleges and maybe moving away from each other, and I was so worried that somehow she might not know how much I still needed her. That she was the only person I really had in this world. My feelings for her radiated in my chest until I thought it would burst and I had to find some way to show her. Something like this, a battle cry of love and allegiance sent forth into this dark neighborhood of assholes that didn't cherish her the way I did and always would. She needed to know that I would always be there for her and stand up for her, that all my feelings could barely even be contained in that loose and flimsy word: *friend*. I would show her, and it needed to be dramatic, explosive, incendiary.

Reinspired, I began spraying lighter fluid all over some big ugly bush right on the edge of the lawn. There was a big stretch of grass between it and the house and I figured it would stop any fire from spreading too far, but I didn't want to think too much about the technicalities of all this. It was the gesture that was so important.

"Oh man, that stinks." Gaby waved her hand in front of her face. "Reminds me of my uncle Antoine."

It did stink. The awful smell of gasoline was rising as I sprayed, squeezing the plastic bottle until its sides caved and it made a little gasp to refill itself with air. Then I sprayed the remaining liquid. "Okay," I said.

"This is some dumb shit, Rosemary. You know that, right?" she said. Then she smiled and struck a match. I reached out to hold her hand as she dropped it and warmth burst over us in a fiery wave and it was everything I hoped it would be, a searing circle of flame, and then just when I had started to enjoy it, just as quickly, it sputtered out. We both looked at each other surprised; the silence only lasted for a second before we began to laugh again. "Oh wait, I think plants have to be dead to catch on fire," I said.

"Of course they do. You're such a fucking idiot," she said affectionately, squeezing my hand and then giving me a little shove that sent me bumping into her car door where I slid down and rested, hanging off her cracked side mirror.

2

JANUARY 6, 2004
TWELFTH NIGHT
THE FRENCH QUARTER

I stared hard at my phone as if just the force of my desire could make it suddenly light up with her number, the flash of her calling me back. Her home number a particular pattern that I knew by heart in the way I will only ever know phone numbers from my past: my mom's, Gaby's and United Cabs for emergencies. The contacts of anyone I had met in the past few years would always be transient, as easily lost as my cell phone where they were stored. But those other numbers were a part of me, imprinted in my body. I could feel the melody tapped out on the small glowing squares of our '80s landline, the receiver too big in my small hands, the Southern politeness that had been burned into all of us. "Hello, Mrs. Parker, may I please speak to Gaby?"

I figured Gaby had a cell phone now, but I didn't know the number and anyway, she still lived with her mom. So, the only way I knew how to reach her, across the estrangement of the last few years to our childhood, was through her mother's old fuzzy answering machine where I had left a rambling, incoherent message. Maybe not making the most persuasive case for why she should call me back.

We hadn't seen much of each other since I had dropped out of college and moved back to New Orleans, and it made sense. She was working hard toward a social work degree and I was fucking around in Quarter bars and selling underwear at a fancy lingerie shop. But beyond circumstance, our relationship had grown sharper and more sour after a few drunken fights about a year ago, and she said she needed a break. I had been too drunk and too surprised to argue and my hurt feelings had made it easy to stay away for a while. I wasn't planning on calling her tonight. I hadn't been expecting how the need to hear her voice had reached out from under all the petty bullshit going on between us with the sudden insistence of a muscle cramp. I let the phone rest on my thigh and blew my nose on the tissue disintegrating in my hand. I needed a new one. I needed to get up and wash my face, find a glass of water, start getting ready for my show. But I was having trouble moving. My body was heavy and limp, stuck to the sagging plush of this old armchair. I checked the phone again without thinking and then felt embarrassed and pathetic. One of Ida's old chew toys, a monkey who had lost an eye a long time ago, winked at me from the fireplace where he lay crumpled up under the legs of the old gas heater that stood there now. It was covered in a thick layer of dust and dog hair. Why hadn't I ever thrown it away? She hadn't bothered with toys in years. It even looked a little singed from the heater, which I had apparently been turning on all winter without noticing the very flammable plush toy wedged just underneath. What was wrong with me?

Ida. Sweet Ida. Twelve years she had been with me, more than half my life measured out in the skittering of little nails across hardwood floors, of hours passed in the gentle rhythm of snores, of her funny, squat little body waiting at my ankles in constant attendance. She was deeply suspicious of everyone that didn't belong to our pack of two, of which she was the self-designated defender. She faced the world and everyone in it but me with an irritable defiance. It was a trait we shared. Was it true that dogs began to take after their owners or did people just gravitate toward similar souls? I didn't pick Ida out—my mom found her by a garbage can one day, a baby Chihuahua barely old enough to walk. But we sure did take to each other. Maybe it wouldn't be so bad to not have this familiar following me everywhere, letting everyone know what a touchy little asshole I was inside.

I had probably been sitting like this for an hour at least. The light of day was quickly fading behind the slanted roofs of houses around my apartment. The chimney swifts were making their last scattered dives through the darkening sky, chasing invisible bugs. All the creatures of the evening rustled in the balcony, the trees, the courtyard below. The living, breathing night waking to movement outside made the stillness in here feel even more terrible, more unavoidable. I was really alone. Maybe it was good Gaby hadn't answered. I wasn't sure how to put it all into words, to explain to her that all the stuff we had been fighting about didn't matter right now. That tonight, I just needed her with me, the cocoa butter smell of her nearness. I needed her to come over and tell me what to do in this tiny apartment that now felt so big and empty. She always knew what to do. I needed her to laugh at me and shake her head; and in her bemused expression, I would be absolved. She had been my company and my consolation in everything since we were six years old.

Louise Brooks pouted at me from the poster above my narrow mantel, and I tried to shake myself out of it. It was probably clear by now that Gaby wasn't going to call me back. I was just going to have to get on with my night. Like that sullen show girl looking down at me, with the same bangs, same black hair as me, I could get it together, make other plans. This was the life I had chosen, a life where all kinds of heartaches could be subsumed in the glossy sheen of satin and rhinestones. I was a burlesque dancer now. I had a show to get ready for. I couldn't just sit around here moping. I had costumes to wear, acts to perform, men to seduce. Thank God I had somewhere to go. The silence of this apartment would swallow me whole if I stayed much longer. I stood up quickly, glad to have something, anything to latch on to. I would dance, and there was bound to be someone in the audience to spark my interest, and if not, I could always find someone somewhere to spend the night with. There were always men to be had as long as you kept adjusting your expectations, and tonight I would settle for anyone with a warm bed and enough desire to distract me from my thoughts. As I stood, I accidentally glanced toward Ida's bed in the corner and had to quickly look away. In my hurry, I tripped over a pile of laundry on the way to the bathroom.

I hadn't cleaned in weeks and stuff was piling up around me like a hamster in a nest. The box of Triscuits I had for dinner yesterday stood open on the floor by my bed, and I picked it up and absently shoved some into my mouth. Had I eaten today? I had two Hostess CupCakes on the bus ride home from the lingerie shop this afternoon. I could always drink a Bloody Mary for vitamins later. After the last few weeks of boiling chicken breasts and mashing them up into a formless beige sludge for Ida, my appetite for food had been noticeably absent. Remembering the smell of that sludge that

I had carefully spread on my fingertips for her to lick at when she refused her bowl made it hard to swallow the large, dry mouthful of crackers I was still working on. There was a flat bottle of mineral water on the pile of books I used as a night table and I managed to wash down the crumbs.

When I got to the sink and looked in the mirror, I had to laugh in spite of myself. I looked terrible. What a fucking mess I was, but then part of the advantage of dyeing my hair so black was that it didn't really show grease. Once I pulled it up under a hairpiece, who would know the difference anyway? I couldn't imagine how women who looked more natural did it. What about when you were just having a really, really shitty day? What did you hide behind? With this hair, red lipstick and false eyelashes, I could have the plague, and no one would know the difference. Somehow the absurdity of stripping in this condition made me feel better. That was why I liked the vintage, pinup look. It required enough makeup and fake hair that I could slip into actually being that celluloid simulacrum of a woman and leave behind the messy hesitancy of my bare self.

I splashed cold water on my face and shut an eye, squinting to make out my lash line. Would eyelash glue even hold against lids all puffy and soft like pudding? Oh well, I would find out. I started to brush foundation across my cheeks with a little sponge and my usual color left wide streaks against the mottled flush of skin. Compacts clicked open and shut and I worked efficiently, concentrating, satisfied to see all my disorder disappearing under clean, sharp lines of well-applied concealer. Once I had started on the path to escape, it was hard not to rush through this familiar routine, so many discrete steps between me and the door. I had a new act tonight, that always perked me up, and there was an undeniable pleasure in doing something that I was unquestionably good at. I was very good at dancing, I had discovered. I used to think I would do something smart with books or history, maybe be a teacher, but since I gave that up with college the irresistible, consoling appetites of the body had come to dominate my life. I lived in a sparkling present, just like the one I felt on-stage where everything bad or complicated fell away and it was just me, a layer of rouge and the insistent pleasure of my body moving through space. I moved quickly now, eager to be done with my appearance and on my way out into the town.

When I finally left my house, painted up and shimmering like a Borscht Belt Jane Russell—my nose always gave me away—the gate clanged shut behind me, and I turned the key in the lock, so relieved to be outside, to be shutting myself off from that silent apartment. I wasn't going home anytime soon, that I had already decided.

Tonight, I didn't even mind the crowd milling around my door, I was almost oddly glad for their company. My build-ing was a popular tourist spot on the ghost tours that trun-dled through the French Quarter all day and night. A bony man in a top hat and orthopedic shoes was pointing at my house with his furled umbrella, braying some gruesome non-sense about Madame LaLaurie who tortured her slaves, and everyone turned toward me curiously. I knew this story, we all did, but he had the wrong house. Not that it mattered to anyone—reality bowed before the lazy exigencies of tourism around here and piling up the bodies paid more than incon-venient accuracy. I knew we were all so full of shit, but still. These were real people he was talking about after all.

But everyone here looked at me as though I were somehow responsible, and I wanted to yell back, *I hear your accents, ass-holes, I'm pretty sure you've got Confederates in your family tombs,* but I decided for once to try to hold on to a little dignity. I was starting to suspect that my insults and kooky outfits might inadvertently be giving these tourists their money's worth. When I stumbled out for milk or cigarettes in the morning, cursing them, all they saw was a hungover young woman in a thrift store kimono with the mouth of a sailor and her arthritic, half-blind Chihuahua in a pink sweater. I was delivering New Orleans to them tied up in a bow. What a bohemian, but whatever, fuck them, even in the tropical heat, my little Ida was always cold.

I shivered a little thinking of Ida, but then put her out of my mind as I had to physically push past a woman in Christmas tree earrings and matching sweater who stood staring, as though I was part of the tour, while two teenage girls jumped out of my way like I might turn on them next. The boys who were with them laughed, that dumb pleasure men always felt in the presence of women's fear. I gave them all the finger as they finally parted around me. The tour guide sent an apologetic look, wanting to establish the solidarity of locals, of those of us stuck in the French Quarter service industry, for whom these loud, pillaging philistines were our only source of income, but I looked away. I wasn't offering absolution tonight, especially to sad old ghoulish chimney sweeps in cargo shorts and spats. Tonight, I was a show girl and show girls don't care about guys like him. There is always a hierarchy, and I got another jolt of relief at this reminder of my place in it. I thought again how I would soon be onstage. I couldn't imagine ever going home again, but that would be hours from now. For the moment I was free, a bird in gaudy plumage, out in the streets.

It was too early to go to the club. I wasn't ready to explain myself to the other girls. They would immediately notice that something was off with their trembling girl antennas. Those busty, bawdy, Technicolor strippers could intuit tragedy. Too many overdoses and abusive boyfriends, temporary evictions, accidental pregnancies and unpaid bills, the girls of burlesque would cluster around heartbreak, moths beating their tender wings against this sadness shining through me, and I couldn't face it.

So, I found a stoop a few blocks away that didn't smell too strongly of piss or vomit and set my duffel bag of costumes down to pass some time. I already felt better being here in the street than I did an hour ago. A carriage rolled by and six overheated tourists cackled over big plastic cups of sweet alcohol. I felt sad for the poor mule, tongue lolling against his bit.

A couple wandered by staring at me and I knew I looked weird, but it was calculated. I had this idea that my sloppy clothes, dirty jeans and a hoodie would somehow negate the demand for attention of my stage hair and makeup when I walked to shows, and kept people from staring. It didn't and the contrast probably just made it worse, but I hated being looked at on the street. I loved attention, I wanted to be noticed and seen and admired, but I wanted it on my terms. That didn't seem unreasonable to me. It was also a funny trick I learned that worked well for picking up men. Sloppy clothes made guys think you didn't care about impressing them, but since I was already made up, ostensibly for my performance, not them, I got to have it both ways. I looked superhot but couldn't care less. Catnip to the right kind of man. Men watching you from behind the bar with a smirk and a cold heat in their gray eyes. Men like Jonah.

Jonah. In all my terrible afternoon, I hadn't thought of him once and I wasn't quite expecting the funny little thrill it gave me. I was glad I was alone, feeling sure anyone could have seen the quick, embarrassing flutter I felt at his name. That was perfect. Jonah. I hadn't let myself see him in a while, a self-imposed banishment after I had made the mistake of seeming too eager, too grateful the last time we hooked up. But it had been a few weeks, weeks that I was lost in my own private sorrows, and now I could say hi without sacrificing my cool. I deserved it. I could allow myself the pleasure of one quick dunk in his flirtations.

A bunch of church bells started pealing and startled the shit out of me. You'd think I would be used to it after thirteen years of Catholic school, but it still surprised me with the sheer excessiveness of it. The sound went on for an unusually long time. The big low bells of the cathedral were tolling but also the higher, more discreet bells of St. Mary's. It definitely wasn't for a wedding, some kind of holiday instead, the celebratory end of some hours-long mass that all the crazy old ladies would be at. It only took me a moment to realize it was January 6, Twelfth Night, which I also remembered was the Feast of the Epiphany. I couldn't tell you when Passover was, but I knew the exact date of the fucking Feast of the Epiphany. That was my mom's fault. Was it one Epiphany or epiphanies in general? It had something to do with the wise men, which I knew because I really like king cake and it was all mixed up together somehow. There was some comfort in the thought that it was the start of Carnival. This day was the official opening of the season, the parties, parades, the general delirium would all start to accelerate now, the feeling that life itself had been put on hold, that real life would have to wait for eight or ten or twelve weeks while the whole city took off and got stupid. Soon the entire town would be keeping me company in a drunken, festive avoidance of any unpleasantness while we ate and drank and danced. No one was sad during Carnival. Our divisions were mended—black, white, rich and poor, we all participated in this glorious munici-pal round of primal therapy. Sure, our parades were presided over by the Uptown men who paid for them, resplendent on horseback in the same velvet capes and satin hoods they had worn since the nineteenth century that bore an uncomfort-able resemblance to Klansmen's robes. That's the thing about traditions, the past still clung to them like barnacles, and our history was dark, but we didn't talk too much about that stuff. And when the sinister dukes passed quickly, any discomfort in their wake was swallowed up by bands and floats and an infectious joy. And beer. It was all very strange and com-plicated. I was suddenly viscerally grateful for it all. I could theoretically stay drunk from now until Ash Wednesday and no one would find it odd. What a wonderful city, to be so cheerfully complicit in all your worst instincts. It was utterly broken, but full of charm. There was a reason I lived here.

The night was warm and misty. The fog that settled in every January added to my feeling of restlessness. Even though I'd lived here all my life, there was something about the un-seasonable warmth and the early dark of a Southern winter that gave a sense of nervous excitement, of foreboding. It was the kind of night to get into trouble, to kick beer cans with indeterminate emphasis, to fall into bed with a stranger. It was the kind of night to drink, to lose yourself in a temporary exhilaration and see where it all took you. It was a wild free-dom, the downward plunge of a roller coaster. It was a feel-ing that I associated again with Jonah. Everything would be okay. I would go find him and see where our night might lead.

It was also the kind of night that would destroy my hair. I felt it puffing up already in the humidity. We had an early show, 8:00 p.m. instead of the usual 10:00 p.m. to try to catch the convention crowd, but I needed to get out of this mist now, before my smooth bangs turned fuzzy and indistinct. It would make the line between my real, increasingly frizzy hair and the sleek perfection of my hairpiece way too obvious. Everything else might be bearable tonight, if only just barely, but I could not get through it with bad hair.

I got up to go to Deadman's Cove. My hair would be safe in the stale, ammonia-scented air-conditioning of that dirty, dreary bar. A bar where you had an ongoing flirtation with the very attractive bartender was a sanctuary like no other.

I hitched my bag up on my shoulder, and a boat sounded its horn on the river, a low, loud, aching call pouring suddenly through the street. And I winced, a sudden stab in my chest that made it hard to breathe. Everything felt suddenly full of secret meanings, the smell of the wet air, the gray of the concrete, the painful slash of hot pink flowers in a cracked planter on my left, the boat's echo drifting softly into the night sky, and some faulty valve in my heart opened up, leaving me helpless in the face of this flood of incoherent but overwhelming grief.

I closed my eyes, waiting for it to pass. A similar thing used to happen a lot at college in the months before I dropped out, when I would get stupid drunk out in the woods by myself. This terrible urgency and confusion that felt physical, like a long, slowly expiring breath. But maybe I'd just always been like this. Shitty with feelings. When my mom had made the decision to let me keep Ida, I could barely look at her for the first few days because her tiny, perfect feet made me want to cry. But Ida hadn't cared or noticed, just wiggled her warm body up under my chin until I could feel my pulse beating against her neck, slowing to the rhythm of her hot, smelly breath.

A metallic taste lingered in my mouth and I tried to calm myself in the presence of familiar streets, geographic landmarks. An uneven curb, the smooth marble of a dirty threshold, the black iron spirals holding open weathered shutters, this was my home. But the feeling persisted, and I decided to hurry toward Deadman's Cove and Jonah. I'd spent my childhood alone, making do, pickles for dinner, brushing my own teeth and putting myself to bed when Mom worked at night, but tonight I needed company. If I couldn't have Gaby, then maybe the company of a coldhearted man with pretty eyes would do. Maybe that was even better.

I found some reassurance just in the sound of my footsteps, a steady slap of rubber on concrete. Maybe one day I would just dissolve into this city, into my books and the flowers and the people I passed in the street and the bullshit stories we all told each other, finally disappear, join the ghosts, sink into history. But in the meantime, I knew that glitter helped hold me in place. Sequins. The sparkle of ice in a glass lifted to someone else's mouth. Dancing in rhinestones and fringe. Bars like the Sugarlick and Deadman's Cove.

Someone sneezed from inside an open window as I passed, and it startled the hell out of me. I could hear *Wheel of Fortune* playing quietly over the sound of grease popping in a frying pan. Open windows and closed shutters were the most deceptive form of privacy. And the smell of shrimp frying could soothe any sorrows.

3

1992
BROADMOOR

Gaby and I were coming back from a slow walk around my neighborhood. We had originally intended to jump rope as we had found a two-for-one set of jump ropes on sale at the K&B. Ninety-nine cents seemed like such a deal, the two wrapped up in their thick plastic bag like rainbow snakes, that we abandoned the Big League Chew we had been planning to buy, that we were currently obsessed with, and had come home with them instead. But they were cheap and too light, and it made it impossible to jump, so we were just dragging them behind us as we walked, talking about *Saturday Night Live*. We were old enough to have sleepovers, but too young to go anywhere, and this show had become the highlight of our week, a way of measuring and ordering the endless slog of the school year. First in the excitement and anticipation of which of our favorite sketches might come on and then the days after, as we remembered and rehashed the funniest parts for another week. If for some reason one of us couldn't sleep over, we would still watch the episode together over the phone, held in the quiet of each other's echoed breathing until the commercial breaks when, by instinctive agreement, we would begin to talk again.

We stepped over a river of suds from where my neighbor's teenage son was washing his car and somewhere someone was listening to Led Zeppelin and Gaby stooped down to pet a tabby cat flicking her tail in a patch of unmown grass. "Careful, she's mean," I warned her.

She ignored me and the cat purred against her hand. "I'm just saying, it's been two weeks since she was on, there has to be a new one coming up soon." Church Lady was our absolute favorite. We didn't get half of the jokes, but every time Dana Carvey showed up wiggling his eyebrows in a tweed suit, we just fell out, rolling on the floor and choking on popcorn. A Church Lady sketch could keep us happy all week, something to mouth to each other wordlessly in the silent halls on our way to chapel, to revisit endlessly as we walked our wide circles around the edge of the playground, keeping a safe distance from the other girls' games.

I watched her pet the cat a little jealously—the creature had always hated me. "I mean, I would settle for Toonces, I guess. Those are always pretty good." Gaby voiced a begrudging agreement.

When we rounded the corner to my house, I was surprised to see shapes on the porch. My mom usually worked a double shift on Saturdays at the Royal Bourbon Hotel in the French Quarter, where she was a concierge. It helped her stay close to the action, she liked to say. I pulled Gaby along. "My mom's home."

"Really?" She could always be counted on to be as interested and curious for any unexpected event in my life as I was. We shared everything that way. "I wonder why."

"Hey, Mama Rose," Mom called to me, waving me closer.

She used to have an old Broadway recording of *Gypsy* before our record player broke and used to like to sing "Everything's Coming Up Roses" to me and the name stuck. "Come see what I found."

She was lying on our plastic outdoor love seat holding a beer in a "Who Dat?" Koozie, her bare feet in Greg's lap. Greg was her latest boyfriend. He played the saxophone in some funk band, because she also liked to say that after my dad she swore off drummers. He had very dark skin and a tattoo that said Denise 1986.

"Hey, you two." Greg nodded at us. I wished he would talk normally instead of that fake extrasmooth way he slurred all his words together trying to be so cool, but sometimes he brought over homemade jambalaya in a big Tupperware and since no one had ever cooked more than grilled cheese or scrambled eggs in our house, I kind of forgave him for it. Also knowing my mom, he was bound to be temporary so that helped too.

"What are you doing home?" I asked my mom. I saw Greg nod at Gaby in that special way he always said hello to her.

Mom threw her hair back over her shoulders. She was always tossing around the almost waist-length black hair that made anything she was wearing look like she had just wandered out of Woodstock. Even the purple polyester blouse with a gold name tag that she was still wearing from work. "I was on a smoke break and look what I found. I called Greg here to give us a ride home." She turned to Greg. "Every time I tell that man I have cramps he sends me home. He always gets so embarrassed, it's almost too easy," she said, snapping her fingers.

"You know that's not why he lets you get away with murder," Greg said, and she laughed appreciatively, poking him in the side with her toe.

I wasn't paying attention because I looked where she pointed and somehow, I hadn't noticed a tiny puppy who had half crawled inside the overturned can of Alpo she was furiously eating. Faint slobbery grunts were coming from inside, but all I could see was a little butt with a tail like a shoelace sticking out and whipping back and forth. Gaby and I squatted down, not wanting to disturb it. The can was slowly scooting across the cement floor of the porch as the puppy inched its way closer to the bottom.

"It's so small," I said, concerned.

"It's a Chihuahua," Greg informed me even though I didn't ask him.

"I'm pretty sure it's a baby." My mom finished her beer and tapped Greg on the shoulder with the empty bottle and he got up and went inside. "She was stuck in a garbage can on that little alley behind the hotel. I was smoking when I heard something. I didn't see a mom or any other puppies, so I guess she got left. Poor little bitch."

"Mom," I said fiercely.

She lit a Virginia Slim and waved me off. "Back me up, Gaby, y'all have a dog. That's the word for it."

"Yes, ma'am," she said and then she whispered to me, "I would never call her that even if it's the right word."

"My mom is the B," I whispered back and we both giggled.

Then, like she heard us, the puppy pulled her head out of the can. The disproportionately big dome of her head had a little ring of dog food on it, even behind her ears. She looked at Gaby and me and then ran over to investigate some dead leaves that were rustling in a corner. She had a wobbly, unsteady run and her belly, now distended by her large meal, stuck out under her as round as a tennis ball. "Oh my God, she's so cute."

"She really is," Gaby agreed with authority. Gaby always had dogs. It was one of the many things I envied about her house, besides her sisters, her cable television and the fact that her mom made things like freezer cinnamon buns. "Are y'all going to keep her?" she asked me cautiously. She always avoided speaking to my mom directly if possible. She could be strangely shy around grown-ups like that.

"Mom?"

"Sure." She stretched her legs and arms and sent the bunch of gold bangles cluttering down her wrist. "She can be our guard dog. Keep you safe while I'm at work."

"That is not a guard dog," Greg said emphatically, reappearing and handing Mom a beer and a green plastic Mardi Gras cup which I knew would be filled with rum and Coke. My mom always smelled kind of deliciously like Coca-Cola and limes.

"You don't know. It's the little ones who are smart, like Rosemary." She indicated me with the cup and the ice rattled. "We should call her Ida after my mom," she said, suddenly sentimental, and then looked at the dog thinking and added, "Or Biscuit, 'cause she looks like one."

My mom almost never mentioned my grandmother, whom I had never met, nor the rest of the family she left behind in Pittsburgh when she cut out, a groupie to some bad rock band that dumped her in New Orleans, or "fucking paradise" as she called it. The puppy was now chasing a lizard along the edge of the porch under the railing, pouncing like an unsteady boat in a strong wind. I picked her up, her back legs hanging down and flailing against the air and she squinted at me, narrowing her funny giant bug eyes. All her parts seemed like the wrong size, like she was a collection of bits from different dogs all hung together awkwardly on this tiny frame. "Ida," I whispered to her.

Her head bobbed on her small neck and her eyes narrowed, then popped back open, surprised, then slowly began to shut again. I held her to my chest, and she nestled up under a fold of my T-shirt, pushing the fabric to one side then another roughly with her forehead until, finally satisfied, she sank her head down and curled in my arms, and immediately fell asleep. I looked at Gaby in wonder and she nodded sagely. She understood the incommunicable fullness of the moment. "Watch out though," she whispered, "she still might pee on you."

4

TWELFTH NIGHT 2004
THE FRENCH QUARTER

Deadman's Cove rose to meet me as I entered, dark and dingy, like a hug with a whiff of body odor. It had been nautical themed once long ago, but years of dereliction had covered everything in a coating of sticky dust and familiarity, and it all just blended together into a sort of generic "Bar." There was a scuffed black-and-white-checkered floor and a pool table in the back. Posters for long past punk shows and cracked tiki mugs and souvenir hula girls so coated in muck that they looked like gargoyles filled the shelves behind the bar. A sickly blue light illuminated the booze from underneath. A vanity license plate that read WAIKIKI and a broken ship's wheel hung from the ceiling. But the decor didn't really matter. Deadman's Cove distinguished itself just by surviving. It had always been here, and it always would, the last to close and first to open. It was the bar where other nights came to die in the blaze of morning. I actually couldn't imagine what it must feel like to work the day shift. You had to have a hard stomach to minister to the types that drank their days away here, but I guessed the bright light of the afternoon never penetrated the blacked-out windows, so maybe it was fine, just never-ending night. *Perfect for vampires*, I'd heard Jonah say before with a smile.

André Williams was playing on the stereo. Some garage rockers had rediscovered him and now his music was always playing, everyplace. Or at least the places I went, and his raw, magnetic voice was wailing vulgar hymns to pussy and marijuana, and I couldn't tell if he was making fun of me or himself or where my abasement ended and his began. But this music, as it always did, filled me with rough, thumping exhilaration and I was glad I had chosen to come here. I threw my bag onto an empty seat at the bar. A poorly duct-taped rip in the fake leather scratched me through my jeans when I sat down, and I hoped it wouldn't leave a mark that could be seen later on stage.

I hadn't even had time to look for him before Jonah materialized across the bar in front of me. "Well, hello there. This is an unexpected pleasure." I smiled at him, but in a bored way and certainly not in a way that let on that I was suddenly so fucking glad to see him I wanted to throw my arms around his neck. *Jesus Christ, Rosemary, get a hold of yourself.*

Still, this greeting seemed a good sign, an indication he was in an expansive mood. I had been right to stay away for a while—scarcity sharpened Jonah's appetites. Nothing made him more disdainful than a woman's interest. He could ferret it out with an almost uncanny accuracy. Luckily, I was almost as good at hiding it. "I was worried we had lost you to the path of virtue." He set an empty glass on the bar in front of me. "I've been waiting for an adult to show up so I can have an honest to God conversation. Just see what you have left me with." He looked pointedly down the bar where two girls in poorly fitting black latex were watching us, uneasily sizing me up as competition.

I smiled again, still with reserve. Right. He always did this, the setting up of the hierarchy of customers to make you feel special, but also let you know that you weren't, there were others in line for his attention.

I had seen it before and I didn't trust it, but my stomach still got warm. That's the thing about guys like this; it didn't matter. I was glad he was here now. The bar towel hung at his waist, a strip of gray against the black of his clothes. The forward tilt of his hip, the way his narrow chest seemed to slide down, all flat planes of geometry toward his heavy brass belt buckle. All of it made me embarrassed by my desire and I looked away. Jonah had pale skinny fingers and the careless haircut and well-chosen shirts of someone in a band, but a slightly greater hopelessness hung around him, marking him always and forever a bartender. He was young looking for thirty, so older than me, but also old in the way long nights and alcohol will suck the shine right out of anyone and replace it with a clammy sheen that is somehow even more inviting. Perhaps a bartender is just a metonymy for the seductive obliteration of his wares.

"If I'm following any path, I think we both know it's not the path of virtue," I said.

"So, where have you been? What have you been up to, mysterious lady?"

"Oh, this and that, hexing the living, raising the dead. You know how it goes."

"God, I love it when you're witchy." He smiled and a spray of club soda shot into my glass and then stopped with a little gasp of the nozzle sealing off again. He remembered. I always drank a lot of club soda. I pulled it toward me and took a sip feeling a kind of glow.

We had hooked up quite a few times, nights when alcohol and cocaine had turned me into a hard, shining creature of sexual nonchalance. Black underwear and smudged eye makeup, I enacted the woman of his teenage fantasies, dark and troublesome, laughing and unconcerned. Sex was easy. He spanked me, hard, while I admired a row of Day of the Dead figurines on a shelf above his bed and wondered who was the more revealed, he in his fetish or me with blue handprints across my flesh. It had happened again, easy, cold. I didn't have his phone number, but I remembered the smell of his hair.

He poured me a shot of Jameson unasked and I nodded my thanks. I paused for a quick moment as I held the glass to my lips. The smell seared my nose. I knew that the wonderful hammer of whiskey could blunt all these exposed nerves, all these cilia that tingled with emotions I had no words for. This is what I should have been moving toward all day. How had I gotten so distracted? I drank it all in one gulp. All at once I went hard, like I had gone from being water sloshing and surging and overtopping my boundaries to smooth, contained, delicious ice. I stretched my arms and flexed my claws savoring the transformative power of alcohol so similar to looking at the world from under the slant of fake lashes. My inner terror retreated, and I became that other girl I sometimes was, cooler and in control. What a relief. Now I could be the girl on the cover of a pulp novel with a tight dress and a smoking gun. I was fishnets and rhinestones, safe in the armor of femininity gone just a little bad. I was going to be okay. Everything was going to be okay. I tapped the glass so he could refill it, which he did with a promptness that made me know almost for certain that he wanted to fuck me tonight.

He put the bottle down and leaned on the bar. "I've been thinking of you…" he paused to let this rare acknowledgment settle "…because after our last—" he cleared his throat suggestively "—evening together. I went out and got this. I've been waiting for you to show up again so we can chat about it, but you disappeared." He reached under the bar and held up a torn paperback, *All Quiet on the Western Front.* I went all hot inside. "It's a pretty good book," he continued, oblivious to my embarrassment. "I never met a girl who was into trench warfare before." He was smiling, but he held the book carelessly as though it might just slide out of his fingers, the gesture inviting a response and yet also somehow distancing. It was always surprising to me how men actually liked to talk about the things that interested them, never thinking of the ways it might only serve to set them apart. Jonah wanted me to know all the books he had read. I confessed the ones I had, drop by drop, breath held, afraid to scare him away.

I tried to think back. Had we been talking about that book? I had a vague memory of him in his underwear describing a season of *Black Adder* to me in monotonous detail. I must have been really drunk.

That book had been a favorite of mine in high school. It was assigned, but for some reason Gaby and I got super into it, crying and crying and crying when poor little Paul dies at the end. We had decided he was very cute, and took it all very hard, and then after it was just sort of connected in my mind with the idea that maybe I wanted to study history in college. Then I fucked that up so badly and all these things felt somehow connected and tied up in this book that Jonah was now flipping through with a quick whir of pages. It was like he was holding my hair while I puked. The experience was mortifying, but also intimate. But still I needed some veil of protection between me and the sudden pounding of my heart. I worried about my thick careful black eyeliner wings against the abrupt watering of my eyes. "Oh man, I must have been smashed if I was bringing that up. What a fucking nerd I am sometimes." I almost wanted to apologize to the book as I talked, like I was trampling the feelings of a precious friend.

Jonah looked hurt, just for a heartbeat. He yawned and tossed the book onto a shelf under the bar and shrugged. "I wouldn't know, I slept through most of high school. But Motörhead has a song called '1916,' do you know it?" I didn't, but this was safer. We had retreated. I trusted the masculine delight in his own interests to pull him further from the uncomfortable vulnerability of mine. I managed to subtly wipe the corner of my eye and took a deep breath. A wet black streak came away on my finger. I was a mess. I remembered talking about this book with Gaby, the deep safety of a female friend, that communion of shared language and silent compassion, a world of feeling that men would never experience, could never understand. "Speaking of Motörhead," he went on. "Did I ever tell you Lemmy came in here once? Sat two seats down from where you are now, drinking pint glasses of Jack and Coke. That guy's got a constitution. He's like sixty years old or something..." His voice trailed off as the girls at the end of the bar called to him again, and I was glad to have a minute to recover.

I weighed my options and tried to watch him surreptitiously. He was listening as one of the girls explained something to him, and I could tell by the tilt of his head, the way he leaned his arm on the bar, that he was being called to settle something. Some debate or question that required his expertise and I commended them for having already learned how to stroke a man like that; you could practically see him rearing up at the question like a cat arching its back toward a caress. Men in bars loved nothing more than explaining things to you. I'd almost come to believe there was no question more infallibly seductive than, *So who was Jack Kirby again?* At least at the bars I frequented. Questions about bands, Quentin Tarantino or Trotsky also seemed to do the trick.

But he kept looking over at me with a knowing smile, almost a wink, that bound the two of us in a shared superiority and it felt so good. Such comfort, like we stood together against all the dumber, less well-initiated travelers through our world. He would be coming back soon. I tried to gather my thoughts. The book thing had been a definite invitation. He wouldn't have done something like that unless he felt something for me. For a minute I was furious at myself for avoiding him, when he had clearly been ready to make these feelings known. Was it possible there was more to Jonah than all this dumb flirting? Could I trust him?

Eventually he came back. "What I was going to say," he continued as if our conversation had actually been interrupted by the demands of his job, and not a power move, "at the risk of sounding unchivalrous, is that you kind of look like shit. I mean, as much as anyone as hot as you possibly can. Is everything okay, Rosie?"

He had never called me that. The affectionate diminutive canceling out the insult. He always used my full name, drawling the *Rosemary* into almost three syllables, the formality of it somehow a kind of gentle mockery. But now, the hint of concern in his voice felt like he had just reached out and caressed my cheek, a tone and touch too gentle, too disarming. "Why are you always such a dick?" I said with a laugh, purposefully misunderstanding him. A confident, bantering tone was vital. I knew him. Despite all these marks of regard, the slightest quiver from me and he would turn away forever.

"No, but seriously, you have a look tonight." He was watching me with that unexpected candor that made all my nerves tingle. If he was going to be this nice, I didn't know how to play it. If I started to weep big snotty wailing tears right here at the bar while a song called "Pussy Stan" thrummed through the room and he watched me with those cool, appraising eyes, I would be lost. But then, the book, the unexpected friendliness, maybe I could trust him with more than a place to crash for a few hours tonight.

Almost before I could stop myself, I found I was speaking this terrible weight off my chest. "My dog died." I shrugged. "She was pretty ancient though."

He thought about this for a minute. "I'm more of a cat man, myself. I always felt dogs were just too obvious, I mean, where's the challenge in something that feels affection for rocks?" he said, dropping into the more caustic tone with which he liked to expound his theories on things, but then, as if catching himself, he stopped. "But that sucks, I'm sorry to hear about it. I'm down to help if you want to try and *Frankenweenie* him. Sew him up and bring him back from the dead."

"Yeah, no thanks." This was all very exciting, but I still wasn't ready for jokes. I looked away and drank my soda.

But then as if he could hear the something in my voice that I hadn't been able to completely disguise, had noticed the tiniest tremor of the electrical current in my response to him, he let his friendliness slide from him, disavowed. "It's a great short," he said. "The best of Burton's early work." And he moved back toward the pair of girls still hungrily watching us at the other end of the bar. "Another round?" I heard him ask followed by the fluttering sounds of their assent, and I tried not to feel it like a wound.

This was fine. This was our thing. We were both good at it and I wouldn't choose to be nineteen like those poor girls for anything in the world. I could wait. He and I were both so adept at the parry and deflection of romantic intent that once we were fully in it, what we did almost ceased to be flirting and sometimes just verged on rudeness. I still had a lingering advantage because I hadn't tried to see him in a while, and so even though I had told him something unbearably personal, the fresh aura of ambivalence still shone around me, I was pretty sure. I could still play this in his language. I wondered sometimes what he would do if he knew I had dreams about him, ridiculous dreams where we were laughing and holding hands, and I was wrapped in the penetrating warmth of his regard. I felt that hard knot in my chest shift at the memory.

For now, he had won because I was stuck on this stool with no one to talk to, trying to look relaxed while my heart still raced in the memory of his recent presence. I picked at a sequin accidentally hot glued to the sole of my sneaker and rehearsed my choreography for the thousandth time in my head, realizing he had never actually seen me perform.

A peal of laughter came from the other end of the bar and I purposefully didn't look over. It was so important not to provide him with confirmation that any girl coming to the bar was doing so just to flirt with him. He had a whole coterie of fans, young women that clustered under his supercilious gaze, baby chicks in dark lipstick and dyed hair, blinking in the fresh dazzle of burnout New Orleans nightlife and preening for his attention. But he and I were different, right? We had an understanding. And I suddenly knew he would know it too, he would feel it incontrovertibly in his bones once he had seen me dance. We were always meeting at places like this, where he had the advantage, but once he saw me onstage, I was sure his last reserve would fall. I was *that* good, and my new act tonight was so especially to his taste, he wouldn't be able to help getting knocked sideways by it. I was basically pretending to be everything he had ever wanted from a girl. He would only see the reflection of his vanity. He would only think it was cool.

"It seems to me if you're going to walk around town in a cloak, you should really be familiar with 'Bela Lugosi's Dead,'" he said when he returned with a roll of his eyes. "Please do not come to my bar and talk to me about Marilyn Manson."

This gesture of inclusion, this moment of shared condescension made me feel reckless and I made my move. "Speaking of our black hearts and shared interests," I said.

He raised his eyebrows in curiosity. "As I usually am."

"I'm doing a pretty goth act tonight. Want to come see me strip off a bunch of black crepe and ostrich feathers like a Victorian catafalque come to life?"

"Did you just say 'catafalque' instead of 'hearse'?" he laughed. "My God, Rosemary, where have you been all my life? A vocabulary like that *and* you're easy on the eyes. Say it again."

I obliged. Guys were so easy once you knew their buttons. My hair was dyed black and I had enough of a spooky aesthetic that when I wanted to, I could certainly play it up. Men's desires were so conveniently set into caricatures already, it made it easy to slide in and out of whatever their pinup fancy was. If you cared to. The light of possibility shone in his eyes and a kind of acceleration took over me. I was racing toward the place where I would be warmed in the fire of his interest. I needed this. I needed him. "I'll give you my plus-one if you come to our show tonight. You get off soon."

"Will I?" The heat in his look flared higher and he poured me another tumbler of Jameson and one for himself. "You girls are at the Sugarlick, right? You dance with Elsa?"

I nodded. Elsa had, in fact, been the one to give me a ride out to Carnival Time, the strange store so far upriver that Uptown became the suburbs. There the roads were filled in with gravelly oyster shells and the levee wall rose high above low ranch houses, where you could buy ostrich feathers in any shade and fringe in any length, and the wildest, silliest of flights of imagination became tactile and possible. It was the pilgrimage we all made when putting together a new act. I went again when the end started coming for Ida, and I knew I needed to put myself in mourning. All I knew how to sew was the half-made and flimsy bits of a burlesque costume, so that was what I did.

He sighed loudly. "Well, for you, maybe I will make the sacrifice and go to yet another burlesque show. Although God knows I've seen enough tits in this town to last a lifetime."

"Liar." This line was common in our circles where so many of the women worked in the industry that all of the guys affected to be bored by it. No one wanted to look like a john.

"You're right, I am lying."

"And anyway, I think by chance you have never seen mine. Onstage," I clarified. I smiled and took out a cigarette, waiting for him to light it for me, which he did with the flick of a tarnished Zippo. The last of my nerves settled in the rush of smoke. "You promise to come?" My voice sounded different, softer.

"Scout's honor."

"You were never a Boy Scout." I stood up and shifted my bag onto my shoulder.

"True. They're all a bunch of fascists."

I laughed. "Okay, see you later, then." As I left, I heard him return to the girls at the bar, but now it didn't matter. They could enjoy his attention all they wanted; he was at work. But after, his night, his trajectory arced back to me. The graffiti-covered door of the bar slammed and for just a moment my knees got weak with relief. I didn't have to go back to my apartment. I could go home with Jonah. Especially once he saw my act. I mean, he had a big poster portrait of Death herself all punked up from the *Sandman* comics up on his wall. Who else would I end up with tonight? The synchronicity was perfect, a gift from the evening. I felt lost in a wave that could only be described as love and gratitude. I pulled my hoodie carefully up over my hair and fled out into the night. I wanted another drink. I wanted to see the girls. I wanted to put on my pasties and fishnets and hear those first few bars of music that called me to the stage. I felt like myself again. I was ready. I almost tripped over the legs of a man passed out in the next doorway.

5

1991
GENTILLY

Gaby was confidently pouring oil into a measuring cup while I sat across from her at the small round kitchen table, reading from the back of the Duncan Hines box. "Are you sure that's the right kind? It just says vegetable oil. It doesn't say what kind."

Her mom didn't look up from the stove, presiding over a bunch of steaming, hissing pots and pans. "That's the right stuff, Gaby," she said. The room already smelled amazing from the pot of étouffée bubbling away, but now she was also frying thin strips of fish which just seemed wild to me, that you could have two separate delicious things for dinner. Her mom was letting us make brownies because Gaby had aced our last math test, which seemed kind of unnecessary since she always did, but what did I know, maybe they had brownies all the time? I was here because my mom forgot we had a half day for the Feast of the Ascension and so I caught a ride with Gaby. Mom sent me to Mary Immaculata because it was the cheapest private school she could find, but protested my indoctrination with a chronic absentmindedness about any Catholic observances at school. I should have just gone to the McDonough 23 around the block from my house, but on our kindergarten visit, she had seen a big splatter of puke in the halls that hadn't been cleaned up yet and she never forgot it. And Mary Immaculata supposedly was good for the arts. Which it wasn't.

Gaby wore a gold cross around her neck, so did each of her sisters, and her mom never forgot the feast days.

"Can I have a turn mixing?" I asked and Gaby pushed the pink plastic bowl toward me. The batter was the most satisfying consistency. Every time I dragged the wooden spoon through it, big circles formed on the surface before rippling back down into the goo. It was hypnotizing.

"Come on, Mom," Gaby was saying. "Everyone in school wears Wigwams."

"Gaby, I am not buying you ten-dollar socks, I don't care who is wearing them. No one at Tellie's school is wearing ten-dollar socks." Mrs. Parker bent over to watch as she lowered the flame under her frying pan. One of Gaby's older sisters, Estelle, had left Mary Immaculata for reasons that I never fully understood. *She just wasn't comfortable there*, was all Gaby would say.

"Just because she doesn't want them, doesn't mean I shouldn't have them."

I had had this same desperate but hopeless conversation with my mom the previous week as well, getting her usual dumb speech about marching to your own drum that always led her to not buying me things. But Gaby's mom and dad both had good jobs and, in general, Mrs. Parker usually understood stuff like this. Gaby had a Lisa Frank Trapper Keeper, and the right kind of backpack, not like the dumb leather thrift store satchel my mom tried to convince me was so European.

"Gabrielle Jolie Parker, you put those in the oven and go watch TV and leave me and my kitchen in peace. Please."

Gaby frowned as she sprayed a pan with cooking spray. There was a stained glass shade on the light over the kitchen table and it made everything look kind of orange even though I knew all the furniture in here was brown and yellow. I raised myself off my butt and then flopped down just to hear the funny sigh that the cushions of her kitchen chairs made and Gaby smiled at me, indulgent. "You are just obsessed with those."

I had kind of been doing it on purpose to make her smile and was feeling proud when we heard the front door slam and her house shook with the arrival of her dad. He made me a little nervous. I was never quite ready for the way the whole atmosphere of the house seemed to change once there was a man in it. And he also used to like to joke with me. If he saw me drinking a Capri Sun or eating a cookie he would say, *You gonna pay for that? Everybody pulls their weight around here*, and then he always laughed and patted my shoulder, but it made me feel shy and embarrassed and want to put back whatever snack I was eating. He was tall and their house was small, and he seemed to reach the ceiling of whatever room he was in.

We could hear him taking off his coat and banging around, and I thought he might have said "Goddamn it" a couple of times. Gaby and I looked at each other at his cursing and I laughed, but Gaby said, "He's been having some trouble with his job."

"Hush, Gaby," her mom interrupted her. "That's not polite."

She shrugged and I wanted to somehow convince her mom that I could be trusted, but before I could say anything, Gaby glanced at her mom and a kind of silent understanding passed between them.

Then her dad came in, loud and a little sweaty. "Goddamn it, Elizabeth, do you know they are going to promote that son of a bitch over me again?"

"Charles," Gaby's mom said warningly.

He noticed me and stopped talking. The air felt suddenly hot and still. I could hear the oil in the pan popping and fizzing. Her mom also looked at me. I didn't know what to do so I played with the puffy seam that ran along the side of the cushion I was sitting on.

"Let's go talk in the bedroom," her mom said, putting down her spatula and turning off the stove. They left the room.

We put the brownies in the oven and Gaby set a timer on the counter. "Come on," Gaby said. "It's too hot in here with the oven on."

We walked into the den where her sister was on the couch doing homework with headphones on, most likely listening to Janet Jackson. Gaby and her sisters were obsessed and the room she and Tellie shared was covered in *Rhythm Nation* posters. When she saw us, she said too loudly, "Y'all can't sit here, dummies."

But Gaby pulled her book away and pointed at the next room. Tellie dropped her headphones around her neck. "What?" she asked, annoyed, drawing the word out as long as she could. Then she stopped and we all listened to the raised voices coming through from the bedroom. The walls in Gaby's house were thin and the wood paneling didn't really muffle the sound at all.

"Well, even if they don't ever make you a supervisor, what are you going to do? Quit after all this time?"

"It's the goddamn principle," her dad yelled. "They just can't stand to see a black man get ahead of himself."

The voices got quieter as Gaby's mom murmured something in response.

"Do you think Dad's getting fired?" Gaby asked, worried.

"Don't be stupid." Her sister looked sternly at her. "You have company, Gabrielle. Stop getting in people's business. Y'all watch TV." She moved aside to give us room and looked down at her book but didn't put her headphones back on, and you could just see the back of her head straining toward the noises in the other room that had started to escalate again.

I handed Gaby the big remote next to me that I didn't know how to use. "My mom and her boyfriends always get like that. That's quiet even, it's when they start throwing stuff that you have to worry."

"My parents don't throw things," Gaby said, but she didn't look comforted. She turned on the TV but didn't look at it.

"Your dad said he didn't get promoted, that's different than getting fired," I tried again. "My mom's been at the Royal Bourbon Hotel for, like, ten years and I don't think she's ever been promoted once." Both she and her sister looked at me then, and I saw that comparing her family to mine wasn't helping. But I desperately didn't want her to be sad. "Do you want to play Crazy Eights?" My mom had taught us a few weeks ago and we were pretty obsessed.

"I don't know," she said.

But I was already up. I knew where they kept their playing cards, in the top drawer of the desk in the corner, along with all the stacks of bills and dead pens and old maps from the World's Fair. I found them and sat on the shag carpet at Gaby's feet. The cards were from a casino in Biloxi and pictures of poker chips flashed as I shuffled. "Come on. It will be fun. I destroyed you last time. Now's your chance to prove yourself."

She slid off the couch and sat across from me. "You did not. I won two out of three."

I already knew I was going to let her win. If there was one thing I was good at, it was finding ways to ignore grown-ups yelling in other rooms. Gaby had less practice. "If you win, I'll give you that pack of Now and Laters in my backpack."

"Grape?"

I nodded.

"You're on," she said, taking up her hand of cards and leaning forward. And then we were playing and the sounds of slapped cards and teasing and laughter filled the air between us like smoke, and Gaby didn't even notice when the timer for her brownies went off in the other room until her sister yelled at us that something was burning.

6

TWELFTH NIGHT 2004
THE FRENCH QUARTER

I almost ran to the Sugarlick. It felt like home, if home were a 1950s, mob-run bordello, and I entered it with a buzzy, breezy cheer. My actual apartment had a pretty similar decor so there was a comfort in it. Everything in here was shades of red. Christmas lights glittered around the mirror behind the bar, reflected in rows and rows of bottles. Chantal was presiding there, like a saint surrounded by stars, a bloodred hibiscus behind her ear that matched the walls. "I expected you earlier, Rosie," she said, handing me a soda with lime. "Those lazy coworkers of yours beat you here for once."

"I got distracted along the way," I said. "I stopped to talk to Jonah. You look nice."

She ran her hands over her curls. "Thanks. I had another fight with Ernie, so I did my hair to show that asshole what he's missing tonight."

"Men. What are you gonna do?" Then I laughed because it seemed like a dumb thing to say. I wasn't sure why, but everything seemed funny. Now.

"Sure," she agreed, but looked at me carefully from under an expertly arched eyebrow.

I wanted a glass of the shitty prosecco we drank for free at shows and I wanted it quickly before the last fiery trails of Jameson floated away. I took a sip of soda and the bubbles made me hiccup before I slid it to the side. "I think I'll just have what the girls are having, if you don't mind. It's been that kind of night."

She looked at me for just a second. I didn't want to have to explain myself, and then she shrugged, pouring me a small plastic cup of cheap champagne. "I hear that," she said, and a deep vein of unspoken sympathy thrummed between us. The sugar skull on her forearm also wore a blooming hibiscus. Chantal Morales had come to New Orleans from LA and dressed like the Mexican gangster she swore her grandmother used to be. She loved true crime stories and platform heels, and her whole look was both a celebration of and a fuck-you to every stereotype she had ever dealt with, and I was a little bit in love with her. She was nominally in charge of our troupe.

"Elsa's back there already. She's having some kind of issue with her G-string. Maybe you can help her with it. And Tammy has a head cold, but I made her a hot toddy. She says she can make it through. And I don't know where Becca and Colleen are. Probably shooting up somewhere. Glad we're keeping on brand as the Quarter's most ragtag burlesque." She flicked invisible dirt from her spotless black cardigan, buttoned just at the neck and embroidered with two swallows. "And I assume you're doing some batshit performance art tonight as usual?"

"I wouldn't say my routines are batshit," I offered. "Eccentric, maybe." One of the ways I had been dealing with my crushing shame of having dropped out of college was by basing my acts around famous women of history. Things didn't have to be so clear-cut, right? Success or failure, education or stripping. I thought if I could combine the two, I would maybe be forging a new path, but when I tried to explain this to my mom all she muttered was *all that private school tuition, for fuck's sake*, and we dropped the subject. She didn't really mind. All this Quarter nightlife was why she had stayed in New Orleans in the first place.

The first performance I had done was as a nineteenth-century Russian nihilist girl with a bearskin coat and blue stockings. The whole act had ended with a papier-mâché bomb that exploded glitter all over me when smashed. It went over like gangbusters, although I think that was because everyone thought I was doing Natasha from *Rocky and Bullwinkle*. When I explained myself, I tended to get a lot of blank looks, but I didn't care; it all made sense in my head. I had been planning on doing Florence Nightingale next, but then once Ida had started to weaken, during those last three weeks of medicines and vet visits, I lost my enthusiasm for nurses. Instead I bought piles of black fabric. I bent over the slow pinning and stitching of black fringe and velvet, sequins mounting in slow, laborious, glinting rows, while she watched me from her pillow in the corner as if she knew I was weaving her shroud. And I knew that she knew, and we sat and waited for the inevitable together in silent communion, the house reeking of boiled chicken and dog piss.

"Anyway, tonight, it's just black," I answered. "That's my whole concept. Black and some ostrich feathers."

"What, like a vampire?"

"No."

"Are you sure you don't want to throw on some fangs? Tourists eat that shit up."

"Nope. Just like a lady in mourning." I didn't feel like elaborating.

She was cutting up more limes. "That'll do, I suppose. As long as you think a bunch of medical supply salesmen will go for it. I think that's the convention in town this week. Either that or psychoanalysts. *They* might be into it. They probably like gloomy shit."

I looked around. "Audience approval might not be much of an issue."

She sighed. "Yeah, it's pretty quiet. There's a Flaming Skulls show later, so I'm hoping maybe some of the guys will stop by here first." She waved off discussion about the crowd with the lack of concern that made her so pleasant and so unremunerative to work for before returning to her previous thought. "It's cool. I like your weird acts. I think it keeps us authentic. Some of those old Bourbon Street girls came up with some pretty nutty stuff."

"I think my landlady used to dance with a parrot."

"If only any of you were talented enough for animal acts," she said wistfully.

"I think she used to have it whistle Dixie and make racist jokes."

"Oh right." She adjusted her cardigan again over the bright swirling floral of her dress and resumed cutting. A bright citrus smell filled the air and her knife made decisive little whacks on the cutting board. "There's always that." Eventually she shrugged. "So long as it all ends in pasties, I don't guess anyone cares very much."

I liked being around Chantal. Nestled under her wing, I felt like I became more of the same kind of girl she was. Fearless, hard-knuckled. With her, here in this bar, I was a performer. I was part of the fabric of the place. I belonged unquestionably. So many of the things I had been trying to figure out just seemed to matter less when I was back inside the red walls of this bar. Most of the people I met here hadn't been to college, but they all seemed plenty smart and everyone was broke. People like Jonah or Chantal, who read about history and watched old movies because they were weird and interesting, liked to hold forth on barstools. Gaby had treated college like the fucking center of the universe, but here I felt vindicated. Here I wasn't a failure, I was just a girl who could hold her liquor and look sharp doing it. Being a regular at a bar offers the most profound kind of comfort. Sometimes I came here in the afternoons when Chantal was working. When the summer sun was blistering outside, so bright it took my eyes a minute to adjust to the soft cool shadows of the bar, the open door cutting a bright pane of sun on the floor. I would sit on a stool and drink beer, colder than anything seemed possible after the muck of humidity outside. Everything had the calm of a faintly remembered dream and I had never felt safer, more at peace anywhere in my life.

It was funny, but my mom had also hung out here. In the '70s when she spent all her time chasing the artists and musicians of the Quarter. It had a different name then, but it was the same bar. It's remarkable how spaces carry on their own lives in this town. Someone has probably been drinking gin at this address for three hundred years. *I can't believe you kids hang out at the Old Black Cat*, she had laughed when I moved back and started dancing. But I didn't like talking about it with her.

"So, how's life?" Chantal asked, not looking at me but wiping her nose with the back of her wrist as she kept slicing. "You've got a little bit of a vibe tonight."

I didn't feel up to confessing my sorrows again. It seemed

pointless to keep unearthing all that misery, especially now when I had champagne in front of me. "Sometimes a girl just needs a drink." It had a delicious tang, battery acid with a lingering finish of apple Jolly Ranchers.

"Champagne for my real friends, real pain for my sham friends," she said in return. A lime slid away from her and she disappeared behind the bar to retrieve it. She rose back into view, hibiscus first. "The last guy I dated actually had that tattooed on his leg. And when I tell you that was the most original and well thought out one that he had, you can just imagine. And you thought Ernie was bad."

"I never said anything about Ernie. I mean, at least he can fix your car."

"Don't you patronize me. You have your way of making your feelings known," she said, but she grinned as she threw the dirty lime in a graceful arc into the trash can at the other end of the bar. "Anyway, time for you to get backstage and get all that Elvira drag on or whatever. And see if you can help Elsa with that G-string. Hold it together with chewing gum if you've got to. This show ain't legal if her bottoms fall off."

"I'll try." I started toward the stage door on a current of champagne and elation. I loved Chantal. I loved the Sugarlick. I loved performing. Onstage everything melted into bright, shining action. I didn't have to think onstage, I didn't have to worry. I couldn't be too much. I didn't have to constantly modulate all the nerve-racking increments of interacting with other people. I was free. And finally, Jonah would see it, this wonderful version of myself. Everything was under control.

Backstage was the usual frenzy before a show. Tammy was kneeling in front of Elsa's butt, trying to safety-pin a broken strap of her G-string. Colleen was squinting in the mirror applying a fake eyelash while Becca was on her hands and knees looking for a dropped earring. Ostrich feathers shook with the girls' movements, beads rattled. Sequins snagged fishnets and scratched the delicate skin of underarms as bras were clipped and hooks fastened, all to the high enthusiastic chatter of already-tipsy Southern women. "Oh good, you're here. Help." Becca pulled me down next to her on the floor. "I can't find it anywhere, looks like this." She turned her head to show me a large rhinestone hoop and I began fumbling across the filthy carpet with her, looking under the piles of street clothes left in puddles where they had fallen.

"Has anyone seen a set list yet?" Elsa was trying to watch Tammy's movements over her shoulder. "All I know is that I'm not first. Who's first?"

"I am. Shut up, you're making me nervous." Colleen sighed and pulled off the lash she had just applied in order to try again. "These fucking things. I mean, look at how much my hands shake." She held up the feathery lash, trembling in her pale fingers.

"Come here," Elsa commanded, "I'll do it." Colleen obediently rose and stood in front of Elsa, with her eyes closed handing over lashes and glue.

I found Becca's earring and we both tried to take Colleen's place at the mirror, but since I was further behind in getting ready, Becca ceded it to me. I watched them all in the reflection of the glass, their bodies glowing in the harsh fluorescent light of our dressing room. Not for the first time, I envied the shitty men that would take possession of these beautiful shapes later in the night. We made such a lovely display in our feminine variety, from plump Elsa to rail-thin Colleen. There was something so freeing in this common nudity. It made me love my body in a way I never had before when it stopped feeling so secret, this thing I had to hide, shown only to select partners with great ceremony and waiting for their judgment. Now I stripped down with the rest of these girls and in our bored community of female bodies, the casual backstage practicalities of professionals getting ready for a show, I felt at ease. And then later onstage when I bared myself to everyone, it was like I had pried that moment of judgment away from any one man in particular to men in general, and therefore no one really. I set the terms, I announced myself an unquestionable object of desire. And they just accepted it. There are very few places in this world where you get to decide the terms. Not like you do onstage. I hurriedly pulled parts of my costume out of my bag and slid out of my high-tops to finish the process of transformation. I felt as sleek as a snake shedding its scales.

The lights came up. A trumpet started high and then crawled into the plaintive registers. The call was sharp, a demand that slid into desire and ended with an entreaty, which I felt at the base of my jaw. A drumbeat began quietly. I moved my hips, but only barely, and the ostrich plumes on either side of my waist began to sway. Bundled into bunches, when I pulled them from their snaps, the velvet of my skirt would split down the middle, and then I could swing them, two feathery scepters trailing streamers, or fling them to the ground. But that came later. Now I stood alone in the spotlight. I felt the audience beyond the stage, drawn in by the intimate hesitancy of my first few movements, a calculated shyness. Then I let them wait. Jet beads hung from my bra and at each small movement of my hips, they trembled and bounced against my skin. The drumbeats passed, tension mounted along the side of my rib cage and crept across my breasts, arousing, but impersonal like a cool breeze. If, beneath my bra, they weren't

caught in rhinestones, immobilized by spirit gum, I knew my
nipples would rise. I held the pose one more second, drawing in a breath like a diver about to jump, and then because
I was good at this, I waited another beat. More instruments
crashed into the music and I broke my pose, striding across
the stage, high heels cracking time on the plywood floor.
Relief rose from the darkness, cresting over the stage. It had
begun. I gave them a smile—triumphant, exhilarated. They
recognized its sincerity, and they loved me.

I moved ahead. The act passed quickly once it started, a
blur of action. I slinked out of my skirt. One of the clumps of
feathers caught a gust of wind from somewhere and when I
flung it into the air, it fluttered just into the darkness. I would
have to remember to go get it after. You would be surprised
at the way people would try to keep things that slither into
the audience. I dropped to my knees. I leaned back, my hips
jutting forward as if an invisible lover was pulling me toward
him. But there wasn't anyone and tomorrow the muscles of
my thighs would be sore. I tilted my head far back until long
fake curls brushed the ground. My arms extended at my sides.
I leaned back and pulled myself upright, then again, back and
forth, a pantomime of apprehending and resistance. Kneeling,
I could suspend myself with misleading ease. I swayed unsup-
ported, graceful but unbalanced, like silent movies, someone
leaning too far into an invisible gale. I dropped my hands to
the heavy beaded fringe around my hips. A pause, a wide-eyed
look of innocence, and then I ripped my belt off and flung it
into the air. I could see it whip in slow circles overhead and
hoped I had thrown it far enough that it wouldn't land on me.
It was small but heavy and the beads hurt. I dropped to the
ground, flat on my back, my knees wouldn't do this forever.
Splayed, flattened, I felt an uneven nailhead in the floor that

I hoped wouldn't snag my fishnets when I got up. I didn't stay long, the gesture was one of such surrender that you couldn't let them savor it, or the disinterest that followed possession would set in, the suspicion that I had played all my cards. In one fluid motion I pulled myself up with my thighs, drew my ankles behind and underneath me, and without using my arms, pushed myself to my feet with those mysterious reserves of strength of a young female body.

I could relax a little—all of the perils of the act had passed and came off successfully, hooks that could stick, beads that could tangle, hems stepped on. Now the air was cool against my bare skin. I rotated my hips in slow wide circles letting the rest of my body follow until I was facing the back of the stage. Hands clasped overhead, my shadow was a figure eight against the red velvet behind me. I rolled my hips down to one side and stopped short at the crest of the arc. Then to the other. The fringe echoed each halt in momentum, swinging from side to side just below the curve of my G-string. The audience had gotten very quiet; the hooting that followed each lost article of clothing had faded away. They were wait-ing. And I knew they were waiting. In the distance I caught sight of myself in the mirror behind the bar. I marveled at my body like that of a stranger, round and smooth, glow-ing and desirable against the dark emptiness of the stage. The music grew more frenzied and I got more deliberate. I slowly reached around and unhooked my bra. The straps slid off my shoulders. Pressing the velvet cups to my chest, I turned around with the same slow gyrations. A raise of the eyebrows, an unspoken challenge, and I tossed the bra over-head. My rhinestone pasties shattered the spotlight, casting hundreds of bright slivers on the walls and ceiling of the dirty little club. I stood in a puddle of black fabric and feathers, the rise and fall of my breath so visible, the bones and muscles of my chest exposed, while applause and desire rolled over my pale, goose-pimply flesh. I was perfect.

The great thing about burlesque was that it didn't end when I left the stage. When I changed out of my costume and back into my jeans and sneakers, I moved through the crowd, beaming, electric, filled with the magnetism of so many eyes reflected back over me. My hair and makeup were too much trouble to take off backstage and I liked leaving this reminder for a while that I was different, special. Sometimes this intoxication lasted all night and I could spend hours in a swirling haze of confidence. I laughed too much, I responded to jokes too quickly. I could perform this brighter version of myself until I got home, pulled off my eyelashes, and unclipped the wigs and pins from my head.

The room had filled up a little as Chantal had promised. Rockabilly guys stood in clumps, arms crossed over their chests, frowning in carefully maintained masculinity, following me with their eyes. A table of blonde girls with ponytails and expensive watches stopped me as I passed by. "Oh my God, you were so awesome." One wearing a sweatshirt with Greek letters on it grabbed my arm. They were all drinking vodka cranberries, and I thanked them, trying to suppress the proprietary feeling I always had when Tulane girls came downtown. Jesus, what a crowd. I couldn't wait to make fun of all of them with Jonah. He would know in that unspoken way we had between us. He would just know that even though all these people were here, I had been dancing just for him. I looked around and caught Chantal's eye instead and she blew me a kiss to compliment my performance, so I headed to the bar, still searching. He was usually easy to spot, the particular slope of his posture, the narrow hunch of his shoulders. I didn't like to admit to myself how well he was inscribed in my memory.

It was strange to think, but by now Jonah and I had technically known each other for years, ever since I was an underage seventeen-year-old, just dipping my toes in the filmy grease of French Quarter bars, their specific blend of punks, weirdos, hipsters and addicts. That final year of high school, when my college applications were done and my tests all passed, I'd started coming here, alone, the atmosphere of unruly revelry slipping onto my shoulders like a favorite sweater. Gaby was panicking about getting into college, and had become a little distant, a little short-tempered, and the punks and losers I found in these bars offered a different, simpler companionship. Easy, comfortable, homey, we liked the same bands, wore the same clothes, it required no effort. And there was Jonah. Always around. Whom I watched from a distance. I wasn't interested in his handsome dereliction then, I was leaving. I was going north to start fresh, to make something of myself, and I was going to leave behind my mom, her ways, this haunted town, the hopelessness that sometimes felt like my birthright.

But things didn't turn out like I had planned. And it turned out I came back. I came back even to the same fucking bar my mom used to drink at. I ran into Jonah here one evening. After a flicker of surprise, he just raised his chin in greeting. "Welcome back." I had never even thought he had noticed me before. But he had. He had seen me all along and he knew, knew I would be coming back. And in the special way that this town accepted failure, the way the stagnation parted slightly and welcomed you in as though you'd never left, I was home. And grateful. We understood each other.

We had found each other. I could have him for as long as I kept drinking. It seemed fair.

But I still didn't see him tonight, so I ordered a beer and sat at the bar. Chantal was too busy to talk so I lit a cigarette and smoothed my hair, happy that I looked so good. Happy that all I had to do was wait. Happy that beer was delicious and that every time I had a show it was like releasing one long exhale I had been holding. Maybe Gaby was right. Maybe I was a drunk.

Our last fight had been about that, here even, at the Sugarlick, fittingly while we were both wasted. It had caught me by surprise, Gaby was so rarely judgmental with me. I wasn't ready for how raw, how angry she had seemed. Getting drunk was something we had always done together, had fun with. There was always booze to be had at my house without my mom noticing and Gaby often allowed herself to be persuaded. I could see her now giggling on the laminate floor of my bedroom, SunnyD and vodka in a repurposed Slurpee cup. *Girl, don't touch my hair. Stop. You're going to mess it up.* I used to take such pleasure in teasing her, pretending I was going to rumple those laboriously set curls. Our world of number 2 pencils and Jolly Ranchers, mean girls and petty humiliations, our childish lives, just became sweeter, easier, laced with the oily promise of vodka and oranges.

I winced and couldn't help but dig my phone out of my bag and check it again, just to make sure she hadn't called me back. I spent a fair amount of time in my head going over that fight, trying to understand what had gone wrong between us, but tonight the memory felt different, intense. These thoughts of Gaby came on me hard, undefended, and each moment of remembering felt like I was falling underwater, everything too vivid, too painful. Loss had made my mind sharp and also scattered, a "floating in time" feeling I didn't like at all. I took another sip of beer. And then another, and I looked around again for Jonah.

Chantal placed a new, fresh glass in front of me. "Have you seen Jonah tonight?" I asked her as casually as I could. She was already taking someone else's order and shook her head as she turned away. I scanned the room again, standing up on the rung of my barstool to see better, but there was no sign of that slouchy, ghoulish frame. Fuck. Jonah wasn't here.

I sat back down. I thought I had been so slick, but he had seen right through me and played a better hand. Of course he had. Oh God, it was mortifying. I could stop this ridiculous looking around. He wasn't here. I could feel the room empty of the one presence that could ignite my evening. Now that I was admitting it, I had known all along he wasn't there. A bar without your crush in it was just dead air. I had gone too far with my invitation earlier. I messed everything up. This feeling I had been trying to contain all evening, that quiet, latent hysteria was making me do all kinds of dumb things, make errors in judgment. I knew better.

I licked my lips and could feel my lipstick dry and cracking, and my nipples itched from the spirit gum that had secured my pasties. Onstage, Elsa was finishing her act, shaking a giant spray of tail feathers, a garish pink flamingo, and music clattered from the stage, an annoying climax of too many cymbals. The stupidity of it all made me cringe. It was still ridiculously early and my plans for the night had evaporated. What a fucking joke. I was a fucking joke.

I turned back to the bar. At least I had a full beer. At least I wasn't weathering this humiliation sober. I drank hard and then watched it settle. Cheap, delicious Pabst Blue Ribbon festering around the edges of the glass and following its own internal life of carbonation and frost. My thoughts got very dark for a moment, sinking down into purposeless, vengeful reflection about Jonah. What an asshole.

"So, hey, that was some weird shit." A voice spoke at my elbow and I glanced up. A smooth pompadour, a hard jaw, a dumb boyish expression. "I mean, you're smoking, but are you like all spooky or something? I want to buy you a drink, but do I have to watch out because you're going to get all witchy, like tell me you're a vampire or something? I shit you not, I have had two girls tell me, all serious, that they were 'undead.' What is up with this fucking town, you know?" This guy laughed and shifted as if dodging something, it wasn't clear what—these vampire women? But under his white T-shirt, his body was lean, and his arm rippled a little, the kind of muscles that didn't come from exercise or anything so unattractive as effort. Just the twisting armature of strong young men.

"I'm not."

"Yeah, no, that's cool and all," he continued, not listening. "You know, you have like your thing and it's kind of sexy, you know, artistic and whatever. So, hey, can I buy you that drink, 'cause you are way too hot to drink alone. It's a thing of mine, that I just can't resist a woman drinking Pabst Blue Ribbon." He stepped in closer and it didn't matter anymore what he was saying because I could feel the desire rolling off him in waves and it was so clear and straightforward, and I sank into it like a freezing person into warmth. I think I remembered reading somewhere that was also what it felt like when you froze to death, but what did I know? I grew up in New Orleans and this guy would suffice. I made room for him next to me and he waved for Chantal. He didn't ask my name but I let my weight lean slightly into his high, hard shoulder and he accepted it without a shudder.

7

I was waiting on my porch, leaning back in the flimsy white plastic chair, and looked into the empty planter on the windowsill behind me. It still had a little tag stuck in the dirt with a picture of blue flowers that said "Morning Glory" though there hadn't been any in years. Gaby pulled up in her boxy white car handed down from her older sister and honked even though she was looking right at me.

She adjusted her rearview mirror in a way that I always thought made her look like she was trying to act grown-up, but mostly I was glad just to be in a car. My mom got rides to work from her boss and I was stuck with the bus or my bicycle, unless I was with Gaby. "I cannot believe we are dragging our lazy asses Uptown again. I am so proud of us." Gaby glanced at me as she pulled into traffic.

"Better than studying," I answered.

"I was reading somewhere that regular exercise can even help with mental tasks. We do this enough, you can get that math grade of yours up."

"Shut up," I said. Gaby was steering with her knees as she

pulled her hair up into a high ponytail and I reached over to help. "I just hate geometry."

"Girl, I hate Sister Denise watching over my shoulder like I'm a shoplifter, but I still get my shit done." She sighed and took back the wheel. "You've always got one excuse or another."

"Oh my God, I'm here, doing this torture with you, aren't I?"

It was spring, and we were on our way to jog the paved running track of Audubon Park. City Park was closer to both our houses but in our recent attempt at taming the growing lumps and curves of our teenage bodies, the track felt more official. The Uptown ladies speed walking in pearls and sweating out last night's white wine, the rich Tulane kids in drum circles on the ground, the neat landscaping and broad two-mile path broken up with funny '80s pull-up bars and exercise stations, it just made us feel both fancy and athletic, two feelings we both found hard to come by, and considered worth the drive.

"Want some?" Gaby handed me a jar of bright green liquid as she looked behind her to change lanes.

"No." But I took it. "What is it?"

"Pickle juice. I heard on the radio it was good for cramps."

"This is pickle juice?" She nodded. "Gross. You're too trusting."

"And you should consider doing some research for yourself. I'm sick of having you lap me because of these stitches I always get." She took the jar back and, unscrewing it carefully, took a sip. The car filled with the sour smell of brine. She made a face and then shrugged and replaced the cap, tucking the jar between her legs as she drove. "It's not that bad." We had both been surprised to discover that I was strangely good at running, easily falling into a fast but steady pace, and I think it got on Gaby's nerves. She was used to being better than me at things. And she had just started stressing about her thighs, or at least complaining about them a lot, and this drove her to keep exerting herself in ways I couldn't imagine bothering with.

The windows were down and the breeze spun in and, as we hit the fancy houses of St. Charles Avenue, azaleas surrounded us in big fluffy mounds of hot pink and coral. New Orleans was as warm and soft as a kiss. "Do you think we will miss it here when we go away to college?" I asked, holding my hand out of the open window and letting my fingers flutter in the wind.

"*If* you go away to college."

"Oh my God, my mom would kill me. There's no way with all the work we are doing that either one of us gets stuck here."

"I mean, I think I'll probably come back at some point. I want to be close to my family. Maybe after graduate school I can come back and set up a private practice here."

"You really will be such a good psychiatrist."

"I spend enough time listening to your problems," she agreed.

I started to argue, but then changed my mind. "Okay, fine." I rested my head against the door to feel the breeze in my face. I couldn't wait to get to the park, to feel that wonderful rhythm of my heart and lungs, my whole body taking flight and moving without even thinking about it. Just breath and blood and the smell of grass rising up in the damp air. I didn't have to worry about my grades or college applications or the rising feeling I had been having lately that none of it mattered, a crushing ambivalence that was making it hard to do even the simplest things. Sometimes I just stayed in bed all weekend, alone in the house with the blinds drawn, Ida asleep on my belly, feeling thick and heavy and unable to do much of anything. These runs with Gaby were the only times I'd felt alive this year. *Jogging?* My mom had been mildly horrified. *Don't you want to take up dance or something at least?*

"It's making me gag, every time I watch you take a sip of that stuff," I said to Gaby finally.

She waved the jar in my direction. "You're just worried. Watch out, girl, Gabrielle Parker is coming up from behind." She wagged her head at me and her short ponytail shook. "Oh, that reminds me. I got us something to get pumped. There was a *Rocky* marathon on TBS last weekend, and I got inspired."

"I'm so jealous that you have cable."

She popped a cassette in the tape deck. "Eye of the Tiger" started pounding through the car and I hollered my approval over the synthesizers. She was tapping her finger on the steering wheel and singing along to the first verse which I didn't know. When the chorus arrived, I couldn't help punching the air and singing too.

"Fuck yeah, Apollo Creed, baby," Gaby said, turning up the volume.

"Didn't he lose?" I yelled over the music.

"Now, hold up." Gaby hit Pause and turned to look at me in the sudden silence of the car. "No, he did not."

I laughed at her seriousness. "Are you sure? I've never actually seen the movie, but it's called *Rocky*, not *Apollo Creed*."

She kept looking back at me as she turned into the park and stopped the car. "Isn't that some shit? It *is* called *Rocky*, and he fucking lost the fight."

"I don't think that can be right," I said. "That doesn't make sense. I feel like I've seen him, like, holding up his arms like he just won."

"Girl, one of us has seen this movie quite a few times and one of us hasn't, now…" She paused.

"Okay—" I shrugged "—whatever, I don't care who won. Put the song back on."

"I just think it matters," she said, but after a few seconds just staring at the tape deck, she turned it back on and soon we were both lost, caught in the pounding momentum of the silly pop song, as the mansions of Uptown stood sentinel around us and the sun shone on the live oak trees and the glorious noise kept us laughing in the shared exhilaration of a loud, loud song.

I leaped out of the car, excited to be outside and moving. Gaby had to deal with a blonde lady and a jogging stroller who was yelling at her about her parking or something, saying she needed a permit, which wasn't true. But eventually she extricated herself. "Lord, I need this right now," she said.

"Me too," I agreed, and after a few peremptory stretches, we took off together, in step, gliding fast across the pollendusted asphalt.

"I just think it's fucked up that you could think that Rocky won that fight," she was still muttering, frowning slightly to herself. I didn't know what to say about it anymore so I let her lap me and congratulated her later on the remarkable effects of the pickle juice.

8

TWELFTH NIGHT 2004
IRISH CHANNEL

When I rolled away from him and hung off the bed to rummage in my bag for a cigarette, it took me a minute to place the smell—pleasant, like soap and hair polish. Oh yeah, Murray's. By now, I was pretty good at recognizing the smell of different pomades. The smell of a man, of his room, on the sheen of his pillows when I lay naked in the darkness of his bed; the odor that followed me when I left, clinging to my skin in a sticky residue of perfumed grease, these stayed with me much longer than faces or names. Murray's pomade had an acrid note, earthy and animal like petroleum and fresh sweat. Royal Crown is lemony and clean. DAX is powdery, almost feminine. They were all the smell of night and submission and unfamiliar sheets, and a certain kind of man whose slick surface and dumb availability allowed me a place to hide for a minute. Rockabilly guys were so easy to attract when you were a dancer. This was not the first time I had hid for a few hours in one's bed. And I was vaguely grateful that he had picked me up. How could I worry too much about Jonah when there was always another option, another guy, another grease-soaked bed?

He leaned back, hands behind his head on a red pillowcase that was stained with pomade. He looked good like this. The rolling underside of his arms where the curve of his bicep twisted down toward the hard side of his ribs was all muscles and strength but also kind of helpless like a rabbit hung upside down. "That was really weird," he said. Was his name Mike? I thought so. "Weird shit happens like that all the time to me."

We had left the Sugarlick quickly. Mike had seemed almost surprised at the ease with which he had pressed his case; I agreed before we had even finished our beers. But I was acting under a dark influence, a familiar feeling that pressed me toward anything that offered a moment's oblivion. What else was I going to do, sit around and think about how much Jonah had embarrassed me? How much I had actually been hoping he would come? Sex, like dancing, had an immediacy that pushed everything else into insignificance. Or at least for as long as it lasted.

I was hurrying us toward that end, steering his bulk out of the bar and toward his car from under the heavy weight of his arm, when some drunk, toothless man with a hard, bony face started pointing at Mike and yelling, "He's a fucking ghost. That was me. I'm not dead. You're not real. I'm not dead yet."

"Okay, old-timer," Mike said, trying to gently move us past, but the man had the wide-eyed look of deep alcoholism and stood his ground.

I felt I was often running into people like this. It wasn't all that uncommon an occurrence in this town, but there was something about his insistence that I found especially unpleasant. I was starting to take it personally. He was getting in my way. "You're drunk," I said stupidly, and obviously.

He looked at me like I had just hurt his feelings, an exaggerated grimace of betrayal, but he stepped aside.

"Don't come back," he'd whispered to Mike as we passed. "You're not real. You're a ghost. You died in high school. You're not real." His voice echoed behind us in the street. It was chilling, running into an ancient mariner when you're just trying to get home for a hookup. He looked like he had been drinking rubbing alcohol or something.

"I mean, you do probably look just like he did fifty years ago." I found a pocket in my bag that I hadn't opened in a while and inside there was a small white half an oval of Xanax and a pair of earrings I thought I had lost. It was like a gift from my former self, left for a night I would surely need it. It scratched my throat as I forced it down. "I can see how you might be confusing to him if his brain is already pickled. You do look very old-fashioned."

He shook his head, unconvinced. "One time I came home and found a cat skull or maybe it was a rat or something, some kind of skull on a stick pointing right at my front door. Like some crazy voodoo stuff. I shit you not." He fiddled with the small silver medallion around his neck. "It was like hidden in the bushes across from my door. I just attract this kind of weird shit. St. Christopher protect me." Then he actually kissed the medallion, which is exactly like what I would expect someone that looked like him to do.

This boy was smooth and pale against the red sheets. Red sheets, how disgusting. I moved closer to him and he handed me a beer can for an ashtray. It wasn't empty, and I wondered how long it had been there. A sacred heart bristled on his arm. The lines were too bright and crisp to have been there for long. A little higher up, a naked girl rested against a palm tree. She had black hair and bangs and if you squinted, she looked like me. I was interchangeable. Wasn't that the point? How nice to be on a desert island somewhere, a palm tree against my back, the humid salty air a caress ruffling my hair.

He picked up another beer can, shook it, then felt the just visible line of condensation. "I think this is the one from earlier," he said. I took it and drank, relieved that it was still cold, and so was in fact probably relatively new. "I'm all kinds of superstitious," he continued with a dumb grin. A little sweaty, one strand of the lacquered crest of his hair hanging free, he looked kind of like a puppy and kind of like a juvenile delinquent. "Better safe than sorry, right?"

He didn't wait for my answer and rambled on about other brushes he'd had with the occult, all of which made it sound like he was maybe a victim of recurrent practical jokes. Although maybe it explained his anxiety around witchy women. He had a picture of Johnny Cash on his wall, and I looked at it while I waited for the pill to kick in and cover me in the smooth warmth I was waiting for, grateful to be here in this apartment that wasn't mine. Johnny looked just a little uncomfortable, smiling for the publicity photo, one arm awkwardly propped on his bent knee, and I thought about his crazy voice. I always envied singers. To be able to put heartbreak into sound like that and release it out into the world seemed like such a magical gift. No wonder my mom was such a sucker for deadbeat musicians. How did emotions become things of beauty like that? These strange creatures that shredded you on the inside and made you unable to behave like normal people. People that go to college and get their degrees and move on with their lives. I was going to be that person. I was going to pay my bills and live in some clean, northern town where everything made sense, and Ida would have a yard to play in and I would do yoga or something. I was supposed to be this upstanding citizen that my mom was so determined that I be, even if she was a total mess of dumb men and poor choices. But instead I had come back. Instead I was here listening to guys like this.

"I even tried, like, sprinkling some holy water around, like they told us to in school," Mike droned on. "Have you ever had weird shit like that happen?"

When I turned to him again, his eyes were floating around in his face and as I looked closer, I saw with deceptive clarity that little roman soldiers in crested helmets were marching toward his jawline. He moved his head, and I saw it was only a shadow, but now I was pretty sure what I took was half an Ambien and not a Xanax. Maybe that was even better, and I settled in for the ride. "No. I'm Jewish," I said, maybe not exactly to the point.

He started, and then embarrassed, tried to cover it up by grabbing my arm with an affectionate grasp that he didn't know what to do with and so awkwardly shook my arm for a minute. "What? That's a new one. You must not be from here."

"No." I thought I wasn't slurring, but it was hard to tell, and who cared anyway. "There are Jews in New Orleans. You've probably even met some before. I mean, I went to Mary Immaculata but my mom is Jewish and that's what counts."

He shook his head. "No, I'm sure I would remember if I had met one. I'm pretty sure they wouldn't let them into a place like Immaculata. That's a good school. Those girls are good girls, like from good families. They were out of my league."

His certainty was so dumb it made me smile. And he had a point—it was weird that I went there. It's not my fault that parochial schools were so popular here. It's not my fault my

mom abandoned her hometown and her nice Jewish upbringing to live in this Catholic city and run around like Nico from
the goddamn Velvet Underground until she got knocked up.
I didn't ask for any of this. But I suppose there were consola-
tions everywhere, and it looked like I had succeeded in finding one tonight. He sat up, watching me, arms resting on his
bent knees, so lean and hard and pretty. I gave him maybe six
more years of beer before this was lost forever but for now,
he was majestic, like a gladiator at rest. And for the moment
he was mine and I was safe here in those hard arms anytime
I wanted. His attention and the drugs were like a nest that I
could curl up in and stop the terrors of possibilities. I didn't
have to ask why this guy was the only person I could turn
to on this night of all terrible nights, because now it didn't
matter. He was here, and that was all that counted, and he
thought I was so hot. A man would do anything for a girl he
thought was hot. There was no safety like that of being de-
sired. He practically had me tattooed on his arm and this felt
filled with an indistinct significance. "She looks like me." I
pointed at his hula girl.

"She does," he agreed and made her dance by tensing his
muscles.

I watched her sway and wobble, hypnotized by the motion
of ink and skin, this girl's flushed pink cheeks and smile so
innocent, like a friend I wanted to giggle with and whisper
secrets in her tiny cupped ears. I felt like we already knew
each other. She was warm to my touch, and soft.

"Hi, sweetie," I said to her softly and I was going to share
more with her, I had so many things to tell her, but he gave
me a funny look and I stopped, suddenly aware I was sliding
over regular parameters of sober behavior.

He decided to ignore me and returned to our previous

conversation. "It's cool though. I'm cool with that," he said mysteriously. He paused for a minute and then tried again. "Even my skinhead buddies will admit that Jewish girls are hot. Pretty green cat eyes like you have."

"What?" I asked. "Yes," I added, confused. "Thank you?" He stroked my arm and I wasn't really sure what was going on anymore unless I was about to get involved in a weird Nazi sex thing. But as I looked up from his tattoos, I noticed those little soldiers again, moving around behind him in the shadows of the trees outside. They marched in perfect formation, such discipline, such force of numbers, the glory of an empire that doesn't know it's already dead.

When he climbed on top of me again, he hurt me. My arm was stuck behind my head, but his shoulder was leaning hard on me and I couldn't figure out how to free myself. There was an inevitability about it, his weight, the pain, the radiant heat from his body that sank over me. A patch of moonlight sliced the wall near his closet, and it took me a while before I noticed Johnny Cash had been standing there the whole time looking at me with that mournful gravity of his and I could tell he knew how inevitable this all was. That actions, once started, must follow their own sorrowful course until they stopped. He was humming "Streets of Laredo." I always liked that song and I asked him why, and what else he could tell me of that sad, young cowboy as cold as the clay.

"Can you stop?" The face above me suddenly came into focus. I had forgotten about this guy. "You're talking to all kinds of people that aren't here and it's kind of freaking me out."

"Sure." I nodded to appease him and as his attention wandered away again, I smiled to myself and sank back into the community of ghosts that was keeping me company in all the shadows of the room.

9

DECEMBER 24, 1997
BROADMOOR

I was trying to wrap the lights around our Christmas tree. I had grown in the past year and I could finally look down on the top of the fake tree that usually lived in a box under the couch.

Mom was in the kitchen flipping through a tattered copy of *River Road Recipes.* "How can they not have a recipe for brandy milk punch in here? If there's one thing I'm betting the Junior League knows, it is alcohol and parties, and it seems to me that brandy milk punch is the quintessential combination of the two."

Ida kept pouncing on one end of the strand of lights and then dashing away with it in her teeth, a movement that threatened to knock over the tree every time. "Mom, I need help. Can you grab Ida?"

"Ah, here it is," she said. "Nutmeg? Who the fuck has nutmeg lying around?" I could hear cabinets opening and shutting and the sound of a stopper pulled from a bottle.

"It's just us, who cares? Come help me with this tree."

"We want to be festive," she called. "It's the night of our very own mother-daughter Jewish Christmas."

"We don't even do anything," I mumbled.

"But we do nothing with style," she insisted. She was wearing a blue-and-white caftan that she called her Hanukkah robes even though it was covered in Chinese dragons. She came in and handed me a teacup. "Cheers. Now, where's that cassette?" she asked, riffling through a big milk crate where she kept all her tapes.

I gave up on the tree and curled up on the couch drinking the sweet milky concoction. Fifteen-years-olds could drink in Europe, she always said when anyone asked. *And Rosie's the most mature person in this house.* I wasn't going to argue.

She found what she was looking for and soon Elvis was crooning carols from our boom box. "'Blue Christmas,' otherwise known as Hanukkah," she laughed. She did this every year in a series of rituals that kind of drove me crazy. "Oh come on, sweetie," she said when I groaned. "This is our thing."

"I would rather just get a bunch of presents."

"Presence is presents. Someday you will look back on this and think what a wonderful unmaterialistic holiday of togetherness I invented. Anyway, you know I have to work tomorrow. And now, tarot!" She pulled the deck from her pocket and sat next to me on the couch. Her long silky sleeves kept getting in the way as she tried to lay out the cards. She had to keep reaching up toward the ceiling to puddle the sleeves around her armpits before they slid back down again. She took a big sip from her own teacup and set it on the floor next to us. "Okay, this frowning lady here is the sullen teen who can't wait to get out of the house and start paying all her own bills for some reason." She flipped another card. "And this—" she looked at it "—um, is the upside-down donkey." Making up tarot was one of my mother's favorite jokes.

"Which means the tarot reader is an ass," I giggled. The punch was very strong but went down very easy, and I started to feel festive in spite of myself.

"For that, you can be the one to rewind the tape."

I did and after a brief whir, "Blue Christmas" started over again. It wasn't such a bad song. Even if she did make us listen to it all night practically. "Come back and let me finish your fortune," she said, wrapping her fingers around the teacup before setting it down by her feet again. "I think this next card means you're going to marry a sailor in the next year. Either that or maybe just go for a swim?"

This and Mardi Gras were our best nights together. Mardi Gras day we always did our own thing. I went off with Gaby, begging rides from her sister to the parades and getting drunk on beers bought by older guys. Who knew where my mom went, likely doing something similar. But then we'd meet again at night on this couch, both drunk and tired out from the sun and the excitement. We'd put on our pajamas and watch the meeting of the courts on TV, Ida snoring belly up between us, the procession of debutantes bowing and curtsying on-screen as the night drew in and the city fell silent around us.

"Mom, Ida's drinking your punch," I yelled.

She leaned over and shooed the dog away from her teacup. "I don't blame you, girl, it's pretty delicious."

"Oh my God, Mom, is she going to be okay? Dogs aren't supposed to have alcohol."

I rushed to pick her up, but Ida just looked at me, tilting her head curiously and blinking. "She'll be fine. I knew a dog once that used to drink beer all the time." She went to refill her teacup, robe fluttering behind her.

"You never take anything seriously," I yelled after her, really angry.

I set Ida back down and watched her, worried. After a few minutes she started to lean over a little and then caught herself and straightened up. Then she did it again. Then she yawned, making a little squeak and showing me the tender bridge of her palate, and then curled up and went to sleep. I was terrified that she might stop breathing, so I sat down and held her in my lap. She rolled onto her back, pink loins exposed, and fell into a deep, snuffling sleep, her head draped upside down over my arm. But at least I could see her ribs expand with each breath, and I knew she was alive. I carried her into my room and lay on my bed, curling up around her, and watched her tiny little snout hairs flutter with each exhale.

"What, we're done in here?" my mom called, disappointed. I didn't answer and pressed my cheek against the velvet curve of Ida's head, one ear transparent in the lamplight. A few minutes later our phone rang, and I knew she would be going out soon or some man would be coming over to laugh too much at her bad jokes, brandy milk punch dripping from a dumb moustache, bedroom doors closing with a hard bang.

I slid Ida down against my side so I could reach my bookcase. It was a night for *All Quiet on the Western Front*. The cover was missing, dog-eared, crunchy from being dropped in the bathtub, but it didn't matter. I started at the beginning like I always did but quickly flipped ahead. Hot, consoling tears began to drip down my cheeks. It could have been the punch, I guess. Ida sneezed hard in her sleep and a fine spray of droplets scattered across the page.

10

TWELFTH NIGHT 2004
IRISH CHANNEL

When I opened my eyes again, the red numbers on his digital clock had stopped dancing. Jesus, it was still early. Nights used to pass in the blink of an eye, a haze of laughter and chance acquaintances, the sun slanting around the blackened windows of a bar before it even seemed possible, time rising and bursting like an evanescent bubble. But not tonight. Impersonal hours kept to their own implacable rhythm. Or maybe a girl could just get a lot done when you shed your clothes at eight instead of ten.

I felt pretty rested from my nap though. I slid out from under a colorful arm and looked around to see if everything in the room had lost the sneaky animation of Ambien yet. For a moment everything was still, as if the posters and furniture and shadows hadn't been conspiring to make me feel like a crazy person, but then I noticed a small tremor, an unsureness around the outline of things, and if I turned my head too quickly, they started to blur again. But at least Johnny Cash had the empty smile of a stranger, which I found myself taking personally.

This guy, Mike something, rolled onto his back, his arm splayed out across his greasy sheets, chest rising and falling with a deep animal sleep that I watched enviously. I slept curled up on my side and often woke in the very same position, all the covers around me smooth and undisturbed. Which was oddly disheartening. I wanted to sleep with the loose ease of a large cat too instead of the tense, furtive rest of rabbits everywhere.

Even though I was pretty sure he wasn't the kind to notice, I snuck out quietly. I brought my clothes into the living room and got dressed between a Social Distortion poster and one with the lurching figures of *Romper Stomper* on it, again annoyed. If this guy was a skinhead, what was he doing wearing a pompadour? Wasn't that supposed to be the point of all these subculture badges, easy instant identification? How else were sad, roaming show girls supposed to pick out the bad apples and the racial purity guys from the Link Wray rock and rollers? I knew there was probably more crossover than I liked to admit.

If I wanted to fuck people with decent politics, I should probably just fuck hippies. But I hated marijuana and wanted all my songs to end after three minutes and how could you fuck someone who wasn't full of rage? Human beings were the worst. I guessed it was the pretending I couldn't handle. Even my shoulder which still hurt from this dimwit's fucking felt like a badge of honesty. The hate, the rage, the helplessness— what else did we have? There was a coffee maker on his kitchen counter with some cold coffee in it and I drank it straight from the carafe to clear my head. I wondered how much caffeine it would take to shake off just enough Ambien from my system. I mean, I didn't want to get too sober, but I didn't want to be stuck here waiting it out.

I noticed one of my shoelaces was wet, which was always a terrible sign in New Orleans. Who knew what disgusting effluvia it had been dragged through, but I tied it anyway and wiped my hands on my pants. I sank into his couch and just for a minute longed for home. My apartment tucked into its courtyard and hidden from the street, the windows gold and glowing broken up by the narrow mullions of the French doors that ran the length of our space. The torn Persian rug on the floor that Ida liked to sleep on, the ratty blue velvet armchair that groaned when I sat, stretching out a toe to rub the silky curve of her offered belly. The scent of orange water and vetiver that I could only smell when I walked in, a moment's fleeting pleasure before it faded into the oblivion of everyday breathing. Toast with honey, stacks of old books, their prices inscribed in faint pencil—two dollars, three dollars on the end papers—their fragile jackets tearing and fluttering to join the dust lining the corners of the room. The lullaby of dog snores. I wanted to go home. I wanted to go home to that apartment. That apartment didn't exist anymore. Not like that. Without Ida it was just two empty rooms. I could feel tears begin to well in my eyes, but the Ambien left me oddly disconnected to the process. It was kind of like watching a rainy gutter fill and overflow. I still didn't want to cry here. Not now.

Hanging around the place of a man you just fucked and wanted nothing more to do with was a recipe for despair. When I found my bag, I couldn't help but reach for my phone. I knew Gaby wouldn't call this late. It was a weekday. She had work in the morning. Her life was broken up into more reasonable blocks of days and nights, rhythms held together by responsibility and working hours. I hated this needy feeling. Standing in front of cupboards and hoping against hope that my mom had remembered to go grocery shopping, that I might open the door and see the shelves lined with all the snacks I saw advertised on TV even though I knew it would just be melba toast and canned olives. I hated this old, searing helplessness. I flipped the phone open anyway.

A text message: @sl were r u?

In my surprise, it took me a moment to decode. I wasn't much of a texter. Was it her? I didn't recognize the number, but then I didn't know her cell. Why would Gaby be at the Sugarlick? Why would she be waiting for me there? Had she somehow figured it all out? Did she remember I performed on Tuesdays and had come to find me? The ads for our show were in the listings in the back of *Gambit*—if she wanted to, it would have been easy to know where I was tonight. That kind of sounded like her actually, she was kind of a genius. In school she watched me struggle my way through math and science with a friendly exasperation. This was so like her, now that I thought of it. She always came through, *Saving my messy ass*, she used to say, sharing her lunch, getting her mom to give me a ride home from school when mine forgot me, letting me copy her notes. I knew I was right to call her. The sensation that she was coming to get me, that she would tell me what to do with this awful night, that I would be able to close my eyes and grab on to her, the size and shape and smell of her body, a hug that I could feel in the deepest part of my stomach made me close my eyes for just a second.

Then I quickly texted back. coming

The answer popped up almost immediately. can I watch ;)

I looked at the phone. That wasn't right.

Was it a wrong number? But what were the chances of someone being somewhere with the initials SL? That seemed too unlikely. It had to be for me. And then a thought occurred to me, but I recoiled almost instinctively. I wasn't going to be made a sucker twice in one night. But still, just maybe, I had to wonder, was this Jonah? Could it be? I didn't even think he had my number. I certainly didn't have his. Had he gotten it from Chantal? I actually had to close the phone again to think this through, trying to hold down an enormous relief rising in spite of myself.

If it did turn out to be from him, it wasn't just the text itself which seemed so monumental, an undeniable proof of interest, but almost more important, that he had to get my phone number. He would have had to ask someone else, a public admission of desire. That was serious. We had never actually spoken on the phone before—all our hookups had been preceded by an accidental meeting at some random bar. This private transmission from phone to phone felt a million times more intimate, the gesture was so personal, so impossible to deny. He couldn't pretend he was just hanging out or talking to a friend. This was intentional. This was deliberate. This was the equivalent of stepping forward into the line of fire. He wanted me. He liked me. He was letting me know. What on earth was he doing?

I opened the phone to read the message again, wanting to take my time, to make sure I hadn't missed any hidden meanings, any indications that this could just be a joke of some kind. He was at the Sugarlick. Why was he there now? Why hadn't he come before? Why stand me up and then do something like this? Was it strategic? If he had come to see me dance, he would have been just one in a room full of men wanting to fuck me. But now he had the upper hand. He liked games of control, dominance and submission. I looked at the message again as if it might tell me what I should do. He had only sent it a half hour ago. Ten thirty.

Then I realized. I was an idiot. I had forgotten to tell him it was an early show. We usually danced at ten.

He had come on time.

I let the golden pleasure of it roll through my body. Even this moldy apartment was momentarily transformed by this wave of joy, like the sun breaking through clouds. I was saved.

I typed, be there soon

He answered again quickly. The way one does when a phone is just sitting on a bar in front of you, waiting, alert, ready. l8r

I smiled. It was enough. A thread of hope. All I needed was the next stop, the next circuit, experience passing like falling dominoes. I could leave this place that smelled like unwashed sheets and the vinegar that Mike told me he had to douse his head in to cut the grease enough to wash his hair. Why was pomade so gross and yet made them look so good? It was some awful reverse natural selection. I could catch a bus back downtown and be there in half an hour, maybe less if I didn't have to wait too long. I needed change. Stupid New Orleans buses that didn't take dollars. I rummaged around a table by the door, found a bowl of keys and some coins. The bus cost a dollar twenty-five. I knew because I took it to work every day. I found five quarters, figured it was the least Mike could do, got my stuff and let myself out.

His building was built around a courtyard, one of those big old Victorian things that had been cut up all kinds of ways into apartments, and had weird eaves and extensions and balconies and stairs, all sagging and smelling of rotting wood. The brick steps down from his doorway were slick with mold and I almost slipped—Converse have the worst traction—and I grabbed on to his door frame and got a nasty scrape down the side of my hand. From where I stood, the orange bulb of the security light was almost blocked by the leaves of a huge Elephant Ear plant. A frog croaked softly somewhere, and electric things hummed, mysterious. I let myself out of his gate, the razor wire above trembling as it slammed shut.

I had no idea where I was, so I started for the corner to look for a street sign. I tried to gauge the safety of the street, although any street Uptown was not a great place to be walking alone at night. It looked the same as everywhere around here anyway. Pretty little shotgun cottages and big rambling mansions, some a little run-down, some in ruins, some with grand pianos in the windows. I figured I was in the lower Garden District, probably close to Magazine Street. I started trying to tell if I was on a black block or an Irish block, and then felt guilty about the impulse. I would look out of place either way right now. In this town, poor people just kind of ended up next to each other. No. Not quite. The divisions just got smaller and narrower, those Irish housewives of a hundred years ago hanging out their laundry wouldn't have stood for it otherwise. One block for us, one block for them. Those kinds of demographics stuck around here. People had their ways. Gaby lived in Gentilly with all the teachers and mailmen and police officers. I lived over by Broadmoor with the other teachers and mailmen and police officers. No black people lived on my block. No white people lived on hers. Now it seemed strange that we had never mentioned it to each other. I guess some things are just too obvious to bring up. And anyway, we didn't talk about stuff like that.

A car cruised by too slowly, the unhurried menace of a shark slicing through an unresisting ocean, and I ducked down behind a parked car so it wouldn't see me. I didn't have anything to steal, but still. While I was squatting there, watching a big palmetto bug move slowly along the curb, away from me, thank God, the posture reminded me of her. Gaby often peed on the side of the road when we were drinking in high school and it was such a funny contrast to her usual composure. I always cheered her on because I liked to see her be carefree and wild. When we were drunk, we were like two parts of a single organism, bound together in a haze of shared jokes and shared drinks. We finished each other's sentences. We followed each other to the bathroom. We knew intuitively that the rest of the world and everyone in it existed only to make us laugh, ridiculous people that lived in the cold chill outside of our friendship. We would have pitied them if they hadn't been so funny. I wanted to be getting drunk with her tonight so badly, it hurt. I pulled my jeans down and peed on the grass next to the curb, in her honor, not realizing till that moment just how badly I needed to go.

When the elation and relief, since I'd probably had to pee for hours, subsided, I noticed a dark spot in my underwear. I had a sudden lurch in my stomach. Had we used a condom? This was the kind of thing I was always doing that would have driven Gaby crazy. *It's time to grow up now, Rosemary,* I could hear her say. *Have some respect for yourself.* But after I ran my finger across my pussy, it came up shiny and dark. I exhaled. A circular for a grocery store was fluttering against the wheels of the car next to me and, for a moment, I considered stuffing it into my underpants but didn't. I stood up and went on with my search for the Magazine Street bus but moving now with a kind of delicate urgency as if by walking carefully and not jostling myself, I could somehow coerce the blood to stay inside me. The first night of my cycle was always pretty light. I had a few hours. At the intersection, one of the street signs was missing, but the other said Camp

Street, so whatever cross street I was on, I would hit Magazine in another block or two. At least I was close, and I kept slide-walking my way forward through the pretty streets and houses as a dog barked a loud, angry protest into the darkness somewhere.

The grocery on the corner was a beacon of fluorescent lights. They shone through the dense grill on the windows, lighting up the whole sidewalk, and I moved toward it like a moth. When I came out into the busier, broader expanse of Magazine Street, the world rearranged itself into an immediate and unexpected familiarity; I was less than two blocks from the lingerie store where I worked.

It was unsettling to be someplace so well-known and yet have it all look so strange. Daylight was different. Then, the whole street hummed. Skinny little kids from the projects, arm in arm, going to the corner grocery for snacks after school. Uptown moms on their way to antiques shops, big purses on their arms like shields, blonde and distracted, intent on the business of spending money, all in the same slacks and flats and blousy button-downs that made up their uniform of casual affluence. The skinny boys that worked at the burrito shop on the corner and played in bands and treated girls poorly when they ran into them in the days and evenings of mornings after. The noise and bustle and bikes and cars, all lit up by the swelter of the Southern sun. I was there too, flipping the pages of a magazine behind the counter in the cool shade of the store, where I spent too much of my paycheck every week, consoling myself for the hours of boredom in the caress of silk slips and nightgowns, taut across my body, bought with a discount and savored later in the solitude of my bed.

Mannequins floated in the windows of the vintage store across the street, strange, ghostly. A car honked, and a guy yelled something at me out of his window, and I decided not to linger here on the corner. We probably had some tampons at work. I had my keys. I might as well check.

The door creaked on the way in and I locked it again behind me. This block of shops was old, and everything in the buildings squeaked and sagged and leaked, threatening the expensive panties and bras that now took the place of whatever Irish groceries and dry goods it had been built for. The building gave all our bright-colored silks and feathers a strangely temporary look. No amount of paint or carpet could fully cover the lovely old gray walls and floor that seemed on the verge of reclaiming the space for some dusty past. I didn't want to turn on the lights; they would make the shop too visible to anyone passing outside. I could see well enough with the ambient light from the streetlamps that made a shadowy twilight. The big striped dressing room tent, the fainting couches and feather boas, all of our "immersive boudoir experience" as my boss called it, now in the dark looked like an abandoned circus. Ooh La Lounge was a ridiculous-looking place in the daytime as well, but now without Eartha Kitt and Dean Martin crooning, all these headless torsos cinched in corsets and dismembered hands waving rhinestone jewelry looked ghoulish. A shop at night has to be the stillest place on earth, besides maybe a graveyard.

Then I noticed the rolled-up bag of Doritos I left behind the counter earlier that day and, suddenly hungry, went to open them. Standing next to the register was a more familiar vantage, and as the store got a shade less strange, I sat on my usual stool, glad for the crinkle and crunch of chips. That had been my lunch of sadness earlier, a bag of Doritos and a Diet Coke. It was strange to think I had been here only eight hours before. It felt like a lifetime ago.

This afternoon I had organized the underwear drawers, refolding dozens of panties into tiny squares, finding relief from my growing despair about Ida in rows of neat, secretive creases. My manager Katie walked by and pretended to be in shock. "Damn, Rosemary, if you start actually working while you're here, we might have to start paying you more." Katie was blonde and normal. She cheerfully upsold the Uptown girls and debutante brides and I covered the hipsters and strippers biking up from Bywater, ready to spend their easy money. It was kind of satisfying to see that an appreciation for fancy bras could unite us all, otherwise so different, but then, that was the point of capitalism, wasn't it? Katie rolled her eyes when I said stuff like that and gave me Camel Lights and knew all the best sites on the internet for funny cat pictures. That afternoon had been slow, and she had tried to cheer me up using our POS computer to find pictures of overweight cats with funny misspelled captions. And it was then, looking over her shoulder—she smelled very distinctly of Aveda shampoo—at a cat that was expressing ungrammatical consternation at the too-small box she was trying to fit in, that I knew. Just all of a sudden, it washed over me with an icy clarity that it was time. I would have to go home that evening and in the few precious moments between my return home and my show, I would have to say goodbye to Ida.

It had been almost three weeks that she had been declining. Three long weeks of boiling chicken breasts to tempt her to eat and coating pain pills in peanut butter and holding her while she trembled, wrapped up in my old cashmere sweater. But she hadn't taken any food or water in two days. I was going to take her back to the vet, but she hated it so much and she already looked so weak and scared. It felt like such cruelty, and so I kept putting it off. But I knew she was suffering. Then, while Katie snickered, reading me silly captions in her bright, Southern accent, I felt an internal swelling, a boundless love for all these silly cats and a sense of the awesome responsibility it was to love something so much, and I knew what I had to do. I asked if I could leave early.

I realized I didn't want any more Doritos. I closed the bag and my stomach gurgled. Oh, where was Gaby? Mike hadn't been enough, distraction wasn't enough. I needed to tell someone. I needed Jonah. He was dark and strange. He liked me. He wanted to read books with me. He would have to tell me it was okay, that I had done the right thing.

Thinking of Jonah waiting for me at the Sugarlick, I didn't want to linger anymore. I went to the bathroom to look for a tampon and was annoyed to find an empty box until I remembered pretty clearly that I'd used the last one last month and forgotten to tell anyone or replace them. I washed leftover cheese dust from my fingers with rose-scented soap and moved to leave. On my way out, I pulled a length of receipt paper from the register and wrote a note that I wouldn't be in tomorrow. Wherever this night led, it would not have me out of bed and in kitten heels by ten in the morning. I deserved that much at least. My note would confuse the hell out of Katie when she opened the store, but who cared? I quickly left and locked the door and turned to breathe in the fresh diesel air of the street outside.

The impersonality of the bus stop made me feel a little better, until a truck slowed to a stop so the driver could yell obscene things at me. I decided to wait inside the corner store, where I would still be able to see the bus arrive.

A bell bounced from the top of the door, announcing me, and the store had the same smell of white bread and stale vegetables that they all seemed to, but I was glad to be in

the company of humans again. I nodded at the man behind
the register and took an Atomic Fireball. I unwrapped it and
sucked, stalling, pretending to search the shelves. Everything
was glistening cellophane and cold aluminum. I got a Coke
from the refrigerators. The guy at the counter was punching
in lotto ticket numbers as a woman in pink curlers was calling
them out. She ignored his growing hostility and calmly continued reading him the numbers she had written on a scrap
of paper hidden in her hand. I tried to smile politely but she
looked me up and down and turned away with the slightest
shake of her head. I blinked. One of my eyelashes was falling off, tilting into my line of vision, and I could tell by its
uneven weight that my hairpiece was crooked. The woman
was in pajamas with Tasmanian Devils on them, I thought
defensively, at least I was wearing clothes, but she and I both
knew her matched suit of faded flannel was infinitely more
respectable than whatever hot mess I was in.

I wanted to follow her home and see what her life was like
and whether she lived alone and whether she watched TV and
whether she would let me sit with her, drinking my Coke
and watching whatever it was she liked to pass the long, long
night. What color was her couch? Did she have any pets?
Were there report cards taped to her refrigerator, drawings,
a school picture of a son or nephew grinning through the gaps
of missing teeth, and would she tell me about them, and let
me hear the pride in her voice? And what thought had pushed
her out into this empty night, in her pajamas, to ask for these
specific lotto numbers? She gathered her tickets and the metal
bells on the door clanged after her.

The guy turned to me with a smile, obviously preferring
my company, still a little high on sleeping pills, to his usual
customers. "Bus? It's too late for you."

I shrugged, wanting to refuse his concern, unwilling to establish myself in his hierarchy. "No choice." I wondered what had brought him here, I guessed from Vietnam, to this corner grocery store in Louisiana where he stood deep into the night, angry and maybe afraid of the people he served.

"You wait in here," he said. "Not outside. It's too dangerous for you."

He was right, I didn't actually want to wait outside and so I grudgingly accepted his hospitality. "Thanks." I put my Coke on the counter and only then remembered with terrible regret that I didn't have any money. I had left the Sugarlick without my cut for the night and he was not going to let me buy a Coke with a maxed-out credit card. All I had were my stolen quarters for the bus. "I'm so sorry. Never mind. I don't have any money." I tried to speak around the Atomic Fireball that now felt like it took up my entire mouth and was making me drool bright cherry red. "I'm so sorry, I took this." I pointed to my mouth and swallowed hard, the cinnamon burned like fire. "I forgot."

He shrugged and made a wave that felt like a caress I didn't deserve. The back of his hand was crisscrossed with scars, faded but still pale against his skin.

"Thank you," I mumbled and hurried to put the Coke back, sick and embarrassed. I stood right next to the windows, as if by pushing myself right up against them I would somehow be using less of his generosity, and watched for the bus. I didn't want him to like me more than the lotto ticket woman or treat me differently, but I was glad he let me stay. Who knew how we ended up the way we had, and was there really anything any of us could do about it? The Deep South was a web that held us all.

A bus finally lumbered to the stop, creaking and squealing deliverance and I was on my way back downtown. Across from me a woman surrounded by rumpled shopping bags was muttering to herself.

It was a comfort to remember the Sugarlick didn't disappear when I left. It continued its strange liminal existence, a loose confederation of strangers and sometime friends careening on their separate paths of intoxication like charged atoms. I would find Jonah. That special fusion of two lost particles slamming into each other. That had been one of the worst parts about college. I got there and realized that I wasn't so special, just poor and socially awkward and, without Gaby, I was alone in a sea of strangers. In college when I got drunk, I had nowhere to go and nothing to do, and took to walking the wooded paths through campus, unused to the deep, creepy silence of the countryside. Even the plants felt different, high sharp pine trees and the cold inky heights of a starry sky. I was so homesick for the warm night and the humidity and light pollution that kept even the darkest nights a gentle purple. If you only wanted to go back to the place you'd spent your whole life planning to leave behind, well, then you realized that there really wasn't anywhere for you in all this whole dumb world. And then the drinking got sharp. And lonelier. And I started stealing water glasses from the dining hall and smashing them on the rocks to watch the blood seep out from my closed fist. And I thought about Gaby, back at home, paying in-state tuition and living at her mom's and the way her voice sounded different now when I called her on the phone. It wasn't my fault. We had been going to leave together. It wasn't my fault I got a scholarship and she didn't.

The bus groaned to a stop and the doors opened, a rush of warm air breaking through in the air-conditioning, still blasting even this time of year. A man got on in a UPS uniform. He had a dollar sticking out of the back pocket of his brown shorts and I wanted to let him know that it looked like it was going to fall out, but then he sat down across from me and unwrapped a tuna fish sandwich that looked even smaller against his big, rough hands and I thought the last thing he probably wanted was some drunk white girl interrupting his food. It was cut into triangles and his bite almost consumed the whole half, and he sat there, chewing and staring at the bus floor, and I decided not to intervene. You could never really make the friends you wanted to in this stupid town. I didn't really know how Gaby and I had beaten the odds. Although I couldn't say if we were still friends now. Maybe we hadn't after all. I still didn't know why she had to be so mad at me.

11

APRIL 1988
MID-CITY

The snack handed out by dour Sister Beatrice was still called goûter, a reminder to the girls that they were part of a long tradition and that the order of Mary Immaculata had been here in the city since we were a French colony. The nuns talked nonstop about our glorious Louisiana history and their role in it even though our school building was from the '70s and looked like a crumpled cinder block. At least today was doughnut day, a high point of the week. I waited in line, trying to avoid any accidental eye contact with Emily or Melanie, their shining pigtails and dimples a perfect cover for the cruelest minds. A delicious smell of sugar wafted out from the big box. When I got to the front of the line, Sister Beatrice said "Only one, Rosemary" so sternly, I was immediately filled with shame and guilt even though I would never have dreamed of taking more than one. Embarrassed, I took my jelly doughnut and pink napkin and made my way back around the girls playing double Dutch and toward my favorite bench. It was half-hidden from the play structure and sometimes a whole recess could go by without anyone noticing I was there. I turned the corner past the big oak tree and saw Gabrielle Parker was already there, reading. I really didn't want to sit next to her. We were the two least popular girls in the first grade, and I felt like the two of us together would be bound to attract the attention of Emily or Melanie who were already cruising around the playground, doughnuts in hand, looking dangerously bored. But it was my bench, and I worried that if I didn't let her know that now, I would lose it forever. The only other place to sit was the steps, and they were in full view of the whole playground.

"Watch out," she said without looking up from her book as I was about to sit as far to the other side of the bench as I could.

It was caterpillar season and the ugly things were falling constantly from the oak trees all over school, their thick spiky black bodies lurking in wait everywhere, bushy stingers raised. I brushed one from the seat of the bench with the edge of my book and it landed on the concrete at our feet squirming to right itself.

"Thanks," I said.

She turned a page. "Nasty. I found one on my collar once."

I shivered. "One landed on my head once. I thought it was a leaf, so I grabbed it. Got stung all over here." I opened my palm to show her.

She made a sympathetic face and groaned a little. We all hated them so much. Then as we had run out of things to say, I flipped through my book looking for my place, and started to read, twirling the yarn tassel of my Garfield bookmark between my fingers. I was very proud of being an advanced early reader and these bookmarks were given out as prizes.

"Hey, y'all, I have a question." I looked up. Emily was standing in front of us twirling the end of one of her braids.

She ignored Gaby, everyone pretty much did, unless we were forced to pair up in class. "Rosemary, do you even have a TV?" Melanie next to her started giggling but tried to hide it behind her hand.

It always started like this, some dumb question that no matter how I answered would prove to them whatever they were making fun of me for. "Yes," I said. "Of course I do."

"Do you?" Gaby asked, still not looking up.

"Oh my God, Gaby, shut up, no one is talking to you."

Gaby ignored her, eyes on her book. This sort of thing happened all the time but for some reason today felt a little different. I don't know why but there was something about having someone else next to me on that bench that filled me with a sudden resolve to fight back. A kind of safety in numbers that I had never experienced before.

"You shut up," I said, feeling wild and daring. And then some crazy bravery took hold of me and I jumped up and stamped on one end of the caterpillar. Orange goo shot out of the end closest to Emily, and she and Melanie screamed so loud that Sister came running.

"They're squirting caterpillars at us," they tattled.

Gaby was laughing. "I think you got some on your sock," she said to me.

"Stop this right now, Gabrielle, I've spoken to you before about your behavior," Sister Beatrice said, fiercely pointing her in the direction of the classroom.

I was shocked at this injustice and was going to say something, but Gaby just shrugged and stood up like she wasn't at all surprised. But then when Sister's back was turned, she held up the cover of her book to me. *Look*, she mouthed. Amazed, I held mine up too and she nodded and smiled. We were both reading *Ramona Quimby, Age 8*. And this seemed somehow a totally miraculous coincidence. We took signs like this very seriously in our class—a day's matching headbands were enough to seal two girls in an exclusive partnership for weeks. Somehow this seemed even more filled with wonder and significance. There were thousands of books in the school library. I smiled back at her and the feeling of a secret, new and special and fiery, wrapped us up together. I wanted to say more. I wished she wasn't being led away to her punishment of solitary in the classroom under the teacher's watchful gaze.

The next day, I was waiting for her at recess, two goûters on paper napkins beside me on the bench. "I already got all the caterpillars off."

"Did you check underneath?" she asked. "Sometimes they hang on." I hadn't and we both knelt down, our thick polyester skirts brushing the dirt to peer under the bench.

"I'm sorry you got in trouble for me yesterday," I said.

"Sister Beatrice wouldn't have believed it wasn't me anyway," she said, sitting down. "She hates me."

None of the Sisters were especially friendly, but I tried to imagine having anyone hate you. "Doesn't that make you feel bad?"

She looked at me curiously for a minute. "Did you read the others?" she asked instead, opening and starting her Cheez-Its. "This is my second time. There's seven. *Ramona the Pest* is my favorite."

I hadn't and for one moment I felt a twinge that she was so far ahead of me. "That sounds good," I said, shaking my head and waiting to hear more while I licked orange crumbs from my fingers. Then she went through the book and told me the plot chapter by chapter, and I liked the sound of her voice and felt happy at school for maybe the first time that I could remember.

12

TWELFTH NIGHT 2004
THE FRENCH QUARTER
MIDNIGHT

I paused when I got to the Sugarlick, my hand on the filthy brass handle of the door. The sneaking feeling of doubling back, of circles passing in and over themselves made me stop, self-conscious. What was I even doing? I should go home and get a tampon. I should go home and take a shower. I even considered for a minute calling my mom. She would be at work now. She still worked nights at the concierge desk of the Royal Bourbon Hotel where she could at least watch people out having a good time, close to that life of the French Quarter she had been so in love with. And Mr. Broussard was there, her married boss, his adoration of her measured out in the tiny bottles of Royal Bourbon shampoo and conditioner that had filled our bathroom for years. But I wasn't in the habit of talking to her about my problems.

The strange thing was I had tried. When I first got Ida's diagnosis, I had gone straight to her house, our house, our porch hung with Christmas lights that hadn't worked for years, my Strawberry Shortcake stickers still on the glass of the front door. My mom had found Ida for me after all—

she knew what it would mean to lose her. She had just woken up. "Poor Ida," she said, leaning under her kitchen table to pat her, straight on the head with the flat of her hand, in that way Ida had never cared for. Mom had lost a lot of weight and didn't look so well. I'd tried to tell her about the tests—how the vet said it was in Ida's bones—but she wasn't paying attention, staring into her coffee mug with a glazed expression. She had just woken up, it was the middle of the afternoon for fuck's sake. A musical was playing on TV in the next room and she nodded her head to some dumb MGM song number. I'd left soon after. No. Mom wouldn't be any help. I hurried to push open the door.

The crowd from the show had mostly cleared and all that was left were the stragglers, the usual Quarter detritus. A couple of plump goths in velvet cloaks, a skinny guy in a porkpie hat trying to get laid, some restaurant workers off shift, still wearing their stained kitchen whites, a few barflies sitting by themselves and drinking with quiet concentration, and crammed into a booth at the back, a group of punk kids in black T-shirts jostling and squirming.

Chantal was standing at the bar, counting out bills and separating them into neat rows. She looked up, the hibiscus in her hair now wilting gently against her ear. "For fuck's sake, Rosie, you left without your share again. It's like this girl doesn't want to get paid." She spoke to Jonah, I saw with a flutter, a particular feeling in my stomach, a free fall, acute, but not unpleasant. He was sitting with Mickey. They were both nursing Miller High Lifes.

"Rosie. Rose-Marie, you've got to get paid," Mickey said. He had Malcom X glasses and a Slayer T-shirt on. He ran a Dungeons and Dragons night in another punk bar and had the faintly tired look of black people in this town that spent a lot of time around white people. He patted the stool next to him, and I was glad to have his chatty friendliness as a temporary buffer between myself and Jonah, seated on his other side.

"What, Rosie? She does it for the art," Jonah said in his ironic drawl.

"Art isn't free, my friend," Mickey answered. "Chantal was just telling us about some crazy Rocky and Bullwinkle number you did last month. Very cool. I'm sorry I missed it. Even as a kid I could tell that Natasha Fatale was on fire."

"Is that her last name?" I asked and he nodded, that proud way men liked to inform me of the particulars of movies and comics, cartoon or TV shows.

"Missing your act seems to be a theme," murmured Jonah as if to himself.

"It's a good thing you've got cute tits, Rosie, because that shit made no sense," Chantal said affectionately.

Mickey and Jonah resumed a fight they were having about the deeper logic of *Akira*. Always comic books. I once made the mistake of saying I read *Archie* as a kid. The extent of their disdain would have been funny if it hadn't been so annoying. *Girl comics*, someone had said, and the subject rested.

I was glad for this reprieve though, a moment to settle my mind. My chair was pulled out a little and when I leaned back, I could see Jonah on Mickey's other side. He was standing, one elbow on the bar, a stance that allowed him to casually scan the room without interrupting his conversation. He was wearing a cardigan now, dark gray and moth-eaten, but it fit him so well, you could see the weeks spent combing through thrift stores until he had landed on this one. I liked him even better for trying. Especially when it worked out so well. The dark cuffs of his shirt were rolled up over his sweater and the sides hung open against his skinny frame. My hands met my elbows when I wrapped my arms around him to pull him to bed. His body was as lean and hard as the leather strop for a straight razor.

"You can't talk postwar Japanese culture and not reference the bomb," he was saying to Mickey. "That's like saying Godzilla is about fucking amphibians."

"No way, man, you're being too derivative about this," Mickey sighed.

As he took stock of the room, Jonah kept meeting my eyes by accident and then we both had to quickly look away. It was getting a little embarrassing.

"That book is wide-angle eschatological end times, applicable to any situation. Martial law and death cults, all human progress leading to destruction. Cities going up in flames or giant lizards, whatever your poison. Living your life ten feet below sea level, for example," Mickey answered.

"I still can't believe you forgot your money, in such a hurry to leave with Mike." Chantal shook her head at me. "Although you're back pretty soon. I'm not surprised—Mike never impressed me as being an all-night kind of guy. Not exactly an eight-hour man." She started humming a song we all knew by that name.

I mentally willed her to stop talking. She didn't know, of course. No one knew how I felt about Jonah. Casually fucking Jonah was a common rite of passage among us, the kind of thing you admit to with a laugh and shrug. The way all bartenders ended up being the last resort in the easy exchange of companionable evenings. But tonight felt different. Private. I didn't want her to mess it up.

But Mickey and Jonah stopped their argument. "Not Rockabilly Mike?" Mickey asked. "Idiot Mike? Rosemary, no. He's like a fucking neo-Nazi or something."

I shrugged, taking the stack of crumpled bills and tapping them casually on end to hide my shame. "I didn't know."

"Chantal, what are we going to do with this girl?" he asked.

She was putting her own stack of bills into a pink Hello Kitty wallet that she snapped shut with some annoyance. "Hey, I'm just their business manager. Keeping a bunch of burly-Q bitches from making bad choices? No thank you, it would be like herding cats."

I had all my senses vibrating in Jonah's direction, waiting, breath held for his response. "Making poor choices is a woman's sacred prerogative," he said finally. "I've been so many excellent women's poorly considered option, I can't say a word against it."

"Lord knows that's true. Is Elsa working at Big Papa's tonight?" Chantal asked him.

"Yeah, she asked me to walk her over when she's done getting ready. She thinks it will be crowded because it's Twelfth Night. First night of Carnival," he added, as if we didn't know. Sometimes it seemed like every woman I hung out with worked in the clubs on Bourbon Street. Except me. I didn't have the nerve. I don't really know why, except that being on display felt different than being on offer. I needed the stage, the distance, the control. But it was dumb because they made a hell of a lot more money than I did selling underpants. Ostrich feathers and beaded fringe were expensive.

Mickey snorted, "What do a bunch of Shriners from Omaha know about Twelfth Night? I mean, come on."

"Feast of the Epiphany," Jonah added again, unable to resist that impulse to lecture, always ready to prove his bona fides.

"Yeah, yeah, whatever, you're not even Catholic." Chantal began dunking dirty glasses into soapy water on the other side of the bar. "That's why you're so into that Day of the Dead shit. You dumb gringos all have the same fetish."

I smiled to myself. Chantal had seen the shelf above his bed too.

Jonah started to defend himself, a practiced tangent about certain cultures just being more goth and badass than other cultures, the same theories he had expounded to me at length in his bed, and I sighed, glad to hear him reiterate it. Now, tonight, I needed someone to cast death in this kindly light. Sugar skulls and skeletons in sombreros. I wanted to be with him in this world of aestheticized bones, cool, inviting. I needed to be back with Jonah, tucked under his arm against that hard, white body, safe together. Skull rings and *Nosferatu* posters. The way he dipped into darkness so lightly, like a stone skittering across water. He would make it okay.

Chantal was rolling her eyes at him.

Jonah leaned back away from her contempt, suddenly very interested in the room behind me. I could feel the currents of air spin away from him, charged. The night wasn't over. He didn't care about Rockabilly Mike or any of the rest of them. I just needed to get him alone.

The Cramps thumped over the room, cheerfully wailing about werewolves and I felt my body thrill to a rhythm as familiar as my own heartbeat. I managed to avoid tapping my foot, not wanting to betray my pleasure. I wasn't tired. I was buzzing. This kind of nocturnal life generated its own stamina, a momentum of drinks and sex and pills that made any quiet reckoning seem more and more unlikely. An urgency set in and hit my bloodstream like a cup of strong coffee, these nights in New Orleans that lasted forever and where there would always be company, fellow passengers in the whirl of nightlife. Like Jonah, a cold sun to keep returning to, and who was now scowling at the back of the room, arms crossed over that sunken chest, his shirt stretched tight over the hunch of his shoulders, folding in on himself like a disgruntled crow. "Look at these assholes," he said, and I turned around to see what he was looking at. "Do they think we can't see that they're all drinking forties? I'm annoyed on your behalf, Chantal."

She shrugged, replacing glasses on the shelf behind her. "Cheapskates."

Mickey turned too. "Oh, leave the kids alone. They make me feel nostalgic. You can smell the zit cream and sexual frustration from here. Tell me you didn't look exactly like that fifteen years ago, a patched jacket and half-assed liberty spikes. I can just see it."

Jonah scoffed. "In Paducah, we did our drinking in cemeteries and rail yards like real punks, not bringing forties to bars we couldn't afford and getting on the nerves of people just trying to enjoy a drink. And no, I had better hair than that. Please, Billy Childish, my friend, not Billy Idol."

Mickey groaned.

"Paducah, Jesus, what a name. That's right, I always forget that you're not from here." I chimed in, eager to give him something, a gift that would remind him that I was still there, waiting.

His bored expression couldn't totally hide his satisfaction. "Well, I've been here long enough."

I was lying. I would never have confused Jonah with someone from this town. He felt far too at ease. It was always the people from someplace else that landed and became the center of things. I can see why, showing up in a new town and getting to be whomever you wanted, the best version, rather than dragging all your past selves along behind you like chains.

It's always a stranger, an interloper in the right clothes and a Ninth Ward apartment, eagerly lecturing me about rhythm and blues or Mardi Gras Indians or some other aspect of real New Orleans with an assurance I can only envy. My New Orleans is an unsteady territory I could never hold forth on, a dangerous miasma. Gaby and I spending the summer doing odd jobs, mowing the lawn and cleaning the windows at her grandparents' home in New Orleans East, baking in the sun. I remembered the plastic on the living room sofa and a big '70s Cadillac in the driveway, her grandmother's hair set in high waves and the tense politeness she always used toward me, this white girl in her house. That was my New Orleans. I didn't understand it. But I felt its weight in my body, a strange, invisible pressure.

Or the Mardi Gras Indians. I was scared of them, preening and strutting, owning their streets with an aggressive beauty. I couldn't explain that my fear was a sign of respect. My deference felt like the only gift I could offer them in the face of our brutal, messed-up racial history. That was also my New Orleans, and we didn't talk about it. Everything was unsaid but intuited, our way of doing things, a silence heavy as iron. But the Jonahs, lost in their fresh infatuation, the city like a girl you'd only just met but were thrilled to fuck, loved to talk. To tell me about St. Joseph's Day and Cosimo Matassa's recording studio and all the things I should know about my city. No. Jonah was not from here. But maybe that's why I liked him. It was easier. Mickey was from Queens, I remembered. Chantal from LA. All strangers. They could come and enjoy the intoxication of it all without the shame, the curse that resided deep in your bones. Gaby knew my New Orleans, the million little rules we all implicitly followed. That first question we all asked each other: Where'd you go to high school? That quick recognition of how everyone fit into the fabric of this dumb city, held by a million tiny knots of habit and expectation. Deep bloodred wells lurking under the most innocuous conversations. For one second, I felt earth-shatteringly lonely.

"Do you know I have been coming to the Sugarlick since I was in the womb? Literally. My mom used to come here when it was a different bar before she knew she was pregnant," I said, perversely wanting to remind them that I was different.

"Well, that explains a lot." Jonah smiled. I knew in the way he said it, there was an admiration, and I felt cheap but I wanted it. "Oh shit, look." He stood up. "I knew it. Fucking youngbloods."

Mickey raised an eyebrow at the term, but we all turned to look just as a forty of malt liquor rolled across the floor and a bunch of boys tumbled out the booth, an explosion of loud voices and childish aggression.

"Hey, now," Chantal yelled, bored. "Cut that shit out."

They were hollering, a crash of laughter over a shared joke and my eye immediately went to a little brown-haired guy with a narrow face, wedged in among the others. He wasn't laughing, looking hard at the table instead. There was something about the way he was so clearly trying to slump down and disappear that I recognized with a quick familiarity that he was prey. He was the joke. Something else was said that I couldn't hear and more laughing and then a big dumb-looking guy reached over and flicked the smaller one on the forehead with his thumb and forefinger. The little guy turned red and pushed his way free from the others. He yelled something back, and it was met with more laughter. There was no way for this kid to win. I could see him trembling even from here and nothing marked you in the world of teenage dominance like that kind of involuntary betrayal of feeling. Then he yelled fuck you, and I could hear his voice crack, ineffectual, heartrending. "I don't want to stay at your place anymore anyway."

I couldn't hear the response but the big one flicked him on the forehead again.

"Those guys are being assholes," I said.

I looked over at Mickey and Jonah. Jonah held his beer between his fingers by the neck. "Hey, I'm off duty," he said, catching my worried expression.

"Yeah, crusty dipshits," Mickey yawned. He was standing now, back to the bar, resting on his elbows and watching with a kind of weary bemusement. "Although I'd put five on that little one. The little ones can surprise you. They can be shockingly agile. Also, when kicked out of the nest, these kids go feral."

"As a skinny former punk, I'll take those odds." Jonah extended his hand and they shook. "I got my ass kicked all the time. Just like he is going to in a minute. It builds character."

The kid turned to leave and even in his clear desperation to get out of there, there was something graceful about him, all the contained force of a young deer about to bolt in spite of his high-top sneakers. He was wearing an old and poorly fitting black suit with a bunch of small, round pins on the lapel.

I still wasn't totally sure if they were just being fraternal or cruel. I never understood how men acted together, men were so fucking stupid, but then I saw him stop and look around. Just for a second, I saw in his expression that his world was falling apart, and although ready to run, he didn't know where to go. And in that weightlessness, the free fall of having no next step, no course to follow, the sudden punch in the gut of finding yourself alone, I felt a kinship, a sympathy so profound, I was knocked sideways by the force of it.

This sympathy filled me up, taking me out of myself for a minute and I grabbed at it, eagerly. Someone else was having problems. I wanted to help. I was spraying lighter fluid all over Ms. Mancuso's grass and I was the big *fwoomp* sound it made when it burst into bright, brilliant flame. I was burning with righteousness for Gaby, avenging her mistreatment. Indeterminate love in all its wild, untrammeled ferocity rushed over me. Who cared who this guy was, he needed someone. I could save him.

I leaped off my stool. The room melted away, as glorious forward momentum swept me up and I plunged in, flinging my fists against the first pair of shoulders I hit. The element of surprise made the circle ripple open a little, and in a moment, I was right in the middle, defending a very confused-looking kid. I ran full force against the one that seemed to be the most antagonistic.

He started laughing. "Come collect your girl," he called to Jonah and Mickey as I hit him over and over, ineffectively, in the stomach.

So, I punched him in the face.

It was wonderful to hit someone. Ecstatic. This tall, blond, rangy guy with a smirk like Steve McQueen, all his cheap, confident charisma became just for one beautiful moment a receptacle for all that I wanted to spew forth from my body, all the force of justice. For one second, I wondered if this was what it felt like to fuck as a guy. To just pummel blindly at a body until it takes all the crackling rage out of yours. "You're being a jerk," I yelled at him.

He curled up, arms over his head to defend himself, and I could see, annoyingly, he was still shaking with laughter. He reached a long arm toward me and pressed against my forehead enforcing a distance between us that I couldn't quite breach, so I ducked and punched him in the stomach again. The knowledge that I was too old for this kind of behavior only made it that much more fun.

The moment he touched me however, a response rose immediately from my friends at the bar. "No fucking way. Out of my bar." Chantal was coming from behind the counter, but Jonah and Mickey were already a few steps ahead of her.

He was already backing up, hands raised, still exasperatingly chuckling. "Yeah, yeah, I got you. I'm not going to touch this crazy little bitch. She's cute, but wild, like one of them little badgers."

"Shut the fuck up," I yelled, tears in my eyes. "All animals are beautiful."

He left the bar, and the rest of the group filed out behind him.

In the still unsettled atmosphere of adrenaline and mild confusion they left behind, suddenly Jonah was right next to me and he swung an arm around my back pulling me close, the contact igniting. I was swept against him, still panting, my heart pounding from the altercation. "You are insane," he said. "Batshit crazy. You are a fucking national treasure." Then he kissed me hard and it was over before I could respond, but I was glad to have it confirmed again that he appreciated insanity. Especially in women.

"Jonah, you still walking me? I'm late. I don't want to have to give those assholes forty bucks shift pay." I heard Elsa call from somewhere. "What is going on out here, y'all?"

Chantal laughed. "While you were getting your tits in order, Rosie's been ass-whipping the younger generation."

"Oh good." Elsa gave me a thumbs-up from across the room.

"Coming," Jonah answered, dropping his arm. "I'll see you around," he said to me emphatically and before I could stop melting and grab him to make him stay, to make him understand that I had plans for us, he was already walking toward Elsa. I wanted to call out after him but everyone in the bar was still looking at me and I couldn't bring myself to do it.

He and Elsa left. It was like a game of fucking musical chairs. But I knew they weren't together. Elsa had a terrible boyfriend named Quasar, or so he called himself, who was the tech guy at a heavy metal club, and she was devoted to him. If this was just a friendly gesture, walking her to work, then he would abandon it for me I was sure, but there was no way to communicate all this across this very public space. I would look ridiculous. It needed to be whispered, so he could feel my breath on his ear and remember.

I was still trying to catch my breath. There was a funny disequilibrium in the room, a bunch of charged particles unsure where to settle.

I looked over at the kid who had been the cause of all this. He was staring at me gratefully, a little bug-eyed, a look that reminded me of Ida in a thunderstorm, all her helpless dependency vibrating through her impractical little body. Her certainty that the world was ending battling her unshakable faith that I could fix it. I supposed she was right. I could fix everything. I had. I guess. In his distress, this guy had a glimmer of that same hopefulness and it seemed amazing that someone could be so innocent. He finally seemed to register my look and when our eyes met the innocence retreated quickly like a shade pulled down over a sunrise and he grinned, a cocky, presumptuous smile. "Well, hello there," he said. "You've got a nice right hook."

"Thanks," I said. And since he was still waiting, so clearly hopeful, and since I also didn't know where else to go, I waved him toward the bar. "Come on," I said. "Let's drink."

He sat down next to me, watching me with a covert alertness, quick calculations that I guessed were about my sexual interest and availability. "So, is that something you do a lot? I mean, punching people? Should I be nervous or honored? I mean, it was pretty cool, and you couldn't have picked a better dick to go for. Ryan is an epic asshole. But then aren't we all at times? The wheel of fate spins, we punch, we get punched. Sometimes an angel appears with fists of glory. Are you going to punch me next?"

He was spinning from side to side on the rotating bar stool. At the crest of each nervous arc, he stopped himself abruptly with his foot against the bar and the rubber of his sneaker squeaked loudly against the varnish and I wanted to tell him to stop but even as he chattered, it was clear how easily he might deflate, and I didn't want to hurt his feelings. "Only if you deserve it."

"I probably do," he said and smiled at me. He was maybe older than I had first guessed, but something in the jittery, unconnected way he held his body made him look younger, a scaffolding he hadn't yet grown into. He had one big pimple on his cheek, but his dark hair fell back from his forehead, a smooth, pleasing swoop in spite of a terrible haircut, clearly self-inflicted, too short on the sides that made his ears stick out. "Do you do this kind of thing a lot?" he repeated.

"Does it matter?"

"Nope. It's awesome either way. I just kind of wanted to think I was your first," he said suggestively. "You know how we men are."

"I do," I agreed.

"Damn, Rosie." Chantal placed a beer in front of me on the

bar. She lit a cigarette and examined me through the smoke, and then reached over with the gentlest touch to tap the corner of my eyelash that was coming loose. "You are having a night tonight. I'm starting to get worried. You're enough to make this part-time stripper get maternal." She paused. "Almost."

I could hear Mickey at the back of the room, enthusiastically rehashing the scene with a pair of pretty girls. Bar fights really bring people together. I was glad to have given him an opening.

"Where was Jonah going again?" I asked, trying to sound casual.

"Elsa's at Big Papa's tonight. I guess he's keeping her company."

"Is that the guy you were making out with? Do you guys have a thing?" the kid asked, equally casually. Chantal and I ignored him. "So, can I have a beer?" he asked.

"How old are you?"

"Be nice, Chantal," I said. "Give him a drink for me."

She looked him over and gave him a Coke. He popped his thumbs in and out of the holes of an undershirt hanging beyond the sleeves of his jacket. "So," he said to me.

"So," I answered, and he started up spinning on his stool again. "It sounded like you were having a rough night," I said, immediately overcome with a secret joy at being able to say this to someone else. "What's up with those guys?"

"What, Ryan?" he asked, and then cleared his throat. "He's just got one of those personalities, you know. If he does something, everybody follows and it's so annoying."

"High school is the worst."

"I'm not in high school." He sounded so outraged that I had to try not to smile. "I've been on my own for ages. Well, not on my own. I've been staying with Ryan. He gave me a place to crash when my parents kicked me out, but maybe we're moving past that, you know, and I should get my own place. You can't just have one friend and rely on them for everything. It makes people get weird, you know, to have that kind of power over you."

"It looked like you had a whole group of friends."

"Those guys?" he snorted. "No. Ryan was different. He was just like my guy, you know."

The way he said that made my insides hurt.

"We were in a band together. I've told him all kinds of shit I would never tell anyone else." He frowned and looked at his Coke, pushing the ice around with a straw. "I kinda regret that now, I guess. Life just gets so fucking complicated sometimes, you know?" His voice wobbled and he coughed to cover it up.

"I'm sure you can make other friends," I said, but then we were both silent at this clear idiocy. I knew that often you don't really choose your friends. You just grab on to them like a drowning person. Gaby should have had a better friend than me. Gaby, who let me pick the movies we rented and places we went so discreetly and quietly that weeks went by before I even noticed or remembered to ask her what she wanted, and then felt so ashamed when I tried to make it up to her. But life happens and then we were all each other had. Maybe something similar had happened with this kid. In any case, there was something in the distress coming off him that warmed me. "Can I please have a beer?" he asked again.

"No one wants your fake ID." Chantal examined her nails for chips.

"You guys, I'm twenty-one years old," he said in exasperation. "Why doesn't anyone believe me? Tell your friend here," he asked me, an assumption of solidarity that I had to admit was kind of sweet.

"You guys were in here drinking forties under the table, we all saw you, and it's annoying," Chantal answered. "So now you don't get shit."

He looked embarrassed. "It's just cheaper," he mumbled.

And we waited for what would happen next, he and I caught in the stillness of the night's crosscurrents, moths hovering in a draft.

Chantal did not have the trembling antennas of the wounded and leaned on the bar, oblivious, folding a cocktail napkin into little origami shapes. "I can't wait to get out of here. When I'm done, I'm going home to take a bath and watch like ten *Law and Orders* with His Whiskers."

"That sounds nice," I said and meant it.

Chantal glanced at me again in that searching way and tossed aside a crane that didn't quite come together. "Why don't you come over? I've probably got enough Gallo for two."

I wanted to. If only I could stay in the warm stillness of Chantal's cheerful living room, walls covered in vintage advertisements and pinup girls all smiling their bright, blushing, innocent smiles, but she was still working. How many hours would I have to face the terrible immobility of the Sugarlick? Waiting, waiting for four in the morning to roll around. Just me and my thoughts and a stillness where I couldn't escape the memory of that quiet little body. It was too risky. I couldn't do it. "That's okay. I'm going to head out and maybe find Jonah in a minute. I had something I needed to ask him."

She looked at me like she was going to say something else, but she didn't. She pulled the flower from her hair, tossing it onto the bar in my direction. "Well, the invitation stands." Then she leaned in unexpectedly, and her kiss was soft on my cheek and she smelled of vanilla and sweat. Warm and soft. It suddenly occurred to me I should ask her for a tampon, but then I was too embarrassed in front of this punk who was staring at us. Then I was embarrassed to be embarrassed, how many hundreds of men had seen my tits, but blood was secret, blood was intimate. Shyness, when it struck, was always so startling and disarming.

"Thanks," I whispered. And then she moved to the other end of the bar, and the room seemed to deflate without her. I shivered.

The guy next to me had stopped swishing around and was now looking at me with deep and emphatic purpose. "Do you want to get out of here?" He reached out like he was going to put his arm around me, but then lost courage on the way and settled for just grabbing my shoulder in an awkwardly friendly way. I wanted to laugh but again, he had that strange air of vulnerability, like he was made of spun sugar so ready to crack. I managed not to, and when I looked at him, I could feel myself softening in his direction.

It was the second time a man had asked me that, at this very bar, tonight. And I was suddenly thankful for men and their desires, even hopeless, deluded ones like this one who I was definitely not going to fuck. But they could always be depended on to lead me somewhere, away from the stillness. I had nothing but time. And anyway, this guy, whose pain visibly crackled off him like cinders, appealed to me in a way that I couldn't quite turn away from.

"And go where?" I asked.

"We will know when we get there," he said, lighting up as he saw that I was considering it. And it was that glow, that sudden beam of clearly unanticipated joy that convinced me. It transfigured him for a moment from a pimply, rat-faced little punk into something marvelously attractive. It felt like it had been a very long time since I had had the power to make someone, even just momentarily, that radiant.

We stood up together and I finished my beer in one long swallow and put my bag back on my shoulder and, avoiding Chantal's eyes, gave her a wave as we stepped back from the bar.

"Be careful out there, Rosemary," Mickey yelled from the back of the room in parting. "A girl's only got her good sense to lose."

I raised my hand in devil's horns and he answered in kind while this guy held the door for me, watching the exchange with glowing approval.

13

I burst out of the water and threw my head back, flinging my hair to make a spray of droplets.

Gaby was sitting on the pool steps, slowly dragging her arms back and forth to push a drowning beetle away from her and toward the drain. "No, when Ariel does it, it's like a big swoop. That just kind of rained back on your own head."

I wiped the water from my eyes. "Okay, let me get shallower, watch this one."

We had been waiting all winter, watching while machines pushed piles of dirt around and the Landrys' yard next door slowly became a pool. When it was finally done, they gave me permission to swim there during summer break, and Gaby and I had spent days choosing different sun lotions and tanning sprays in anticipation. We had even found a raft in Gaby's garage from some past trip to Waveland and my hair was full of Sun In: we were ready. Ida was having conniptions, barking nonstop and pushing her face through the chain-link fence separating our yard from theirs, running back and forth, determined to save me from whatever clear danger had befallen me.

I ducked under the cool surface of the water and Ida's bark-ing disappeared. We were obsessed with *The Little Mermaid*, watching it over and over until the VHS tape got fuzzy. I sank down and then pushed off the bottom, propelling my chest up and out into the warm air and flinging my neck as hard as I could. "How about that?" I asked when I had landed.

Gaby kept her eye on the beetle while she lazily kicked her legs out in front of her. "I think your hair's too short."

"Okay, fine, you do it, then."

Gaby frowned at me and then started out toward the raft floating at the deep end in a slow, graceful stroke. "No thank you. I don't even like mermaids that much."

"Yes, you do, come on." I knew she didn't like to get her hair wet because she was the only fifth grader that actually carried an umbrella and would use it every single time it even drizzled. But I still thought it was a terrible waste of precious pool time. I didn't feel wet until I went under and then when I came up, the whole world had gone down ten degrees in temperature, and everything felt fresh and bright and joyful. "I promise you will feel a million times better."

She grabbed the raft and pulled it under her belly cross-wise and slowly kicked toward me. "Five hours it takes under the dryer."

"No way." I knew she straightened her hair but that seemed impossible. "You're making that up."

She was revolving in slow circles. "I watch TV or do my homework. It's not that big a deal, but yeah, about five hours." A cloud passed quickly over the sun and the world went dim-mer and then passed and everything shone again, brighter after the quick reprieve.

I was trying to imagine having the patience to do anything

for five hours. I didn't think I had sat still for that long in my entire life. I ducked under again to do a handstand while I thought about this. Even so, I still wanted her to really swim with me. There was something about her always keeping her head out that made it feel like she was not fully participating in the experience. I wanted to have races or play Marco Polo and it wouldn't be any fun if she kept her head above water. Especially since she hadn't mentioned this the whole time we had been waiting and making our plans, I still kind of thought she must not be serious.

When I came back up, I saw Mrs. Landry watering the pots of flowers on her back steps. It was like the third time she had come out since we had been swimming and she was making me a little nervous. She kept watching us but then when I waved, she quickly went back inside. Even though the reflection of the sun was fierce on the glass, I could just feel her at the windows, watching us.

I splashed a spray of water in Ida's direction and she leaped back in a huge comical bound and then started barking again, although now from a greater distance from the fence. Gaby had her back to me, her pink striped bathing suit making her look like a Starlight Mint and without stopping to think too hard about it, I jumped on her, knocking her off the raft and into the water. She came up sputtering, lifting her hair out of her face and for one terrible minute I thought she was going to cry. " Rosemary! How could you? What did I just tell you about my hair?" She slapped the water.

"I want you to have fun with me. How often do we get to be in a pool? You're wasting it." I was a little nervous now that I had done it but I still felt kind of justified. But she was already on her way out of the pool. "Wait. Don't be mad," I called to her.

"Don't be mad," I said again and pushed a wave of water in her direction. She waited a minute, standing up in the shallow end, and I almost thought she really was going to get out of the pool. So, I swam over and grabbed her hand, pulling her deeper. "I'm sorry, I swear. Come on, you're already wet."

"You just don't listen," she said. "I swear to God, if you ever do that again, I am never going swimming with you."

"I promise I will never do that again." She still waited, hesitating. "But in a way, you have to admit I did you a favor because now you have no choice but to have fun," I said.

"I'm going to kill you," she said, finally jumping up and pushing me underwater by my shoulders. I opened my eyes and my laughter came out in big surging bubbles and I tried to grab her legs and soon we were tumbling in and under each other in circles.

When we came up still grappling, I said, "See, doesn't that feel better?" And then I had to dive away because she came at me again, but she missed. We splashed and kicked together now in careless motions and spent the rest of the afternoon in the pool just as I had wanted, but it didn't feel quite right. Something had shifted and I felt bad, but I didn't know what to do about it now.

It didn't matter, because the next day Mrs. Landry came over and told my mom that she didn't want me using the pool with friends, and my mom got really mad in a way she didn't usually. She even bought me a Slip 'N Slide to make up for it, and Gaby and I spent the summer bruising our ribs and knees, throwing ourselves at the knotty ground and patchy grass of our backyard on the slick yellow plastic. The next Halloween my mom told me to go egg Mrs. Landry's house because she was a racist old bitch.

14

The Sugarlick door swung shut, warped and weathered wood, traces of bleach and mold and thousands of drunken palms, and I was once again on the cracked Quarter sidewalk in the shadow of the balcony overhead.

My fight with Gaby had started so innocuously here and it was strange that so much time had passed, a year of my life now lived without her. I had been excited to show her my dancing, here was this amazing new skill I had discovered that she had never witnessed. I had been crushed at her re-action. She didn't get it at all. Said I was demeaning myself, and even worse, *playing the whore*. That one hurt. It was one thing if she wasn't going to be supportive, but to call me a drunk and a whore, that was too much. It was like having the rug pulled out from under me. Now that she was interning for her social work degree, she had this new authority to her; she sounded different when she talked about things and had certainly never spoken to me that way. In retrospect, calling Gaby a judgmental bitch was not the best way to defend my integrity. No matter how drunk I had been, she didn't deserve that. I remembered watching her walk away from me, arm hitched tightly over her purse.

"It's funny," I said, to distract myself from the memory. "I had a fight with my best friend in this bar a while ago. Maybe it's cursed. Or maybe all bars are like this because being drunk makes us all act like idiots."

"Definitely the latter." This guy was bent away from me, fumbling with a bike lock. "But sometimes there's a silver lining. So," he added, looking up. "Do you have a thing with that guy?"

"Who?"

He gave me a look. "You know who."

"No," I said reflexively. But then I thought about it. "Yes." I tried it out to see how it sounded. It sounded right so I said it again for the pleasure of it. "Yes. I do."

He didn't seem concerned. "Yeah, I know him, he bartends at the Cove, right? He's always got a lot of girls around. Why is that? I think he looks like Steve Buscemi."

"Oh, I don't know, he's got a style."

But this guy wasn't done. "Or like if Mark E. Smith and Hank Williams had a love child, and then that kid became a junkie who paid too much attention to his hair. And he's also missing a pinkie. Did you know that?"

I smiled; our intimacy went way beyond that. "Just the tip of one. He and I have a history. What, have you never dated a bartender? In this town?"

He looked surprised. "Me? Well, yeah, sure. I practically fall in love with every woman who hands me a drink, Jesus Christ. But I'm a fucking loser. You look like you could be choosier."

"Why are you wearing a suit?" I interrupted him.

He turned his head from side to side, cracking his neck.

"It's a long story. I'll probably tell it to you, if you're interested. Why? Do you like it?"

I shrugged my shoulders. "I was just curious."

He finished fiddling with his bike and stood, fastening the enormous chain of his lock around his waist. Its weight immediately pulled it down to slam against his hip bones, and I flinched thinking of the bruises he must surely have. He didn't seem to notice and grabbed his handlebars looking at me expectantly. His shitty bike was covered in duct tape and had a big metal basket on the front. The Quarter was filled with young men in dirty clothes with just such bikes, crisscrossing the streets at all hours, delivering cigarettes and six-packs and half-rancid hamburgers and fried shrimp po'boys, servicing a web of desires. He seemed happier now that we were outside. I knew that feeling. I waited for him to start talking again, feeling he wouldn't be able to stay quiet for long.

"So, what was your fight about?" I asked to get him started.

"Huh?" He was watching a stray cat dart out of traffic.

"What exactly was your friend saying to you in there? You looked pretty upset."

"That? Just the usual bullshit."

"I don't know, getting kicked out of someone's house seems pretty dramatic. You should try me. I'm good with this kind of stuff." I watched his face closely, looking for any returning tremor of that earlier emotion I had seen but his expression was unreadable. I wanted him to tell me his secrets.

"Didn't you just say you had a big fight with your best friend? Maybe you aren't so good with this stuff."

My feelings were hurt. "At least I have a place to sleep tonight." He didn't need to know I was kind of lying. And anyway, I felt like he owed me. This evasiveness didn't seem fair after I had started a fistfight in his honor. "Tell me, maybe I can help," I offered again. I could tell by his very specific interest in the cat now hiding under the wheels of a parked car that he wasn't going to elaborate, and this seemed to break some essential contract between us. Fuck this guy, I had things to do anyway. "Okay, fine. I guess I'll be on my way."

But he looked up quickly, worried, I noticed with satisfaction. "It's just boring. I owe him some rent. No big deal."

"Oh," I said, trying to hide my disappointment. I didn't know what I'd been expecting but this did feel a little pedestrian.

"But I don't know, maybe you can still help me. I need all kinds of things, especially from someone who looks like you," he said, flirting aggressively again.

I rolled my eyes. He was very bad at this, but then as if he realized it himself, he dropped this unconvincing bravado and changed the subject, relapsing into honesty almost as if by accident. "I don't know why Ryan is such a dick when we're out together. He's not like that when we're alone. But he tries to show off in front of the guys because he wants to start a new band. Everybody wants to be in a band. I'm over it. I want to make movies. Do you like movies?"

"Sure." I liked this confidential side of him better. We had begun to walk, for no reason, directionless, while I started to consider my next course of action. I could go directly to Big Papa's to find Jonah. In the crowded dark of a strip club, no one would notice my arrival. The fact that I had followed him there could be smoothed over between the two of us with a joke or a suggestive comment. I needed to let a little time pass though. I couldn't appear too eager. He had come to my show, kissed me even, but then in that evasive way of his, he had slipped away after, almost, I suspected, to keep me from getting too sure of myself. And so now I would have to chase after him, but I would have to do it carefully, with finesse. Once we were somewhere where we could really talk, alone, just the two of us, all this would be unnecessary. Until then, I didn't want to take any chances. He was easily spooked.

This guy led his bike beside me and every so often, he stepped up onto one of the pedals and coasted, hanging on to one side of the bike and wobbling. His chatter rose up again and he was describing some Korean horror movie in vivid detail. I was pretty sure he was on drugs. Amphetamines, I guessed. At least they made you friendly. It was such a gift when other people did all the talking for you and you could just coast, barely existing. This was why I never got along with junkies—they were too quiet. "What's your name?" I asked when he paused for breath.

"Christopher." He looked over at me and smiled. "Patron saint of travelers, sailors, floods, epilepsy and lighting strikes. Also fuckups, losers, delivery boys and guys who cut their own hair because their best friend did and called it a 1930s prison cut that made him, the friend, let's call him Ryan, look like a movie star and that made me look like I should be on the locked ward at Charity Hospital. I'm usually better looking. Not much but a little." He swallowed hard and tapped his finger along the top of his handlebars. I was glad that he was visibly high because it meant that he wouldn't be going to bed anytime soon and that energy sparking off his sad eyes like flint meant he wouldn't be the one to leave first. That was a comfort at least.

"I'm Rosemary," I said in answer to the question he hadn't asked.

"That's a pretty name. When I was little my mom used to make potatoes with rosemary, at least I think that's what she said it was and, man, it smelled so good. Is there anything better than the smell of dinner when you're, like, a dumb little kid and playing with Legos or some shit?"

"My mom didn't really cook."

"I get it, my mom once tried to beat the disrespect out of me with a rosary, but still those potatoes smelled fucking delicious. No, I'm just kidding. She probably wanted to though, I was a fucked-up little kid. A word of advice, while we're talking parenthood here—don't ever send your pussy-assed little son to Catholic school. Those priests will fuck him up good. Literally and figuratively."

I started to respond but he cut me off. "No, I'm just kidding again. Do whatever you want with your kids."

"Okay, thanks, I guess," I said, before his flow of talk started up again.

"Do you ever cook stuff yourself and be, like, it's just me, Rosemary, making some rosemary potatoes or whatever?"

I smiled. "No. Never."

"Yeah, all I know how to make is instant ramen. But if I ever have a house, I'm going to keep those potatoes going in the oven all day. Just for the beautiful fuck of it. I bet you'd make a good mom."

"Are you kidding?" Even on drugs this seemed too unreasonable. "Look at me."

"I'm serious. You have a nice face. And you probably smell really good." He leaned over then and sniffed at me. I was surprised and shied away, and he got embarrassed and all of this made his bike swerve and he had to slide off the pedals to catch himself. "I was just curious. I apologize for myself and the way I smell. Our hot water has been broken all winter so..." He trailed off and started humming tunelessly to himself. "What should we do? What should we do?" He looked around as if the empty street might have any answers.

"You're so fucking pretty," he said. "It kind of makes me want to punch you. But not in a bad way. Just because it's so intimidating."

He was talking gibberish but still the word lingered, *pretty*. Its touch was gentle, the brush of a finger against a cheek, meadows and flowers and sunshine, how nice to see myself in all of those things. And how unexpected. How tempting it would be to follow this boy around and get to see myself through his eyes. Christopher, wearing buttons on his lapel that said, Eat the Rich and Nazi Punks Fuck Off and who talked about roast potatoes and Legos.

I had become accustomed to the icy calculations of men like Jonah, the way Rockabilly Mike had just nodded after my show, *Nice act*. He had said it with almost a smirk. They all had to be such dicks about everything. True, it had led me to Mike's bed, but not because I believed his implicit disparagement, that in his jaded experience he had seen other, better women. The trade seemed fair to me. Give him my body and get to warm myself in the heat of his desire. I didn't need his kindness too. But this guy was just throwing it out there, a compliment tossed at my feet like a gift with nothing asked in return. Or at least not yet. It felt nice.

"Thank you," I said.

"It's just a fact. I hate people that pretend not to notice stuff like that, fucking liars." He brushed me away like it was a discussion long since resolved. "It needs to be something special." He murmured to himself. "What bars do you like?"

This seemed to sum up all one needed to know about another person, but before I could answer he shook his head. "No, that won't do. Bars, bars, so boring, so obvious. You're too special for a bar."

"No one has ever said that about me before." How could

anyone be too special for a bar? I couldn't even imagine. He again brushed it off like it was no big deal. "Well, it sounds like you just got kicked out of wherever you live, and I'm not taking you to my place, just so you know. And I've only got a little while to hang out."

He wasn't paying attention and spun his bike bell by hand, slipping the flat metal sphere between what were clearly sweaty fingers. It made a flat, muffled ding each time. "We should just move. Move, motion, speed. Speed, speed, crash into it like a bus without brakes. Good movie but what a dumb way to kill people," he said as an aside. "Just fucking blow them up." He made a little explosive gesture with his fingers and a noise that reminded me of playgrounds, the kind of sounds boys made all the time with their G.I. Joe figures. He stepped astride his bike.

"Hop on."

"What?"

He pulled on my sleeve, caught some of my fake hair and I had to grab at the back of my head before I lost it completely. "I'll ride you," he said, indicating his handlebars.

I laughed loud and short into the air. "No thank you." One of my mom's boyfriends had tried to do this once and I ended up with four stitches in my forehead.

"Come on," he said, smiling. "I promise I'll go slow."

"No offense but you look like you weigh one hundred pounds."

"None taken. I'm fit." He so clearly wasn't that I laughed again. "Please," he said suddenly, and I saw a kind of urgency in his eyes, in that face all soft and yearning and I noticed he was bristling with energy like a racehorse, a young body bursting with drugs and eagerness and all at once it was very easy to step out into the dark loam of possibility, to hand my

body over to someone, anyone, and he seemed so eager for
the burden. "Have you done this before?"

He nodded. "A million times."

"Fine. But be careful. I'm terrible on bikes. I have no sense
of balance." This seemed true on many levels.

His face lit up. "I spent my whole life on this bike. You
don't have to do anything. Sit here." He placed a steadying
hand on the center of the handlebars. "But you can't put too
much weight on the basket or it will break, so maybe kind of
try to get your legs around it and rest your foot underneath
against the fender if you can. Like if you bend and spread your
knees or something."

The absurdity of his instructions felt appropriate to this
new, unexpected turn in the night. Maybe he was right; Jonah
could wait. The right span of time would make it look more
casual. He would be nicer to me if he thought I didn't care.
And I had learned not to turn away from twists of fate like
this, the little fillips of company that a night in the Quarter
so often offered, a sprouting tendril veering off from the stalk
of a vine. It was a gift to someone like me. Somewhere to
go, an hour to burn. A person to whom my presence was a
gift, even if he was all over the place. Or maybe precisely because he was. Something about him made my shoulders feel
looser, the air around me lighter, easier. There was nothing
outwardly reassuring about him, but for some reason he had
that effect. I didn't want to leave him just yet.

I did my best to climb on as he had indicated, while he
held the bike steady, as steady as he could, and I noticed
again how thin he was and wondered if he would be able to
carry our weight. But before I could ask, with a few wobbling jumps forward, he stood and leaned hard on the pedals
and we took flight.

I gasped, and then the wind, the speed, a mix of terror and delight ripped a shout from my chest, high and loud, carrying up and out into the night as we hopped the curb and flew the wrong way down the bumpy street. He did it. "Be careful," I yelled.

"I got you," he said, quietly and close to my ear.

Brightly painted houses with drawn shutters passed in a blur. Gas lamps flickered in arched doorways and the clouds and the fog seemed to bow low, a purple embrace of the quiet town and our reckless progress. Familiar streets from an unfamiliar vantage passed like a movie. At each bump, his bike rattled loudly, a bunch of spare parts just barely held together, and I gripped the cold steel bar beneath me even tighter, tensing all my muscles to stay on my impossible perch. The bright lights of a daiquiri store flew by, huge machines churning rainbow vats of colored liquids. A dog barked at us from behind a gate, indignant. Christopher swerved around a giant pothole and I shrieked again, and he laughed, breathless now against my neck. The forward momentum pushed me against his narrow chest, his arms wrapping around me. He smelled like dirty laundry and I relaxed against him, shutting my eyes, feeling only the wind and his heart pounding, his breath heavy with effort.

He cut over toward the river, riding through the parking lots behind the retaining wall and crossed up and over the train tracks on a narrow walkway of wooden planks that rattled me and the bike like a set of false teeth. Then with a desperate gasping push from him, we were up over the small hill of the levee and riding along the flat path on top. In the distance, the lights of Algiers twinkled on the far shore, and the big black sludgy expanse of the river rippled between us. The sound of waves lapped at the rocks down below and I breathed in deeply at the sudden vista of sky and water all submerged in the same dark murmuring. After all the narrow streets of the Quarter, the river felt as endless as outer space. "I love it up here," I said, my voice disappearing into the wind.

I think he tried to answer *me too*, but he was breathless and concentrating on pedaling.

"You don't have to go so fast," I tried to suggest.

But he just laughed, and I knew that he knew what a joy there was in all this wind and water, and that he would burst his heart right open to keep the two of us caught in that ecstatic forward blur. Some gutter punks were drumming on the grass, transient, close to the trains that they would hop to other cities and other gutters. Their dog looked up at me as we passed, a sweet-looking pit bull with a soft face like the velvet fuzz of a peach, and I wanted to leap down and bury my face in his broad forehead. Ida had been so frail. Her bones becoming weightless in the last few weeks, like a bird. I wanted to take him home and let him see that some humans took their responsibilities seriously, offering stability and constancy, safety and security to our puppies, a communion of two to shelter together from the harsh world. I was mad that these homeless teenagers with their face tattoos and bongos wouldn't be able to do that for him. My eyes watered but the rushing wind blew away my tears, a single stream that ran back into my ear.

Then, since we were running out of boardwalk, Christopher turned his bike down another path to cross back over the train tracks and into the streets. I was glad he knew that I didn't want to ride farther down to where they had redone the riverfront, turned it into a brightly lit pedestrian destination, where the bricks were all too clean and the landscaping too fresh, the signs too aggressively cheerful. The river belonged to the quiet warp of the old boardwalk and not to the stupid city council riverfront revitalization schemes or whatever. But he knew. And I liked that he knew.

When we burst back onto Decatur Street, the souvenir shops up here were still open and loud Cajun music blared from the propped-open doors of big tourist bars. All the lights were too bright, a searing fluorescent blue. Four women in pink cowboy hats hooted at us as we rode past, raising their drinks and cackling. Somewhere a man yelled something insulting. We almost ran into a couple whose argument had slipped off the sidewalk and into the street. I shrank back against the noise and confusion and the sudden feeling of visibility. My delicate joy withered in the face of all the loud, manufactured fun of the upper Quarter. Christopher, sensing my dismay, asked, "Wanna see something cool?"

That sort of a question was never really a question and since I had already abandoned myself to his strained athleticism, I nodded, my eyes shut against the inflamed pink faces of Southern vacationers. He turned off toward Jackson Square and coasted down the stone ramp, hitting the broad flagstones with another shattering rattle that made me worry about the bike. And then he stopped, and I slid off, hitting my butt against the basket, scratching my ankle against the sharp wire lattice. I felt flushed and shining, my heart pounding. "That was really fun," I granted him.

He was still panting and slipped the heavy chain off his waist and around his bike, locking it to a lamppost with a quick, practiced agility. He smiled a shy apology. "It's no car, but it's not a bad way to travel."

"Did I wear you out? Was I too heavy?" I felt his continued breathlessness almost like a reprimand.

His look was so contemptuous, I didn't pursue it. "Come on," he said.

We crossed the square, the cathedral looming above us, white and stern. I wished they didn't keep it so clean. They had washed all the years off of it, which in such a filthy city made this building a stranger, too gleaming, unreal, something only for postcards and photographs. When I was little, I once asked my mom if going to Mary Immaculata made me a Catholic. She exhaled a long plume of menthol cigarette smoke and told me I was lucky they hadn't set me on fire already. We had never been to synagogue and she kept a Joan of Arc candle on her dresser next to the mirrored box full of cheap jewelry. Religion in general was a confusing jumble.

I watched the back of this strange young man, Christopher, walking in front of me. His boxy suit had faded to a rusty black and the uneven hem of his pants bounced against his high-top sneakers. Watching his skinny ankles, the funny way he rolled through each step, headlong and hesitant at the same time, made me feel kindly toward him. He also kept glancing back at me to see if I was still following and seeming surprised every time that I was. At one point he tripped, and I reached for his arm to steady him, but he slid out of my grasp before I could, and I saw the back of his neck flame red for a minute. He turned the corner to the quieter side of the square and stopped in the shadow of a tree next to the high railings that bound the garden in the center of the square. He looked both ways and then locked his hands together and bent down.

"What are you doing?" I asked.

"Go over. I'll give you a boost."

The garden was locked at night and the railings, sunk into a stone wall that already came up chest high, were another six feet over that.

"Are you kidding?"

"You've got to do it quick though. Here." He held out his clasped hands expectantly.

"Sorry, there is no way." I walked a few feet away and sat down on one of the iron benches in the middle of the square. It was very uncomfortable, colder than I expected, and the narrow, rounded slats dug into my back. That's all I needed. Another run-in with the police. Last time they had given me a pretty inconsequential scolding for trying to start fires, but I was much older now and I had no plan on ever seeing the inside of central lockup. I had heard plenty about the moldy bologna sandwiches and that they took your bra away.

"Ryan and I do this all the time. Trust me. I've got no money, no car, no place to stay, my best friend hates me, my parents kicked me out. My sister, who was once the coolest girl in the whole world, married an asshole and doesn't talk to me because I'm a dirty loser. I've never had a real girlfriend, but you know what? I spend a lot of time on my bike and in the Quarter at night, and I know some cool things, and you're so fucking pretty I can't even look at you, and this is all I've got, so would you please, please just step on my goddamn hands?" At the far end of the square, a group started slowly moving toward us, stumbling and loudly singing a Jimmy Buffett song. "I mean, do you want to run into those guys?"

They did provoke a kind of immediate urge to escape, and as I still wasn't quite ready to leave this guy and the odd instinctive kinship I felt in his company, I stood up. On the opposite side of the square, a police car slid down to cruise slowly around the perimeter. "Hurry up," he said more urgently. "Please."

Despite my one glaring exception, I had never really been a delinquent. An early drinker, yes, but that barely counted

in this town. I had started hanging around the Quarter
senior year, but it really wasn't until I had come back to town
that I realized the immense freedom that opens up to you
once you had failed. The way once you have given up, life
just unfolds all around you in possibility because there are
no rules anymore, because nothing matters. A lesson this kid
had clearly already figured out. And here he was, with his
cupped hands offering me the only thing that still mattered—
company, because the road down was only terrifying when
you were alone. And it was kind of cute that we were wearing the same sneakers. "Fine."

Again, he looked surprised and I wondered why he kept
offering things he didn't expect anyone to take him up on. I
stood up and eyed the distance to the top of the spiky railings.

"Let me help. It's easy once you get some momentum. Just
up and over."

I leaned back and threw my bag over the top. It landed
with a thump on the other side. Once a choice was made, I
always found it easy to throw myself into the follow-through.
Maybe too easy. But this was the part I liked—the doing
without thinking too much about it. I grabbed an iron rail
in each hand and hoisted myself up to the top of the stone
wall. I stood on the ledge for a second, enjoying my height.
The rails were thick and cold in my hands and the square
looked different from up here. I could see all the way from
the noisy buskers still active at Café Du Monde on Decatur
to the silent corner of Chartres Street. In the distance, the
lights of the police car flickered through the hedges of the
garden. The raucous group singing "Cheeseburger in Paradise" got closer. "Yeah," his voice said from below, "that's
probably the worst place you could stop and hang out if you
don't want to get busted."

With a quick jolt of fear, I wedged the narrow soles of my sneakers between the bars and, grabbing the decorative points at the top, pulled myself up, just snagging the crossbar of the top of the fence with my other foot, and flung myself over with a desperate propulsion. I landed with a soft thud in the dirt of the other side, and in retrospect the leap seemed embarrassingly easy. Christopher shimmied up and over with the ease and strength of a young monkey, light and heedless. Thumping down beside me in a crouch, he took my hand and pulled me down and through a row of formal hedges into the deep landscaping all around the edge of the park. And just like that we disappeared.

15

NOVEMBER 1999
MASSACHUSETTS

"Hey," I tried again to break into the clump of girls hanging around the stone wall outside the dining room. "Are all y'all freezing too? I am." As soon as the words were out of my mouth, I cringed. I knew what was coming, and I could hear it too, but the effort of trying to be friendly, the self-conscious agony of greeting a not particularly friendly group of freshman girls made me sound ridiculous.

"Oh my God, 'all y'all'?" someone laughed. "There's even a plural?" They were all wearing the same ugly fleece jackets. Everyone here dressed like Ida's middle-aged dog groomer and I just didn't get it. There followed the usual few minutes of imitating my accent. Since I had arrived, I had been caught in a cycle where the more uncomfortable I became, the more absurdly Southern my voice sounded, and I didn't blame them for making fun of me. I laughed awkwardly and then sat on the wall at the edge of the group. After thirteen years of Catholic school, I was still unused to the idea of talking to boys. Even if this group of girls weren't exactly welcoming, attaching myself to them was better than going into the dining hall alone and having to look around, holding my tray like an absolute ass. These girls lived in my hall, and I could still shuffle in under their cover.

Or maybe I could just grab an apple from the salad bar and eat it in my room. The food was hardly worth all this social anxiety. How could anyone stand to eat things like Salisbury steak and clam chowder? Everything was gross and tasteless and still people seemed to eat it like it didn't matter. Just one more thing that seemed too strange here. Everything was odd in ways that I hadn't expected. People didn't say hi when you passed on the paths. Even the girls I hated at home, we all said hi in the same fake lilting way when we passed each other at school, and while before I hated the hypocrisy of it, now I missed the connection. But more than anything I missed Gaby. I wasn't ready for how much harder it was to face all of this without the consolation of a friend at my side. It had been twelve years that she was my partner in every new experience, and now I was alone on this ugly, windswept hill and the trees were already bare and it felt like the whole world was dying. I was surprised at how terrible just the changing of the seasons made me feel. The sun itself was disappearing and I couldn't stop shivering. "Just wait till February," my roommate said. She was from New Hampshire and had all kinds of practical raincoats and boots and listened to terrible music where every song went on forever and she hated me. I could tell.

All the money I earned from my work-study job at the bookstore I spent on calling cards home. But when Gaby answered, she didn't sound the same. She kept cutting off my complaining about the girls, the weather, the food, with a curt "hmm," when what I wanted more than anything was sympathy. I was sympathetic when she talked about how annoying it was to be stuck in New Orleans, to still live with her mom, or how she was taking eighteen credits or whatever. All I wanted was the same from her about my aching, terrible, unexpected homesickness. It didn't help that my midterms had been a mess. Even my history teacher who I was half in love with and so excited to impress had just scrawled a devastating "clever but lazy" on my last essay. Gaby and I had always been in the smart group together, and now it was like no one noticed me. I mean, I had gotten a scholarship, hadn't I? I was trying in a way I hadn't ever before and maybe the fact that I was trying and still fucking up made it that much worse.

It really was cold on this wall and I thought about going inside just to get out of the wind. The leather jacket Mom and I found at Thrift City was not doing the job at all. A few weeks ago, I had tried to solve the dining room problem by sitting down at the black kids' table, thinking that it wouldn't be weird, but after their initial surprise and confusion, they had been so thorough in ignoring me that finishing my cereal had been one of the most humiliating ten minutes of my life. Even when I'd complained about it to Gaby, all she said was, "Maybe leave them alone," which I did, but it still seemed strange. I thought the north was supposed to be different. I mean, I'm from as far south as it's possible to get in this country and no one thought it was strange that Gaby and I ate lunch together every day. "Well, it's not like there were any other black kids for me to sit with at Immaculata," she had said with a laugh, but it made me feel funny so I changed the subject. I couldn't tolerate anything getting in between us, not during those precious hours on the phone when I could actually talk to someone who understood me. Even when we weren't talking, the silence of the phone line was comforting, just knowing she was there, on the other side.

"Hey, Jackie O." The girls at school had started calling me by this nickname after a party a few weeks before when I had impressed everyone with my ability to consume quantities of Jack Daniel's. The rest of the girls shrieked and grimaced after every shot, all puking within a few hours, and I had made quite an impression by being the last one standing. "There's an off-campus party this Friday, do you want to come with us?"

I hesitated. I had had some vague idea that I would be more serious in college. This was my chance to turn out differently from my mom, to show that I was going to be my own person. I was going to wake up early and get good grades and be some better, cleaner version of myself. But I'd had a pretty good time at the party the other night. All this awful shyness melted away with a few drinks, and I was awesome suddenly; everybody liked me. "Oh, you're from New Orleans," a girl had said, splashing Southern Comfort on her college hoodie. "A girl from my high school went there once and had to have her stomach pumped."

"She was clearly an amateur," I'd answered with a smile and took another shot and everyone cheered. The world was warm in the glow of someone's lava lamp and the *Reservoir Dogs* soundtrack was playing. The knot of tension that had sat in my stomach since I arrived on campus finally eased and I was happy. Thank God it turned out I was good at something. An alcohol tolerance built from ordinary life at home seemed special and impressive here, and since I was proving myself totally unremarkable in every other way, I couldn't pass it up.

"Yeah, okay," I said to the party. I would find some other time to study.

"Awesome." A girl with sandy-blond hair in an ugly scrunchie smiled at me, and I knew in the deliverance of that moment I would probably say yes anytime they asked me.

16

TWELFTH NIGHT 2004
JACKSON SQUARE

Jackson Square. I have a picture of myself here as a baby. In stiff, old-fashioned lace-up shoes, I'm standing on the pebbled path squinting and grinning, balanced on two thick legs, rolls of baby fat squeezed by the elastic of a romper embroidered with pansies. My mom is sitting behind me, thin, young, in big gold hoops and a low-cut '70s denim shirt. She's holding her elbow, cigarette poised near her face and staring at something off camera. Andrew Jackson's statue looms over us. Old ladies used to sit around the square selling birdseed in little packets. Feeding and then chasing the pigeons that had gathered is one of my first memories of pure joy. The whole flock would scatter, rising up into the air, a frantic beating of gray wings that ruffled my hair and made it feel like the whole world was spinning away, uplifted.

Then in junior high, Gaby and I used to beg rides from her mom so that we could come here to wander around the bright, touristy mall of the Jackson Brewery, buying expensive slabs of fudge, high on the novel pleasure of independence. We went to Café Du Monde, feeling like grown-ups. Sitting alone, we ordered from the tiny green menu pasted on the side of the silver napkin dispensers. A dollar twenty-five for beignets, another seventy-five cents for the coffee, sweet and milky that we had already started drinking. We bit into puffy sweet clouds of fried dough. I always messed up, inhaling too soon and then choking on the powdered sugar, Gaby whacking me on the back. "She's fine," she explained to worried mothers from other places. "Now look, you got his attention, and that creepy man's going to come talk to us." There were always men floating around, panhandling, trying to sell a deflating balloon animal, playing a few suggestive notes on a trumpet, as if we would pay him to continue. And to each in his turn, Gaby would direct that excruciating politeness. That smile, a gracious reply to whatever junkie was trying to seat himself at our table until I finally snarled at him to go away. "Why are you so polite to those guys?" I teased her.

"I can't help it," she laughed, but there was something tense in her, and even then, I could feel the blurred outlines of it, something terrible in the way that Gaby lived in a world of particular rules, codes of behavior that never occurred to me. When we were little, she often had stomach aches at school. The only thing that helped, she swore, was to lie flat, facedown, nose pressed into the scratchy carpet of the classroom's "quiet reading corner," her hands cradling her belly. I remembered Sister Agnes's annoyed face when she said, "Again, Gaby?"

I still passed through the square almost every day to catch the bus up to Magazine Street for work, but it had been years since I had come into the garden at the center and the memories it unlocked felt strangely fresh. I had certainly never been in here at night and so all that familiarity, the sunlit days of childhood, passed into shadow, like looking at a stage after someone had turned out the lights. Floodlights angled up from below made the contours of everything stand out too clearly, and Jackson's statue reared against the black sky, enormous. His horse strained its open mouth against the bridle and pawed the air with its front two legs, weightless, helpless tons of bronze. Seen so close, Jackson's rakish salute was kind of terrifying, and I looked away. Christopher was watching me, waiting for my approval. "Wow," I said honestly.

We were in the bushes, a little clearing hidden on all sides by tall plants. On one side, elephant ears rustled between us and the iron fence, their huge heart-shaped leaves shielding the small patch of dirt and roots where we sat. On our other side, manicured box hedges formed a thick green wall. Above, an oak tree's spreading branches turned the streetlamps into dappled spots of light. While I looked around in silent appreciation, the drunk tourists finally passed by, so close I could have reached through the branches and railings and touched them. The cathedral bell rang once for the half hour and the police car flashed its siren, one loud blip, at the tourists. Life swirled around us. And here we were, suddenly safe in the hidden heart of it all.

"Pretty cool, huh?" he asked.

"How did you find this place?"

"Me and Ryan figured this out one night, just being drunk and fucking around and then it's been kind of our spot ever since."

He still talked like a teenager, half-hearted cadences alternating with bursts of sincerity, but it was hard to tell in this town. He was part of a certain life that was remarkably elastic. Punky delivery boys were like bartenders that way and their youth could stretch out the better part of decades. A cheap room and a few friends were all you needed to enjoy the special place the Quarter reserved for people who had stopped living for the daylight hours. I wanted to know where on that arc he was, how far in this light and easy freedom of drugs and minimum wages he had endured. But I didn't want to ask.

Since we had entered this little spot, he had been looking at me with a peculiar directness, and I wanted to keep him talking to put off what was so clearly in his mind. I wasn't about to fuck in the bushes.

"How did you guys become friends?"

He leaned on one arm, shifting closer to me. "Shows, bars, I don't know. Our scene is just kind of like that. You see each other around enough and then suddenly you're best friends."

"Really?" I asked. "I don't think of my burlesque friends like that. I mean, we've never had a real conversation. It's all pasties and guys. Although, I don't know," I added, thinking of Chantal. "I guess there are some who are different."

He lay down, propping his head on his hand and inching ever closer to me. "Yeah, I lied. That's not how it happened."

"Well?"

"What is there to say? Sometimes you just get someone. Life felt easier when I was with Ryan. I like myself better with him. I like myself better with you too."

I could see where he was coming from and in a strange way, I felt a similar involuntary ease, like I wanted to stay with him and his funny loose-limbed manner in this green-domed pillow fort. "You've known me for, like, five minutes," I countered. He didn't seem concerned and just kind of shrugged. I wondered if all that stuff about me being too special for bars had just been to lead me here, the bushes, where a guy who doesn't even have a place of his own brings girls. "Is this where you bring people to make out?" I asked.

He sat up quickly and that flash of discomfort burned in

him again so suddenly I almost apologized. He was awfully sensitive. "Why would you say that?" Then he flopped down on the ground flat on his back on the roots and rocks, not looking at me. "Fuck. Just fucking fuck everything. Why is everyone against me?"

I suspected it might be the drugs making him so careless with his body, but it definitely added to the impression I had of something too young. Like a puppy that hadn't learned the stillness of resignation. "I'm not against you, dude. I'm just making conversation."

He sighed and waited, some internal calculation that I wasn't privy to. Then he propped himself up on his elbow again. "If you want to know what happened between me and Ryan, why he got all weird on me, it's because we hooked up, okay? I gave him a hand job and then he flipped out," he said quickly, watching for my reaction with a certain hostility.

"Oh." I hadn't been expecting that. Had I been wrong about the waves of desire I had been feeling from this kid? I tried to make my face indifferent, but I had been expecting our interaction to be based on his wanting to fuck me, so for a moment I was at a loss. This, however, was much more interesting.

But as I was trying to adjust to this new dynamic between us, he saw my confusion and answered with a frown that was almost a snarl. "I'm not a fag, just so you know."

I bristled. "Why would I care if you were?"

"I'm into girls," he added, again a little aggressively.

"Okay, sure, whatever," I reassured him, and then because I was really curious, asked him, "Was that something you guys usually did? I mean, is that something guys usually do?" I actually knew so little about the secret interior worlds of men. I wanted this kid to keep talking. Were there whole complicated worlds moving behind the blankness of the desire that they turned in my direction? The possibility made me like men in general slightly more.

"No." He shrugged. "I mean, sure. Who cares? It didn't have to mean anything. We're together all the time anyway, it was just a thing. He's such a hypocrite." He paused as though intending to stop there and then almost as if compelled to keep going, I guessed from the drugs, resumed. "You know, what the fuck? We watch porn together all the time, but if I touch your dick all the sudden I'm gay?" He glanced at me again to quickly check my reaction, but then returned to his own internal argument. "It's fucking lame. Especially from a guy who wore a devil's lock for two years. Homophobia is pretty fucking square if you ask me."

He was obviously upset, yet I couldn't help but be a little fascinated. It was kind of thrilling to discover a problem so far out of my experience. People were so interesting. And men. My years of Catholic school and the hookups since then meant that I knew nothing of the murky territories of male friendship. "You watch porn together?" I asked.

"Straight porn," he said rather sternly, but this seemed of little consequence compared to the tremendous intimacy he was describing. "All guys do. It's really not a thing."

"Really? Okay." I was still a little unconvinced. Then I remembered his face in the bar, that sudden quick despair that he hadn't been able to hide. There was more to all of this. "Are you in love with him?" I whispered, but as I spoke, I felt a funny disappointment, as though I had lost something.

"No." He ran his hands through his greasy hair, and it stuck up from his head in sprouts. "God, that's probably what he thinks too. I just need to talk to him, you know, when there aren't like ten of us around. I didn't mean to freak him out." He stared at the ground, his forehead creased. "I just wanted—" He stopped. "And why am I even telling you all this?" he asked in annoyance.

"Because I'm interested."

"That's how this all started with Ryan. I told him things that I had never told anyone before. I'm always spilling my guts and it fucks everything up." His ears got red and he had that sudden look of fragility again, an impression of being made of eggshell, translucent, pale, and I reached out to touch his arm. He startled at the touch and then tried to cover it up by crossing his arms and rubbing his elbows like he was cold. "He makes really good scrambled eggs," he said finally. "And I have these moments sometimes where I start to freak out. It's happened since I was a kid, like I really kind of lose it and he was always good at chilling me out. Sometimes he'd even sit on me, like just hold me down until it passed and, I don't know."

"Like a panic attack?"

"I don't know. If my parents had ever brought me to a doctor, maybe I would know why I puke at all the wrong times and get the shakes like a crackhead, but we don't do that in our family. 'Nervy,' is what they call me and that's that. Whatever. But Ryan never freaked out about it. He just kind of fixed it when it happened. I don't know, he didn't mind." He caught himself as if remembering me and tried to play it all off. "Whatever, it's not a big deal. I can find somewhere to sleep. There's always a punk house to crash in." Then changing his mind yet again, he sighed. "My stuff is at his place. I don't know what I'm going to do now."

"I don't know what I'm doing either," I admitted. "Do any of us?"

He looked up at me, relieved, and for a moment we were

caught together in a glow of understanding, and then he reached out and gently felt my breast.

"Dude." I slapped his hand away.

"Sorry." He shrugged and kind of laughed, and somehow this had the effect of resetting our relations. He began pulling leaves off one of the hedges and tearing them into little pieces.

I felt back on more steady ground. "So." I had been about to ask him if he was from here, but somehow, I knew that he was. So instead, I relapsed into that catechism of new acquaintance. "So, Christopher of the twitchy disposition, where'd you go to high school?"

"Why does everybody ask that?" His whole body stiffened again, and he kicked at a root with the heel of his sneaker. "Why does it matter?"

I shrugged. "Don't you think we should get to know each other better?"

"It's such a bullshit question though. St. Francis De Sales won't tell you shit about me. It was a pit of assholes and sadists and priests copping feels from little boys' gym shorts."

I let that go, but my question had done its work. St. Francis De Sales was the fanciest boys' private school in town. This kid was supposed to be at home on St. Charles Avenue. Not here in the bushes covered in filth and smelling like last week's laundry. I poked his Eat the Rich button. "And this?"

"Yeah, what of it? Fuck those people. Fuck my parents and all their drunk, racist country-club friends. I hope they're all first up against the wall when the revolution comes."

"That may be a long time coming in this town," I said, but he wasn't going to get off that easily. I knew this world existed, the social precincts of Uptown New Orleans, an enclosed terrarium of privilege, the mossy loam of centuries of tradition and wealth. You feel it at Mardi Gras parades, looking up at the floats and the riders hidden behind their silk masks, plastic cups in hand, drunk on self-aggrandizement and noblesse oblige while we ordinary folks raised our hands, begging them for trinkets and beads. Secret societies, balls, debutantes, the rolling tinsel of centuries-old krewes, the old-fashioned masks and capes that made them look like so many multicolored, velvet-draped figures of terror. I had never met anyone who went to St. Francis and I wanted to know more. How did he get here? I had slipped down maybe a rung or two from my barely respectable, vaguely slutty mom, but we existed in the same universe. This guy had bypassed whole continents in his downward spiral. He should be drinking Johnnie Walker in a Perlis button-down shirt and feeling up a deb in her parents' downstairs powder room. If he were gay, or even kind of, that would be a whole thing where he came from.

Once, my boss at the lingerie store forgot her phone on her way to her usual Friday afternoon lunch at Galatoire's and I had to bring it to her. The frosted glass door closed behind me and once inside the bright, icy air-conditioned room, I looked around at the tables, chairs, brass light fixtures, everything frozen, perfectly maintained, like they hadn't been changed in a hundred and fifty years. I couldn't believe what was going on in that beautifully appointed room. Everyone was wasted. Like falling down, "spilling old-fashioneds on white table-cloths" wasted. Women in pearls strolled from table to table, chardonnay in hand, grabbing the backs of bentwood chairs for support, cackling and shrieking their gentle Southern syllables. People sang loudly. Anecdotes were yelled across the room. Waiters splashed streams of flaming coffee into silver urns with long, delicately handled silver ladles. Corks popped, dishes clattered. Men in seersucker jackets sweated

and laughed, pink jowls shaking. Someone stood on a chair
singing the Ole Miss fight song. Strangers joined in, upraised
glasses spilling booze. The long mirrors that covered the walls
spun the chaos into an endlessly reflecting mural while the
tile floor heightened the noise into a clamor. And all of this
was happening at two in the afternoon on a weekday, and it
was all hidden from the prying eyes of the uninvited by the
taut white curtains covering the front windows. I had never
seen anything like it. It was fascinating, especially to a low-
income, self-conscious Jew. "Have you ever been to Galatoire's?" I asked him.

He raised his two middle fingers in reply. "Fuck that place
too. Have you ever seen *Night of the Hunter*?" he answered
instead. "Do you think it would be cool or stupid to get *love*
and *hate* tattooed on your knuckles like Robert Mitchum?"
He didn't wait for me to answer. "I wish so many other people hadn't done it, but it really sums everything up, right?
Crazy that he's supposed to be a preacher in that movie. Bap-
tists are nuts."

"It would be stupid," I answered, but he was looking at his
knuckles reflectively and wasn't listening.

"I used to work at Blockbuster," he continued, changing
the subject. "Movies are just..." he paused and looked into
the branches above us, searching for the word "...they're just
everything. I'd just die without movies," he said finally. Then
he began chewing on a thumbnail that was already bitten to
the quick. "Do you throw a punch with the love hand or the
hate? I'd go for the love, nice irony there."

He was not going to talk about his background, which
was disappointing. This guy had strange priorities of what
he wanted to share and didn't. "I had to turn that movie off
halfway through." He looked up at me, appalled, and I felt

I had to clarify. "I felt too sad for those kids. No one taking care of them." He was about to argue so I shook my head. "I don't like movies where kids are in danger."

"I've been working on a script." He pulled a bunch of crumpled papers from his back pocket and then gingerly unfolded them. The lined sheets were covered in a messy scrawl.

I extended my hand. "You walk around with a movie script in your back pocket?"

He didn't seem to see anything funny about it and handed it into my waiting palm with hesitation. "Careful, it's my only copy. I really like Tarantino."

"Of course you do." In the shadows that flickered over the page, I couldn't make out the words, but I liked looking at them anyway. He had been using a ballpoint pen that kept running out, making him write so hard he tore the pages in places. It was hard to see all that frantic sprawl and not feel a gentleness. "You should write a script about Uptown people. They are so entertaining to the rest of us."

"No thanks. I want to make something that lets people just go away for a couple of hours, get out of their heads, get out of their lives, you know, action films, heist stories," he continued. "I probably watched four movies a day until I started hanging out with Ryan. I still do sometimes. I did," he corrected himself and flinched a little.

I could have told him just how much I understood that desire to escape, but even in the shelter of all these whispering plants, there were some things you couldn't explain. Like how after I had failed out of college, I couldn't even watch dumb comedies. Every time someone got humiliated, or disappointed, my heart shattered for them, a wave of newfound empathy that broke over me and made me turn it off and bury my tears in Ida's indulgent fur. That you can't watch *Dumb and Dumber* because it keeps making you cry is not the kind of thing you can really admit to. I handed him back his papers. "I like when people want to make things."

But he had already slipped from enthusiasm into embarrassment. "Yeah, whatever. It's probably shit just like everything I do." He shoved the pages back in his pocket. "So, Rosemary. Since we're doing it this way, where'd you go to high school?"

I was glad he also knew intuitively that I was local. I was glad for a moment of solidarity. I was glad to be sitting here, on the crunch of dried magnolia leaves in the fresh rich smell of dirt and roots. "Mary Immaculata."

He grimaced. And then, to my utter outrage, I saw a look of contempt cross his face. "Oh. I didn't know you were one of those."

"How dare you. You just said you went to the fanciest school in town."

"Yeah, but I hated it. Look at me. I'm a fucking punk. Immaculata girls are materialistic cunts."

"Yeah, I know they are, you asshole. I hated it too. I grew up with a broke single mom. At least I'm not some slumming rich kid." He didn't even flinch, and I guessed he had heard that before. "Do I look like a fucking cheerleader in designer clothes to you?"

He actually looked at me, considering, and I remembered why I hated this conversation about high schools. "What are you, seventeen?" I asked, trying to find an advantage.

"Twenty," he answered proudly instead.

For a moment this held me. Twenty. Oh, to be twenty and still possess as much awkwardness as this guy had eking out of his bones. Men, men could stay children forever it seemed. By the time I turned twenty, I was as old as I'll ever be and everything since has just been passing the hours. By twenty, I knew I wasn't going back to college. At first it seemed as if they might reconsider the alcohol infractions, and I spent my forced leave of absence pouring badly made lattes with milk that never seemed to foam. It was like I was cursed—all the milk that passed through my hands at that dumb coffee shop refused to give up more than a thin, watery froth. But then the school said no. And that was that. All my potential erased in a polite letter of dismissal. Or a retraction of my scholarship, which amounted to the same thing.

I moved into a tiny apartment in the Quarter that I rented from a racist old lady who used to dance on Bourbon Street and whose windows were lined with an unfortunate collection of pickaninny figurines. *You're just two blocks away from where I used to live before I had you,* my mom had said, a fake cheeriness to make me feel better that was instead a million times worse, before she turned back to *Days of Our Lives.* And now here I was, arguing with a ratty little jerk about who had been more miserable in high school.

And it was obviously me. "You don't know anything about me. I was more punk than you'll ever be. In high school I set my principal's lawn on fire." I was a little ashamed of myself, but whatever. This kid needed to be put in his place.

"Oh yeah?" He raised an eyebrow, and as quick as that, I had returned in his esteem.

"Yeah," I said, trying to decide how much of the story I was going to tell him. "I was going to do her house, but I didn't want to kill anyone by accident. Me and my best friend just tried to burn her lawn. It turns out grass is hard to set on fire, so it was really dumb, but still, I did it."

"That is pretty badass," he said, settling back into a valley between roots and looking at me with a returning warmth. "Did you get in trouble?"

"Yeah, she called the cops." I spoke knowing this would impress him, as well. I remember the look of terror that Gaby gave me when we heard the sirens. I think she almost peed herself. Cops are so scary in theory. Until you see them, and they're just big fat white dudes looking so bored. And you could practically tell he was trying not to smile. He wasn't even a real cop, just neighborhood watch. I teased her about that for weeks. "But they let us go. It was fine."

"Bar fights and arson." Christopher was looking at me very, very softly again. "I think I might be in love with you."

I laughed. This guy was all over the place, but I felt better. I needed that flame of admiration. And in spite of everything, he still seemed like kind of a sweetheart. Something gentle lurked under all this anxious fidgeting. I wanted to help him.

Then as if to prove me wrong, he sprang in my direction. He lost his balance landing on top of me and aiming, I think, to kiss my mouth, but missing and slobbering on the side of my jaw. I hit the ground and felt a stone beneath me jab into my shoulder blade.

"I'm sorry. I'm sorry," he mumbled, instantly apologetic. He was light and uncoordinated enough that he didn't feel like much of a threat. I knew I could shove him off with one push. This ill-considered lunge only brought to mind slumber parties and the play fighting you do as a little kid; he felt like a kitten or something pouncing at a toy. Except that he was now trying to kiss my neck. Again, he smelled of old clothes and I thought about all the guys like him I had been underneath in my time. Those shitty apartments with dishes in the sink, the smell of mold creeping in from under buckling floorboards, guys who would fuck me on a futon without a frame, so close to the floor you could smell the dust. A halogen lamp, posters on thumbtacks, a milk crate full of CDs, maybe records if I was lucky and he had taste. The smell of stale masculinity that didn't care and wouldn't care about you in the morning, and the great ease and rest that came from being disregarded like that. But this kid didn't have any place to take me. "Chill out, buddy," I said, giving him a push.

"Please." His voice was muffled by my hoodie, crushed under his face. "Please. I'll tell you something I've never told anyone."

I pushed him harder and he fell back with no resistance. "I don't want your secrets, weirdo," I said, sitting up and brushing leaves out of my hair. But I wasn't sure that was true.

We looked at each other for a minute. He was still panting slightly. "Please. You're so pretty."

"Yeah, so you said." I could understand where he was coming from. There was something about this den here that had the privacy, the sanctity of the confessional. It made you want to share. I had secrets burning a hole in my stomach too. And I was almost tempted. But then it occurred to me again that I was probably not the first person he had brought here, and my feelings got hurt. Was this just what he did? He was watching me closely, an expression that kept switching between his usual look of a deer caught in headlights and something a little more canny. "It seems like you're having trouble making up your mind," I said.

"I swear I'm into girls." He stared into my eyes to make sure I understood. "Don't get the wrong idea."

"Okay. I don't really care. Is this how you usually get laid? Bringing people here and offering secrets and then making out in the bushes? Is this your thing?"

He flinched and he was all eggshells again. But then I had

a funny flash of intuition and I made a guess. "Is this where you had your thing with Ryan?"

He didn't look at me, but his feelings were so raw and visible in his sweaty face, and all of a sudden I put it all together. "Did this all happen tonight!" He nodded, still not looking at me, and I couldn't help laughing. "Jesus Christ. I thought I was having a fucked-up time but you're really cramming it in. Don't you think you should go home and call it a night?"

"Yes, I should go home, but I can't," he yelled back, annoyed. "Because Ryan kicked me out."

"You're a mess," I said affectionately.

"Yeah, thanks."

We sat in silence for a minute while someone far away played "When the Saints Go Marching In" poorly on a saxophone.

"I hate this song," he said finally. "So, what's your deal?"

"What?"

"You just said you were having a fucked-up time. What's going on? Why is someone like you sitting here in the bushes with someone like me?"

"Ugh," I sighed, unpleasantly reminded of myself again. "I don't want to get into it. But let's just say I've had a really shitty night. You've got no home and I don't want to go home to mine. What a pair. Speaking of, I should go in a minute. I've got to go find my friend."

"No." He grabbed my wrist. "Please don't go. Don't go be with that hipster douchebag. He sucks."

"Well, maybe, but we kind of have a relationship and I need his help tonight. And," I added a little meanly because the way he was looking at me was making me feel bad, "at least he's a grown-up."

Christopher didn't seem to notice. "I'm serious. I've never

felt more alone than I did tonight when Ryan looked at me like that and then out of the fucking blue, you run up and punch him in the face. You're all I have. You have to help me."

"Help you do what? Fuck, I'm the one who needs help." I started to pick a few stray leaves off my pants with my free hand in anticipation of getting up. "Listen, Christopher, I'm sure you will make up with your friend. Misunderstandings happen. Tempers cool. You guys will probably be back to normal by tomorrow."

"Come to a party with me," he interrupted me, urgently.

"What?"

"I was going to go with Ryan. I think he will probably still be there, and I could find him and talk to him, but I can't go alone. I mean, I could, but I can't face it."

"What kind of party?" I sighed, still held in his sweaty grasp.

"For Twelfth Night. It's an amazing Twelfth Night costume party. There's a band, free booze. King cake. That's why I'm wearing this suit. It's my costume. I know you would love it, please."

"Pretty boring costume," I said, distracted. King cake. How could I have forgotten about king cake today? I fucking love king cake. Every year I waited and waited and waited for the sixth of January and then I bought one, only colored sugar, no icing, and ate the whole thing myself. Doughy, yeasty, just sweet enough, it was the one food that I felt I could eat forever. That first terrible year at school, my mom had a bakery ship one to me. I don't know if I was more surprised that she would remember and plan ahead enough to order something like that, or by the intensity of joy and longing that I felt cramming that special texture, light and airy and dusted with sweetness, into my mouth. *It tastes like a cinnamon roll*, my idiot roommate had said, unimpressed with the precious slice I gave her. Then I ate the rest of the cake by myself, weeping with homesickness on the hard, narrow bottom bunk. The cake had fallen in its journey and the grainy stripes of colored sugar had melted, and the whole thing had turned to a thick, gluey mess, made all unguent by the snot and silent tears running down my face.

But fresh king cake was the taste of spring, and mild afternoons, and the rumble of a marching band dancing just a foot away from you, the sharp push of the matrons backing up the crowd to make room for the girls tapping in white boots, huge pompoms and batons swaying in time, of my mom laughing and elbowing me to the front of the crowd. Of no bedtime on parade nights, of joyful anticipation, the two of us walking toward the lights of a parade in the distance, hand in hand, my mom whooping and singing along to the songs pouring out of cars and porches and speakers tied to bicycles. A backpack full of Miller Lite, beads jangling around her neck and wrists, holding my hand and making me dance next to her on these nights when the city became what she wanted it to be again, and I got to warm myself in her reflected happiness.

All I wanted in that one moment was a slice of sweet, fluffy, flawless king cake. I had forgotten with everything that happened this afternoon to go buy myself a king cake.

Christopher was watching me intently and I didn't want to let on how much I could be tempted by a slice of cake. How embarrassing. But somehow, I knew that he knew. He knew that deep, atavistic craving for dough and colored sugar. Still, I had plans. "I can't. I'm sorry."

"You'll regret it. It's a really good party."

"You will find another chance to talk to him, I promise," I said, but he looked away and quickly let go of my wrist.

"You'd like it," he said quietly.

"You're a sweet guy," I said, "but I really do have to go find my friend."

He reached out suddenly and grabbed my hand again just for a second. A gesture that felt surprisingly tender, a kind of innocent grasping. "Well, if I can't convince you, can I at least walk you wherever you're going? Where are you going?"

"Big Papa's."

He made a face that was all snotty punk again. "Gross. Strip clubs are gross. Exploitation is fucking gross."

"Yeah, okay." I stood and dusted off my butt. "Don't be rude, some of my best friends work there."

"Hey, I know, some of my best customers work there. Strippers get hungry at two in the morning, but still. They bum me out."

"Well, you don't have to—" I began.

He cut me off. "I'm coming." He stood, then bent over and offered his back as a step for me to get up over the railings. "I was just saying."

I slung my bag crosswise over my chest for stability. "What about you? Where are you going to go?"

"I'll figure it out." He spoke to his own knees, still doubled up for me. "There's always a new gutter to roll in."

"That's the spirit." I grabbed the railings and stepped onto the curve of his shoulders and, trying not to wobble from the boniness of his back, I hoisted myself over the black iron fence. The drop was farther on this side and I had to close my eyes as I tumbled out of the seclusion of the locked garden and fell to my knees on the hard paved stones in the sharp light of the square. I glanced back at him and he was watching me through the bars of the fence with such undisguised longing that I had to look away. I don't know if anyone had ever needed me like that. A little flame burned in my chest, and I wasn't sure if it felt nice or painful. Then he landed at my side with a grunt and I let him spring up and brush my cheek with his lips. I leaned my forehead against his for a minute. He was cold but sweaty. "Come on," I said.

"I'll get my bike on the way back," he mumbled, reaching around and straightening my bag for me with a quick, deliberate tug, then dropping back to walk at my side.

17

In the short time that I had been gone from New Orleans, this had all happened somehow. The Sugarlick was open, and it was filled with loud, glorious women in red lipstick and tattoos. Unapologetic, excessive, hard-drinking, tough-talking broads radiating sex and glamor. After my internment in that bleak, frozen wasteland for college where no one smiled, and everything was low-key, and people wore corduroy, and the world was as dreary as leftover oatmeal, this place made me feel like I had come alive again. I met Chantal one night by sitting next to her at the bar and one thing led to another, and soon we were drinking Jameson together, while a cute guy I had seen around now seemed to know my name and kept buying me drinks. "Yeah, I can't compete with the girls at the Flim Flam Club," Chantal was saying. "They are like superstar Ziegfeld quality, but I could probably pull something together in this dump. There's always room for more tits and ass in this town."

"That sounds amazing," I said enviously. "I wish I could do something like that."

She looked at me, confused. "Why not? You could totally do burlesque. You've got that thing."

"A killer figure?" the cute guy interrupted. He kept saying very complimentary things but in a very dismissive tone. I had no idea if he was flirting with me or making fun of me but either way, I liked the attention.

"Yes, Jonah, obviously." Chantal waved her cup for emphasis. "But I meant an attitude. You kind of look like you're not really giving anything away. Not bitchy exactly, which don't get me wrong, I mean as a compliment, just…" she paused "…distant. Add that to naked titties and men go crazy."

"It's true," he said. "And you should come by Deadman's Cove sometime. I bartend there most nights," he added, looking purposefully into my eyes and then pointedly wandering off to talk to some other girl across the room.

"Actually, fuck the men," Chantal leaned in to whisper to me and her breath was whiskey-sweet and warm. "You should do it because burlesque is awesome and all the girls in my troupe will also be awesome and you should hang out with us. It's such a feeling of power, when you get up there and you own your shit. It's different from how you imagine."

I said I would think about it, but really, I knew if it meant I would get to hang around with Chantal and her friends, I would totally do it. I would get to come to this bar as a performer, no more anxious moments on the threshold wondering if I would know anyone, the nervous few minutes until I started drinking or found an acquaintance. I would have a place in this nightlife world that had already been exerting such a strong pull on me. I already wanted to be here every night. I wanted to stay this confident, brassy girl I became when the sun went down and I started drinking.

My first costume was emerald green and as I glued silky

layers of fringe and trim to my dress, I felt the same nervous tingling of holidays approaching. My mom loved hot glue and Carnival costumes and was always ready to figure out ways to make our silly elaborate ideas come to life—a mermaid stuck in a net, an Egyptian goddess made from cardboard and gold spray paint. This had the same sparkling distraction as the weeks leading up to Carnival, and it was so easy not to think about my recent failures as I planned and stitched and invented. I found a whole new set of skills as my ideas got more elaborate and I cobbled together ways to make them work. Wire structures for feather headpieces, snaps and Velcro for tear-away panels, it was like a part of my brain sitting dormant my whole life had suddenly blossomed with this unexpected talent I was now discovering. Gaby had been pretty busy since I had come back, and selling underwear had left me with an uncomfortable amount of time to think. Working on my act filled up all the space in my life with a kind of thrilling anticipation and wonderful textures that shimmered and sparkled and covered every surface of my small apartment. I was going to dance as a snake shedding my skin, tulle embroidered with sequin scales. Burlesque was funny and odd and sexy and over-the-top and ridiculous, and all at once I had a place for all these feelings that I didn't know what else to do with.

The night of my debut I almost bailed, but then Elsa, another girl who had recently joined our troupe, gave me a shot called a mind-eraser. I loved the poetry of that. "Break a leg, hottie," she said and gave my butt a pinch, and suddenly I was desperate not to let her down. I threw myself onstage expecting the worst, but the strangest sensation came over me once my music started. A feeling of invincibility. I knew exactly how the next three and a half minutes were going to happen and more than that, I felt this bold new awareness that I was going to own them. A strange, fierce pleasure ran down my arms and into my fingertips and there in the spotlight, poised on my high heels, in my armor bright and iridescent as a beetle's wings, I felt blissfully, confidently in control. I was the fullest expression of myself, no apologies, no second-guessing, and the audience felt it too. They believed this person who I was pretending to be, and in their gaze it became true. So, I began to move, and as I filled up the space, just my body and the music and the beautiful layers I had built myself, I knew incontrovertibly that I was special for as long as I was on that stage. They loved me. And I loved them back with all my overflowing, intemperate heart.

Elsa grabbed me in a bear hug when I came off the stage. "I knew it, you're a natural. Sugarlick Ladies, ride or die. Oh fuck." She noticed and tried to disentangle where our costumes had caught together, my tassel stuck in the sharp curve of one of her hook and eyes. I ripped the tasseled pastie off my nipple and tucked it inside her corset where I hoped it wouldn't be noticed, and she ran onstage for her act. I covered my free nipple with my hand in the dark of the wings, naked except for my G-string and laughed silently but uncontrollably, drunk on success and friendship and cheap champagne.

18

TWELFTH NIGHT 2004
THE FRENCH QUARTER

Big Papa's was in a pretty, old building. The curled iron supports of the balcony, the weathered brick of its facade, its bones were still visible under the neon and tinsel that ran the whole length of Bourbon Street like a poorly applied and peeling veneer. Plastic signs were everywhere offering hurricanes in big hourglass cups—seven dollars and fifty cents, drinks that I only ever saw clutched in the hands of people I didn't want to talk to, or later sprayed over the sidewalk, the distinctive dark pink of regurgitated grenadine. Cheap advertisements jostled each other—Jell-O shots, daiquiris, jazz bands, souvenirs— and yet somehow managed to look so temporary, fleeting. Maybe it was the steps of the threshold, ground down and coated in scum, the elegant marble faintly visible underneath, or the delicate balconies, warped and weathered, unused by the fly-by-night businesses below, but still beautiful; it all stood, a silent counterpoint to the transient fizz at street level. I almost kind of liked Bourbon Street and I could imagine the Bourbon Street my mom used to talk about—jazz clubs and artists and wild nights without all the plastic gunk.

I mean, not really. It really was grotesque, and I usually avoided it, but tonight, I felt the sheer volume of noise and people and ugliness crashing around me as waves of frantic, pleasing stimulation. The hawkers, the buskers, the Southern belles standing sadly in cheap crinolines with filthy hems, holding signs offering 2 for 1 Specials and One Drink Minimums, the groups whooping with the desperate enthusiasm of people trying to convince themselves that they were having as much fun as they had paid for. Here in this world-famous depravity, tourists still thought they might lose themselves at last, until the sickness of booze and unacknowledged disappointment made them stumble back to hotel rooms. And then in the gray haze of hungover mornings, maybe they could forget that they had been conned.

But it was still awe-inspiring to watch. It was like being at a concert that was too loud, and you could only feel the immensity of the music in your body, in the trembling of your bones, in the hollow of your chest. The energy of Bourbon Street felt good after the quiet of the square. We were back on my territory, and despite my detour with this guy and his troubles, I was still myself in this hard, plastic nightlife.

"Man, I hate this place." Christopher watched the sea of people stream past. "Every time I come here, I end up getting into fights. You'd think by now I would have learned, but it still happens every time. What?" he yelled at an enormous man wearing a University of Oklahoma jersey.

The thick-necked reveler was too drunk to notice, but before someone else did, I steered Christopher into the alcove of the doorway and up some stairs inlaid with ornate tile, now so filthy as to be almost invisible. "Can you not do that?"

He shrugged me off. "It's these Neanderthals. What a

bunch of meatheads. Nice beads, asshole," he yelled at someone else behind me. "It's not fucking Mardi Gras."

"Well, you just established that technically it is," I corrected
him. He answered me with a look.

Two girls stumbled by with brassy blond highlights and
feathered boas around their necks. "Y'all know where the
Cat's Nightie is?"

I waited for Christopher to say something else stupid, but
he pointed politely and murmured, "Two blocks down."

A group of big guys stopped close behind them. "Hey,
ladies, looking for a party?"

"Fuck you, assholes," Christopher yelled.

"Nice haircut, faggot," one said, unconcerned, and the girls,
laughing, melted into their group and they all continued on,
caught in eddies of bodies moving like the mop water running the length of the dirty street.

"Hey, Christopher, can you just relax a little?"

He was watching them go, still twitching slightly. "It's like
this every time I have to deliver food to the girls. It's like trying to ride your bike through a sea of fuckheads. I consider it a
sacred responsibility to deliver sustenance to hungry strippers
and I have to dodge all these drunk sportsball fans. When I'm
in a good mood it's like a video game, like *Frogger*, but other
nights one thing leads to another and I get punched. It's cool
though. You can't let the dark side win."

We were talking in front of a larger-than-life-size poster
of a naked woman cradling a giant rope that barely covered
between her legs. Her lovely breasts were positioned right
above Christopher's head, and the nipples had a softness to
them, a gentle spreading that made them seem recognizable,
real as opposed to the eight-by-tens posted just to our left, a
wall of tiny, hard points jutting out of lingerie like weapons.

She had blond curls that draped over one shoulder and round, babyish cheeks and even though she was making that face— eyelids lowered, lips parted—of every other sexy poster on this street, she looked somehow incongruous. Her expression didn't quite achieve the blankness of all the Playboy-inspired spreads all around us, and she remained implacably her own individual self. Someone who I wanted to smoke a cigarette with and listen to her complain about her job in a high, soft voice. But maybe the men felt that way too. Maybe that's why she was out here, six feet high, the promise of an intimacy available right inside the door and for a price.

I looked back at Christopher who was watching me with a sulky resignation. "Well," I said.

"Well." He crossed his arms, the dirty white cuffs of his shirt poking out from his jacket.

"It was nice to meet you."

He stared furiously at a picture of a sexy cheerleader next to us. "This is dumb. That guy is dumb. Don't go in there."

"I'm sure I'll see you around. You know what this town is like. I'll probably see you everywhere now. And thanks for the bike ride," I added and meant it. Maybe it was see-ing someone in worse shape than myself, but I felt renewed, like our time in the darkness of the garden had been a nap or a cool bath. Whatever I was dealing with, I was handling it better than he was. And that made me feel better, the surge of confidence I needed to settle things with Jonah. After all, I was the kind of woman people fell in love with in an hour. I could swoop in and illuminate someone else's tragedy like an angel of retribution. I could face the rest of my night know-ing I had this power.

Christopher looked less invigorated. In fact, he kind of looked like he might cry. It was so nice to be on the leaving side. The not-wanting side. This is what I had been waiting for, ever since I had left the Sugarlick with him. The relief of it filled me up and I smiled, unable to totally contain my rising spirits. "Can I kiss you?" he finally said, still addressing himself to the centerfolds on the wall.

"Nope."

The club bouncer laughed. "Ouch, son." He had been standing next to us the whole time, blocking the door but perfectly immobile. I was startled to realize he could hear us. Even though obviously, he could. "Y'all are obstructing the entrance." He moved his hand to the side to indicate which way we should move.

"I'm coming in."

"No unescorted women," he said.

I could feel Christopher's hope perk up next to me.

"I just need to pick up something from one of the dancers."

The bouncer didn't look at me—his gaze stayed fixed on the wall opposite in a way that was hard not to take personally. "No unescorted women, two drink minimum."

I had never had any qualms about lying to bouncers. It felt expected. "Well, I can't buy a drink because the thing I need to pick up is my wallet."

"You gave your wallet to a stripper?" He almost smiled, and I was torn between wanting to defend Elsa and trying to establish a moment of camaraderie with this person blocking my way in his huge black dress shirt. "Nah, I'm just kidding," he said after a minute. "The girls are good people."

"I mean, do you really want this guy to come in with me?" I indicated Christopher. "Does he look like he's got money to spend? I just need to run backstage. I'll be two minutes. Please."

"Yeah, you look like shit, kid. Why'd you do that to your

hair? You need to get you to a good barber. No wonder she doesn't want any of that."

I braced for a round of expletives from Christopher, but he ran his hand through his greasy forelock. "Humphrey Bogart has this haircut in *High Sierra*."

"That's a good movie," the bouncer said, nodding. "I used to watch that shit with my dad. You know what else is a good movie? *Treasure of the Sierra Madre*. That guy had style."

"Exactly," Christopher said.

I was feeling somewhat forgotten.

"But you know what—" the bouncer looked at him with stern emphasis "—dude probably went to a good barber. He probably went to a goddamn movie star barber. That's why he looked cool as shit and that's why your shit is all fucked up."

A kinship had clearly been established and Christopher grinned. "Hey, man, at least I'm trying."

"Not hard enough, clearly. There's one just around the corner on Iberville."

"That's expensive."

"No. It's not," he said definitively, but he stood aside to let me pass. "I like the girl in that movie. Always looking real pissed, but in a good way."

"Ida Lupino," Christopher exclaimed, excited. "She's the best. You know she directed movies too."

I decided this was a good moment to leave. "Bye."

He looked hurt again suddenly, like a punctured balloon, but then I was passing through the curtained door and he and all his youthful agonies were gone in a fluttering of dusty velvet.

Inside the club the bass line of the music was rumbling deep and loud enough to make my heart skip in an uncomfortable way. A girl was dancing onstage to Nine Inch Nails and she seemed a little bored by it. Strolling from one side of the small stage to the other in a desultory way, she would suddenly drop down to a crouch and swing her knees far apart and then back together in a jerking, explosive motion before standing and resuming her ambling. I was amazed at the shoes real strippers could navigate in, so high and pointed. I wondered if the implicit danger, the threat of injury was part of the appeal for men. Did they want to hold their breath in wonder that these women could sustain themselves in shoes of such desperate impracticality? They probably didn't even notice the easy association of heels like this and bared breasts. That the covert powerlessness they felt in places like this, the terrible vulnerability of desire was mitigated by the explicit vulnerability of women on patent leather stilts. I danced in ballroom shoes, low and stable. Because I was a wimp. And because burlesque was different. Maybe. I didn't know.

I looked around for Jonah, or Elsa, thinking she would know where he was, but it was very dark and hard to distinguish among the different shapes gyrating in front of small round tables throughout the room. And I didn't want to look hard enough to stare. The decor was red. Red and fuzzy, velvet or velour or something, with flickering fake candles, and everything smelled of dust and bleach and the sour scent of sweat and the chemical waft of cheap perfume. A cocktail waitress brushed past me with a tray full of bottles of Coors Light. I had never seen Coors Light in bottles before and the small fact added to the alien feeling of the whole place. The sensation of being in a new and separate world. It was the little things sometimes. "Excuse me, is Elsa here?" I asked. She looked at me blankly, supporting the tray with both hands and I realized I couldn't remember what name Elsa used at work.

"Sorry. Maybe in the back?" She lifted the tray back up to her shoulder with a visible effort and moved toward a large group of men in striped Dr. Seuss hats, yelling their appreciation at the girl onstage. Overhead, a pretty young woman in a tiny flesh-colored G-string swung slowly back and forth on a fur-covered swing. I recognized her. Her name was Taylor and she often came into my store. She was a 36C and I had sold her a nice matching set just a few weeks ago. I waved, but she was staring at a corner of the ceiling, lost in her own world, swinging slowly back and forth and occasionally spreading her legs, all while maintaining the same dreamy expression. I guess it wasn't that surprising that I knew someone here. Big Papa's was famous for hiring girls with lots of tattoos, something the more expensive clubs didn't do, and the overlap of heavily tattooed young women who stripped and went to the same bars as I did and slept with the same guys was extensive. I probably knew half the women who worked here.

Also, the management let you dance to any music you wanted. Which is why Morrissey now started warbling through the club. It was hard to imagine anything less sexy than that aggrieved Manchester whine but the girl stepping onstage clearly didn't care. She sang along loudly to herself, wiggling in the abbreviated plaid of a Catholic school miniskirt, her long black braids swinging back and forth in time to the music. I saw a guy in a bad-fitting suit look at me and, worried that he was a manager, I passed along the bar toward the back of the club, where a smaller, second stage had another girl dancing on it. I was trying to blend into the darkness at the far corner when something moved on the floor next to me and I jumped and shrieked before I could stop myself. In the Plexiglas floor of the stage, an enormous boa constrictor slowly uncurled itself and re-coiled in a different position. The guy behind the bar laughed at me, and Elsa looked up from where she was bent, whispering to a man sitting at a table. "Rosie," she said. She whispered something else to the guy and trailed her arm over his shoulder suggestively as she left him and came over to me. "Hey, how's it going?"

"Is that a fucking snake?" I yelled over the music.

"Have you never been here before? Yeah, there's two." She pointed over her shoulder. "The back's full of mice and chickens. I hate watching them eat." She shivered. "I can't believe you've never been here before."

Since I didn't work at the clubs, I felt like I didn't belong and a kind of shyness had always kept me away. I felt like I needed to explain myself, but there wasn't really any way to articulate this and for just a moment something wavered between us, a kind of distance very different from the affectionate ease we had backstage at our shows. She was wearing a silver string bikini with anchors on it. "That's cute," I said, wanting to reestablish contact with her.

"You don't want to know how many times I've said 'ahoy, sailor!' tonight." She saluted and rolled her eyes. "It's actually less busy than I expected. Which is fine. It's always hard to come in after a show. Guys here are way less into the pinup look. They've got no taste. But seriously, when I'm wearing burlesque makeup, I get like half the money. You know why? It's because Hugh Hefner doesn't like red lipstick. Seriously. That one dude isn't into it, so none of the Playboy girls wear it, so now every dimwit thinks sexy is that gross nude lip. So annoying, but whatever. Come on, I'm going to take a break. I've got something I want to show you."

I immediately felt better to be with Elsa. She had that confident bearing people get at work, the comfort of moving around places that are familiar and which to a stranger, uninitiated into the customs of the complex civilization that is the heart of every unique establishment, is so isolating. "I'm taking a break," she yelled at a guy across the room. He nodded and went back to watching a small portable TV with a long thin antenna that was propped up on the table next to him.

"Hey, is that Taylor?" I pointed at the swing.

Elsa glanced up. "Yeah. I think she might be on ketamine tonight. She's been up there for a long time and usually everybody hates it. I've gotten so many yeast infections from straddling that thing. Fur is not a hygienic material."

"Oh." Again, I felt that immense distance that separated our experiences. What Elsa and Taylor did here was clearly work. The dancing that brought us together was something different. But it was hard to figure out exactly why. We were both taking off our clothes for people's enjoyment, but I felt the distinction, unspoken, unacknowledged and it made me uneasy. Backstage at burlesque shows, in the dingy, overcrowded dressing room, surrounded by the feathers and spangles and half-clad female bodies was the only place I felt less alone. Helping someone pin their stockings to their G-string or passing around a bottle of spirit gum or eyelash glue, it was like I could breathe again, sinking into female companionship like falling back into the softness of a feather bed, caught and held suspended, but surrounded in gentleness.

Which is not to say we didn't get prickly, but the common goal of performing together was like a rubber band that, even when stretched by the small, inevitable irritations, held us together without any effort from me. I wasn't responsible and so I could trust it. Otherwise, you might do or say the wrong thing, and that bond that you'd been counting on to hold you safe might break and you could spin out, alone, lost. Years of friendship dissolved in a judgy fight about stripping.

But here we weren't together in the same obligations, and I started worrying Elsa might somehow indicate that under these red lights the fragile ties of our fellowship didn't hold. "I think I sold Taylor that bra." I cringed, worried she might be able to tell I was trying too hard. Trying to trace the web of connections that bound us, to show I belonged here, even when I knew I didn't.

She squinted toward the ceiling. "Oh man. I would never waste fancy stuff in this shithole. I should come up and see you soon. I need to spend some of this hard-earned money."

"Yeah, come up, you can always use my discount." I felt a flicker of safety. She liked me. She liked where I worked. We were friends. For now.

She pushed open a door behind the bar. The room was small, and the few women already there made it feel very crowded. The air was thick with cigarette smoke. Elsa squatted in front of a row of lockers and started fiddling with a combination lock. A woman in cutoffs and a pink sweatshirt was sitting on a counter next to a sink looking at the brown G-string she was holding up through the smoke of the cigarette in her mouth. "I don't know, can you smell it?"

She held it in the direction of another woman who was reading a book, her glossy red heels propped on the counter next to her.

"Get that funky thing out of my face, girl, are you crazy? And yes, it fucking stinks."

"I keep forgetting to bring it home. Anyone got any Febreze?" the first woman asked.

Elsa handed her a bottle that she took out of her locker. "You know I'd never be caught without it. Rosie, this is Delphine and Nia, or Sugar and Porsche."

"Hey." Delphine nodded at me in greeting. "Your wig is slipping."

I looked in the mirror behind her and tried to hitch my hairpiece up a little on my head. At this point in the night, I really needed to take it out and totally redo it, tighten the ponytail underneath and reclip it but it felt like too much trouble, so I just moved a few bobby pins and hoped they would hold.

"Watch it." Delphine sprayed the G-string in her hand liberally with Febreze.

Nia started to cough, waving her hand against the cloud of scent. "What is that? That is not Spring Breeze."

"No," Elsa replied, helping herself to a cigarette from Delphine's pack. "They were out. It's the purple one—Tropical Fiesta, I think."

"Great, my naynay's going to smell like piña colada, thanks, Elsa." Delphine lit her cigarette for her.

"It was all they had. How long has she been there?" Elsa asked, pointing at a third woman slumped on a bench in the corner of the room. She had a black Bettie Page haircut very similar to mine, but then so many of us did.

Nia turned around. "About an hour. Not the place I would choose for a nap, but I don't know her life."

"Why not, you come here to read books," Delphine said.

"I just ate." Nia whacked her on the thigh affectionately. "I can't shake my thing with my stomach full of fried shrimp. I need to digest a second."

"Can I have one?"

Nia nodded and pushed the open take-out container toward Delphine with her foot. "Y'all, this book is so good." She held it out. *Parable of the Sower.*

"Is it religious?" I asked, and she gave me a disgusted look while the others snickered.

"Nia is always reading about dragons and shit." Delphine swung her G-string around trying to dry it off.

"This is not about dragons or Jesus, Jesus Christ," Nia said, annoyed. "It's science fiction and it's good."

"I liked *A Wrinkle in Time*," Elsa said, reaching over and grabbing a fluffy curled shrimp from the remains of Nia's sandwich.

"Because that's a great fucking book," Nia agreed. "But whatever. I'm not here to educate a bunch of strippers."

"Nia is dancing to put herself through college," Delphine told me.

Elsa laughed. "Aren't we all?" She looked pensively at the ceiling as she chewed her shrimp, holding the delicate tail in long purple nails. "What do men have against a girl dancing because she's good at it and just wants to earn some fucking money?"

I felt silly standing there holding my bag, but I didn't want to leave. I liked being here, this tiny room filled with women's bodies and the chatter of bored conversation. "What are you in school for?" I asked.

"Journalism." Nia turned another page. "I want to be a court reporter."

"Really? How did you get into that?" I've always been amazed by careers that never occurred to me. Which was most of them, and sounded ridiculously self-absorbed, but I liked the reminder that the world was wider than my own dim horizons. In a million years, I would have never thought of being a court reporter, but then I also couldn't imagine having to talk to that many people. I said as much.

"Not as many people as you have to talk to stripping. These

fuckers aren't even here for the titties, they just want to talk
your ear off about their lives and jobs. It's good practice. My
great-uncle was a ward organizer. I might still run for city
council or some office."

Delphine snorted derisively, and Nia closed her book.
"Fine. I probably can't do that after working here, but some
things came up in my life and it's fine. This place is actually
great training for a lot of professions." She looked at me with
slightly more interest, and I felt the other two women stop
listening, settling into their smoking with a quiet absorption;
they had heard this conversation many times before. But I was
happy to listen, glad to have a purpose here with this dumb
bag still on my shoulder. I set it down. "Drunk white guys
will tell you anything if you have your shirt off. It's fucking
crazy. I had a public defender in here the other day and he
was rambling all about his caseload, and I was like, 'isn't that
all supposed to be confidential,' and he just laughed at me.
I had already told him I was studying journalism at Dillard
and he was still just blabbing on, and I was like, 'either you
have had way too much cocaine, or you're terrible at your
job, or you don't think I'm a fucking person with ears on my
goddamn head.' But whatever, someday Tits McGee here is
going to instigate some serious criminal justice reform. Or
something. Maybe."

"That's our Tits McGee." Elsa tapped her on the tip of her
shiny heel.

"While these two bitches are going to be shaking their ass
until menopause."

"Maybe." Delphine shrugged. "Or maybe I'll buy myself
a nice apartment in the East and retire and run a boutique
or something."

Elsa extinguished her cigarette by running it under the

tap and I heard the sizzle. "Rosie works at a really nice underwear store."

"Oh yeah?" Nia asked. "I like lingerie."

"Yeah, on Magazine Street," I said.

"Maybe I'll come by," she said, and I knew from her tone that she wouldn't.

"Yeah, you should, it's great," Elsa continued, and I wished she would stop. Elsa was from Boston. She couldn't hear the chill in the room. The way that I knew that Delphine and Nia were from here and that they didn't go to Magazine Street to shop and the way this wouldn't occur to Elsa and I was jealous of her obliviousness. Jealous of her for being from somewhere else and landing here and being friends with her coworkers and not having to feel that constant line that shimmered between us, the dividing wall of color that popped up in the most arbitrary and stupid ways, like where you bought your fucking underwear. Maybe I was wrong. Maybe it wasn't so insurmountable, but how did you break through an obstruction that no one would even acknowledge? Somehow, I felt it even more in the strange little things, so inconsequential as to be beneath notice, the sensation of geographical doubling, like two maps laid on top of each other that didn't line up. Delphine and Nia bought their underwear in different places than I did. At Mardi Gras, they watched the same parades from different corners, they drank different liquors at different bars and, when we brushed up against each other like now, sometimes we could all laugh and talk like we occupied the same essential city, but then unexpectedly, arbitrarily, the lines would reappear, and I felt ashamed.

When Gaby and I went drinking in high school, we followed the bars along the curve of the river from Riverbend to Bywater, and sometimes there were other black people in the room, and sometimes there weren't. But the rules were always clear between us—those were the places we went because they were nearby or because we wanted to see a band. Until one day she mentioned having gone to a club with her neighbor. It was a club I'd never heard of, and I felt a stab of jealousy at the thought of a life she lived without me. And I asked her, "How come we always go to white people bars? Why don't you take me to the black club?" And she laughed at me. "Really?" she asked. "You want to go to the club?" and I could feel her weighing out the idea in her mind. She never did take me. Maybe she was embarrassed of me. Maybe she didn't trust me. Maybe she was right. But whenever I asked after, she would put me off with that laugh, that laugh that had a chill of distance in it, always polite, always gracious, and I knew she would never let me go there with her, and I knew I couldn't ask anymore. So, we kept going to the same bars we always did and drank until we were almost blind, and the laughter that came in uncontrollable waves drowned everything else out.

I realized it had been too many hours since I had had a drink and a kind of panicky feeling came over me. "Do you guys have any booze back here?" I looked around. "What's she on? Can I have some?" I joked, pointing to the girl with my haircut. Her head had dropped to one side and she was drooling a little, a delicate line of spit against her cheek that in its perfect slackness had regained a kind of childhood. She reminded me of sleepovers and waking up first and watching a friend in a sleeping bag with wonder, envious of the possessive demands of sleep that had taken her so far from you.

Elsa rummaged around the messy counter next to her. "Like I said, I think Taylor's on ketamine. I think her bag was somewhere around here. It was mostly empty. Ah, here."

She picked up a little plastic baggie from under a pile of foundation-smeared tissues. "Yeah, it's empty, but there's like a tiny bit in this corner. At least I think it's Taylor's ketamine, but who knows really?" She shrugged, holding it delicately between long shiny talons.

"One way to find out." I took it from her. I had one bobby pin in my hair that had been bugging me all night because it had lost its little protective plastic tip. It had been poking me in the delicate area just behind my ear, but it would be perfect for this. Without the bulbous tip, the end of the little metal rod was flat and smooth, and I used it to dig out the tiny bit of powder collected in the corner of the fragile bag.

I thought I saw Nia shake her head but then I inhaled and, though it wasn't very much, everything got just a little bit warmer for a minute. A warmth that flowed down through my arms and legs, a thick, delicious porridge-like warmth, and I smiled what I knew was a dumb drug smile.

"Oh my God, I can't believe I forgot." Elsa hopped off the counter and dug around her locker again. "This is what I wanted to show you. Look, I took in a new foster."

We both liked dancing and fringe and Swarovski crystals, but dogs were the true passion that bound me and Elsa and as I looked at the picture of the chubby pug she was holding out to me, that shared enthusiasm spread through my veins, bursting forth, uncontained, pure love. "Oh my God." I took the picture and I saw it tremble in my grip. I held on to it with both hands, embarrassed. His muzzle was going gray and thick rolls of fat cradled his round head, a cushion of flesh that his face was sinking into. "He's so beautiful."

Elsa smiled proudly. "I know. I knew you would appreciate an old dog."

"Look at his eyes. He looks like a weepy sea captain."

"Yeah, he's going blind. That's why they're getting filmy."

"Ida too."

"I know. Whatever. With their noses, dogs don't really need to see."

"Ida can barely smell anymore. She keeps banging into table legs and stuff and then she looks up at me with such blame. Like I put it there on purpose."

"How old is she again?"

"Fifteen," I lied. I couldn't bear to tell her. What if we didn't have anything else to talk about to each other this way, this great shared sympathy. I couldn't lose anything else tonight. I held the picture up to my face and felt I was swimming, lost in the folded pudge of that thick little body. It was like I could feel the warm, steady rise and fall of the perfect pink belly whose curve was visible under his crooked haunches. "I'm dying. What is his name?"

"Stanley."

I felt tears welling up and for a minute didn't care about keeping it together. "That's the most beautiful name I've ever heard."

"Is she crying?" Delphine asked.

"Okay, there." Elsa put an arm around my shoulder and looked at the picture with me. "But I know, he's to die for. Look at that crooked ear."

"My aunt's dog got eaten by an alligator the other day," Delphine informed us, sliding out of her clothes and into the brown G-string.

"You're full of shit," Elsa said to her.

"I swear. They were crabbing out by the spillway, and I swear to God, he just snapped him up. It's okay though, that dog was nasty. He had yellow crusty eyes. Nasty."

"She's full of shit," Nia agreed. "Although, I think one of

my neighbor's dogs almost got eaten once in the park. Alligators fucking love dogs."

I could barely hear them. My whole world had shrunk to the rectangular frame in my hands, this dog, whose ridiculous expression of baleful resignation seemed to contain all the joy and absurdity of canine devotion. I couldn't help the tears that rolled down my face like a faucet I couldn't turn off. This fat little dog was having a preposterous effect on me. I thought my tears had run their course, then I noticed his perfect little black toenails and started crying again.

Elsa took the picture back. "Okay, Rosie. Why don't you get a Kleenex or something? You're kind of all over the place tonight."

Glad to have something to do, I went into a stall to unroll some toilet paper, and I could feel the others were exchanging looks about me, but I couldn't help it. Everything was floating on a cloud of feeling and those feelings were passing through and around me but for once they didn't hurt. Thank goodness for ketamine. I came back out blowing my nose. "I need to talk to Jonah. Is he still here?"

"Yeah, he's around somewhere, drinking, pretending like he isn't interested in whoever is dancing," Elsa said. "It's so dumb, I don't know why he does that."

"Just so long as he remembers to tip." Nia brushed a few crumbs off her lap.

"Men are idiots," Elsa said, summing it up. And I waited, not wanting to go back into the club without her. I felt like I needed to coast along next to her, in the warmth of her protection. She stubbed out her cigarette and readjusted the elastic on her bikini bottoms. "So, if you decide you want a wheezy old pug, let me know. You know Cholula will only

tolerate guests for about a week or two before she starts trying to take an eye out."

"I can't," I whispered.

She looked at me funny again. "Are you sure? You look
like a girl that could use a barely continent dog with nasal
labial problems." She laughed.

And then I almost told her. I almost confided everything to
her, this terrible, awful thing about Ida, but I caught myself.
To make those kinds of confessions, you needed a history, the
kind of understanding of years of quietly existing near one
another. She couldn't help me anyway. She was at work. All
I would do is weird her out and I didn't have enough friends
for that kind of carelessness. "I wish I could," I said instead.

"Well, let me know if you change your mind. Maybe he
and Ida could enjoy their retirement together, two old dogs
farting and enjoying their golden years."

"Get out of here, y'all are gross." Delphine checked herself
in the mirror and shifted her breast inside her string bikini.

"It was nice to meet you guys," I said. "Maybe I'll see you
around."

They both nodded, and Elsa pushed open the door and we
were back in the loud, pounding darkness of the club. "They
seem nice," I said. "Do you guys hang out a lot?"

"Outside of work? Not so much, but they drink around the
corner sometimes after hours if you want to come by." I did
want to so badly but thought it would be awkward.

Elsa looked around. "Ugh, this place. What time is it? I'm
supposed to be here till four. Why do some nights just seem
to last forever?"

"I think it's around one? Or two? Tonight is one of those
nights," I agreed. "But I guess sometimes you've got to see
where it all takes you."

"Yep. Usually that means in the bed of some loser with a drinking problem and a stack of Morning 40 records. But I wish you better luck than that this evening. All right. Jonah's probably lurking around somewhere stage left. Go have your adventures. I'll see you later."

I watched her thread her way through the tables, her silver bikini shining in the red glow. A dusting of makeup made her shoulders shimmer as she passed under the spinning light of a disco ball. I wanted to stay with her. Everything looked softer after the ketamine. The fake candles flickering on the tables had halos and everything was gentle, smoother. The girl spotlighted onstage was a wobbling mass of pale creamy skin, she looked like she was made of marshmallows. I could see poorly drawn devil wings tattooed on her shoulder blades. She shouldn't have done that, I thought. But then I thought, maybe it meant something important to her. Who could tell? Before I left to go to college, I went and got a fleur-de-lis on my shoulder. The guy doing it kept asking me if I was a Saints fan, and I told him I was because the real reason was too silly, too intimate to share. My mom read me *The Three Musketeers* when I was a kid and the villain, Milady, had a fleur-de-lis branded on her shoulder. My mom thought that was so cool and so did I. *Always be that kind of woman, Rosemary. Don't let anyone make a fool of you. Outsmart all those stupid men and do it with style. Especially with style.* Mom had style but she sure was a sucker for stupid men. It always ended with her drinking the French champagne she reserved for breakups and play-ing and replaying the scratched records of the terrible hippie band of the guy who she said was my dad. But not me. I had my tattoo to remind me I was better than that. I turned away from the girl onstage and eagerly looked around for Jonah.

19

Gaby and I had decided to try to make money over the summer by doing odd jobs for our families and neighbors, but we didn't know how to do much, and no one seemed to need any help. Finally, Gaby's grandmother hired us for an afternoon out of pity. It was August and though we had just started washing the windows, we were sweating already. I had lost a coin toss and was working on the outside of the big glass sliding door while Gaby did the inside. She aimed a big spray of Windex at my face and said something that I couldn't hear. I flinched even as the drops splattered harmlessly on the other side of the glass and she laughed, dragging paper towels through the spray while bobbing her head to whatever music was playing in there. I retaliated with my own spray but she just wagged her finger at me, now singing along to something I still couldn't hear.

The sun was blazing. Luckily, I was in a small triangle of shade from the overhang of the roof. All around me the treeless stretch of her grandmother's backyard just baked. Grass and concrete and a low hedge, my impression of New

Orleans East was one of flatness—it didn't have the bumps and oaks and twisty greenery of the rest of the city. Everything out here looked very new and orderly. Her grandmother's subdivision was all one-story houses, wide and flat, driveways and paved paths, the white-hot heat having nowhere to go but into the ground. Her grandfather's Cadillac, old but still impressively huge, sizzled near me in their driveway, the rusty gold color adding to the feeling of me and everything else roasting like food in an oven.

I finished my side and banged on the glass and when Gaby let me in, the air-conditioning sent chills down my spine. I hadn't been to her grandmother's before and the house had the unfamiliar smell of the many different little air fresheners that were plugged into every room. Her grandfather sat in a recliner watching TV, a glass of iced tea on a little table next to him with a doily on it. The muted dings and mumbles of *Jeopardy* filled the living room where everything around him matched, shades of mauve and tan echoed in the drapes and cushions and rugs. It made me not want to sit on anything for fear of messing it up. The women of the family, Gaby's grandmother, her mom, an aunt and a cousin I had never met before, circled around her grandfather. They mostly ignored him, having their own conversations, a buzzing life that only paused every so often to ask if he needed anything, which he shook off with a wave of his hand.

"You look a little hot, you want me to turn the hose on you?" Gaby asked me with malicious innocence.

"No thank you."

"Come on, just a little spritz, to freshen you up?" She acted like she was going to get me with her spray bottle.

"Next time, you're taking the outside," I said, wiping off my forehead with the bottom of my T-shirt.

"Oh no, that kind of weather is only for the stupid or the sinful." She shook her head and whacked me with a damp rag she was holding, and I squeaked.

"Gabrielle, I know you two aren't talking about getting my living room wet?" a voice called from the kitchen and we both mumbled a quick "no ma'am."

"Come in here, I have another job for you."

Gaby picked up our buckets and rags and ambled toward the kitchen with a slowness I was sure was going to get us scolded, but it gave me time to look at all the framed pictures lining the hall. Lots of teenagers in shiny graduation gowns, blue, green scarlet and lots of the proud, toothless smiles of school portraits. I was quietly impressed that her grandmother had ordered the big eight-by-tens. There was Gaby in the big puffy braids she had worn in kindergarten before I knew her, brightly colored pairs of balls knotted around each end, that self-conscious awareness of the momentousness of the event of getting a picture taken and that smile, so serious even then. I could just see her, determined to be worthy of the occasion— it was so like her. Then another picture of Gaby on a balance beam, arms upraised fiercely in a rainbow-striped leotard. "I didn't know you did gymnastics?"

"What? Oh yeah, Lakeside Little Hearts. I did that for years until I hurt one of my ankles."

We had always been so dismissive of after-school activities and athletics of any kind that I felt a little betrayed. "You never told me that."

She turned to look at me. "One, I don't tell you everything, Ms. Nosy, and two, there's nothing to tell, I had to quit."

"It's still interesting. Were you good?"

She turned away. "I was awesome at it, but there's no gold

stars for trying and I had to stop, so what's the point in talking about it?"

"I don't know, it's kind of cool. If I had been really good
at something, I would talk about it all the time."

"Yes, you would," she agreed, and I gave her a poke in
the back but stopped because we were now in view of her
grandmother.

The table next to her was piled with loaves of white bread
and deli bags. Her grandmother smoothed down her cardigan.
I couldn't imagine how she could wear one in this heat, but
it matched the shirt she was wearing underneath. She was all
one shade of light teal. Her hair was set in a pile of gray curls
and she wore a little gold pendant necklace that matched the
small hoops in her ears. I had never really known anyone so
carefully put together and she made me a little nervous. My
Keds were filthy and I was pretty sure I hadn't brushed my
hair that morning. "Girls, I'd love it if you could help make
these sandwiches for my church. We are feeding the needy
this weekend."

Gaby was reading the label on one of the deli bags. "I see
you got the cheap ham for the needy," she said, and I was
shocked, but her grandmother just gave her a look.

"If you want to get paid, Gabrielle, I suggest you start learning how to talk to those that will be signing your checks.
There's a plastic bag for each sandwich. Easy on the mayonnaise."

She pronounced *mayonnaise* in three long syllables and as
I sat, I noticed all the brands in her kitchen were ones I had
never seen before. Nescafé and no-salt seasoning and a little
pile of toothpicks in a crystal bowl.

"She's not going to give us a check, is she?" I asked, when
she had left. I didn't have a bank account.

Gaby shook her head at my stupidity. "That's just how she talks."

"Your grandmother is so elegant," I said admiringly as we started prying thin pink slices of meat from the wet stack and folding them across pillowy white slices of bread.

"Yeah, she's always been like that." Gaby was making faces at the mayonnaise as she spread it, wiping the knife on each piece of bread like she was trying to clean off something disgusting. "My grandpa had his own contracting business. He did pretty well, some city contracts and stuff. Not to hear them talk about it though. 'Gabrielle, how are those grades, you know this school is expensive, you got to try twice as hard if you want to be a doctor,'" she said, imitating her grandmother's careful enunciation. "Girl, you know I don't want to be a doctor. Can you imagine me cutting up bodies?"

"Gross."

"It's always one thing or another, uplift yourself, uplift your community. We're lucky she's paying us, usually she has me doing this kind of stuff for free."

"Still, it's nice that they're here. I don't even know my grandparents."

She thought about this. "Well, then that's one less set of people breathing over your shoulder every week, asking about this test or that quiz, already asking me about college applications. I'm in eighth grade, for God's sake." Then she stopped herself. "I actually can't imagine what it would be like not to have family around. That's strange that y'all can live like that."

"It's not me, it's my mom." I felt a little defensive.

She looked unconvinced and starting humming, then singing "Waterfalls" by TLC. A moment later her mom and aunt came in, looking for something in the fridge. "Ooh, Gaby, you are murdering that song," her mom said affectionately. "You want some potato salad?"

"Oh no," her aunt replied, waving a hand. "I'm on Weight Watchers. Let me show you how it's done, Gaby." Her aunt reached across the table for a lone apple sitting in a wooden bowl and started to sing where Gaby left off. Her mom joined in from behind the open door of the refrigerator while Gaby yelled at them both to shut up, that she could carry a tune just fine.

They ignored her, clearly having fun together while Gaby put her hands over her ears. "Like a pair of dying cats, I swear. This family."

I kept assembling sandwiches, slicing through the yielding bread over and over while they all laughed and teased each other, singing and pulling more food from the refrigerator. I felt very left out and very small. I couldn't help but wonder if Gaby really needed me at all. I wanted to be a part of it all so badly, so I started singing along too. I didn't actually know the words, but I made kind of approximate sounds and I hoped that her mom and aunt were singing loud enough that no one would notice, but they gave me a funny look.

"Some people should learn the words before they start singing," her aunt said to her mom, taking a bite out of her apple and shaking her head a little. I saw them exchange a knowing look. "See how young they start?" I heard her mutter as they left the kitchen, as Gaby's mom shushed her.

Gaby was laughing at me as she pushed aside a stack of plastic-wrapped sandwiches. "You're so stupid sometimes," she said lovingly.

20

TWELFTH NIGHT 2004
BIG PAPA'S, BOURBON STREET

I spotted Jonah in a corner, as Elsa had mentioned, pretending to be uninterested in all the bodies moving around him. Which looked so silly. There were cheaper places to drink than a strip club. I maneuvered my way toward him around tables and dancers and waitresses and pulled up a chair and sat down, suddenly exhausted.

"We've got to stop meeting like this," he said with a smile.

I wonder if maybe it was the ketamine that made me feel like my bones were melting into the hard vinyl of this ugly black chair, or the full body relief that I had finally found him, and we were here, together at last, alone in this pounding darkness. The floor vibrated slightly from the music. I couldn't say anything and just sat, accepting this profound state of dissolution. Unaware that he was the hard-won objective of a quest that had taken up the better part of my night, he tapped a ring against his beer bottle to the rhythm of the Guns N' Roses song now playing, casual and relaxed.

"Chatting with the old ball and chain, I saw," he went on, glancing at the stage and then looking away again.

"What did you say?" I rose out of the warmth of my stupor for a minute. If only we could just sit here in silence together forever.

"Elsa," he said. "Didn't you know she and I are married?" He unrolled one of his sleeves and then carefully rolled it again, pushing it the last little bit past his elbows, checking to make sure it was even. "It's cool, we have an arrangement. She was the first person I met in this town. Every man should marry a stripper at least once in his life." He gave me a rakish smile again. "We aren't even together anymore. It's more a sentimental arrangement, we just never bothered to file divorce papers."

"Why are you telling me this?"

He looked surprised. "Making conversation?"

I could tell from his tone he didn't feel like this changed anything in our relations, but my feelings were suddenly horribly hurt. I was struck by the way I had suddenly fallen to a supporting role in someone else's story. I didn't like it. I didn't want to be a side note, a diversion in his history with someone else. The sudden shift in perspective made my stomach waver, and I took his beer from him and took a sip. No one liked to be reminded of their self-absorption.

"Why Elsa?" I wanted to know what made her so special and why in her elevation, I suddenly felt lessened, interchangeable.

"Why not? She's a good gal. If worse comes to worst, I could always hang up my hat with her and call myself pretty lucky. But as I said, it wasn't a big thing. We were drunk one night and ran into an Elvis impersonator. It just seemed the thing to do. You know how things happen around here."

"But marriage," I argued faintly, "that's such a big deal."

"It is? Rosemary, if I wasn't so well acquainted with your

cynical heart, I would start to think you were sounding like a romantic right now." He was laughing at me and I came to myself quickly.

"I can't help it," I laughed back. "I'm always looking for candidates for my future trail of ex-husbands."

"Yeah, but you're probably going to kill them. I wouldn't marry a merry-widow type like you for anything. My momma didn't raise any idiots. Elsa, over there, she would never poison me just for the thrill of it. Unlike some people I could speak of." He raised an eyebrow at me.

I tensed up at this, but at least he was flirting again. Whatever insecure feeling I'd almost let slip I had managed to cover up. I wanted him to keep flirting with me. I wanted to burrow into that feeling, warm up against his neck and let it wash over me, waves of glorious security.

It was kind of crazy, but I had never had a boyfriend. My shyness about talking to boys had persisted through those few pathetic semesters of college and then once I came back, I started sleeping with them, seeing them as almost a natural extension of my new burlesque hobby. Men were always around; they were always willing. I knew that somewhere, something else existed besides the one-night exchanges I entered into. I had seen movies. I had read books. I knew that there were times when a girl in need, in distress, could find the one, the special one who could offer more. One who could hold me in his arms and talk to me about things both important and not, how terribly fragile we each were in this sharp-edged world of feelings and hesitations. How terribly alone and scared of death we all were. "I would poison you," I said earnestly to Jonah. "If you needed me to."

He tipped his beer toward me. "And that's why I love

you. Always so grimly fiendish." He started humming The Damned, but I was caught on the word *love*.

"So, Jonah," I said, starting to run my fingers through my long fake ponytail, where they instantly stuck because of all the tangles. I pulled a small twig out from somewhere in the curls, probably from the garden earlier, and let it drop onto the floor, hopefully unnoticed. "Do you have any plans for later this evening?" As I leaned toward him, my elbows on the table, it occurred to me I should have maybe stopped at some point to reapply my lipstick. I could still see the droopy end of my loose false eyelash in the corner of my eye and I wondered just how visible of a mess I was and whether it was dark enough in here not to matter. Strip club lighting covered all manner of imperfections and sorrows.

"Funny you should mention it, I don't," he said, willing to allow a glimmer of excitement to pierce his veil of mannered boredom. "Why, Rosemary? What did you have in mind?" Then he paused. "Didn't you already go home with Mike tonight?"

For one horrible moment, I had no idea what he was talking about. Then it came back slowly through the mists of memory like a bad dream from a very long time ago. Oh yeah, I had gone home with Mike. How ridiculous it seemed looking back on it now. Those were the actions of a sad, desperate woman, a stranger almost. What Jonah and I were discussing was something altogether different. It was strange that he was even comparing the two. "What? No," I lied. "Well, I mean, I did go to his house, but only so he could give me drugs. I would never soil myself with those rockabilly meatheads."

He laughed. "I thought it was a little out of character. I think of you as a woman of some taste and intelligence."

For a moment, I wished it had been out of character, but

maybe he was right. Maybe it was. Maybe I was this smarter, more discriminating woman he was alluding to. How nice that would be. "Exactly. I just went to sweet-talk him out of a little crystal meth. You and I understand each other."

"What is it with racists and crank?" he asked. "That's like the number one form of recreation in my hometown. It's so tacky. Who wants to be awake that much anyway? Sleep is great. No offense."

"None taken." I smiled at him. "But if I wasn't going to go to sleep tonight and was theoretically looking for some other way to pass the time…"

"You know, I never could resist a woman with trouble written all over her, and you, my friend, I hope you don't mind my saying so, you look like the definition of *trouble* right now. You look like a girl who's going to be the best lay of your life then burst into tears and try to stab you with a kitchen knife. And I say that in the most complimentary way. Maybe something is wrong with me, but I find that particular feminine type utterly irresistible."

The knowledge of how unintentionally close he was to the truth made my whole body go hot. I was trouble. I always had been. And it hadn't turned him off. Quite the opposite. I had been right all along. He was the one. He would save me yet. "So, I need you to do me a favor, then, before I carve my initials into your back with my fingernails," I said.

I could see he liked that. "Anything for you." He drank some of his beer.

My voice sounded strange and far away. "I need to stop by my place on the way home so you can help me bury my dog."

He managed after a minute's difficulty to swallow his sip of beer and leaned in as if he hadn't heard me correctly. "I'm sorry, what?"

I looked straight into his watery-gray eyes, and noticed wrinkles just starting at the corners. "I need you to bury my dog."

"What?" he repeated. I took his beer back from him again and finished it while he watched me, his face slack with confusion. I started to get nervous. "What are you talking about?" he asked again.

"I told you earlier, my dog died. I need someone to bury her. I can't do it."

He squinted at me and then slowly rubbed his nose. "Rosemary, I thought you just wanted to fuck."

"Yeah, well." I didn't know what else to say. "I do."

"What are you even talking about? When did your dog die? Recently?"

"Yes." I took his wrist and checked his lovely vintage watch. "Eight hours ago."

"What the fuck?" He raised his empty bottle toward the waitress to request another. "And I thought my story about the Elvis impersonator was something. You really know how to top an anecdote."

We waited for his beer to arrive, those funny pauses of waiting for alcohol, when everything is suspended for a minute.

When it arrived, he spun the bottle around between his fingertips, seeming to derive some reassurance from the motion. "I'm sorry for your loss. I had a cat that died after getting into some mothballs. It's not easy. Her name was Boudicea." He sighed. "She was a really good cat."

I wasn't going to be distracted. "You know I do want to. Fuck, I mean," I clarified. I wanted him to understand what was on offer. "I *also* want to fuck. After."

"I'm so confused," he said, looking at me, mystified. "You're talking about doing this now? Tonight? Is this some

kind of fucked-up foreplay thing? Where exactly is your dog?"
He looked down at the label of his beer for a long moment
before he spoke again, uncomfortably slowly now. "Rosemary, is your dead dog just at your house?"

I nodded, my eyes finally welling. "I can't go home. I
need someone to come with me and bury her for me. I just
can't do it."

"Why didn't you call the vet?"

"What can they do? She's already dead. And she hated it
there. I can't send her there, all alone, to get shoveled into
some oven with a bunch of strange dogs she's never even met."

"You're insane. But also, why me? Why would you think
I would do it? That sounds disgusting."

I pointed at the skull on his forearm, a snake winding
through its empty eyes. "The Day of the Dead stuff, the goth
stuff. You're always complaining about how our culture is too
freaked out by death."

"Are you kidding?" He just looked at me. "Can you really not see how this might be different? I like animals. I'm
not a ghoul."

I looked at the table. "I thought you would do it for me,"
I said quietly. There was an uncomfortable silence. "You just
said you liked fucked-up girls. You said I was irresistible." I
was almost whispering now, my voice fading with the in-
creasing knowledge that this wasn't going like I had planned.

"Jesus Christ, I like little statues of skeletons drinking beer,"
he said, ignoring my last point. "Just because you listen to
Bauhaus doesn't mean you want to bury someone's fucking
dog, for fuck's sake."

"Well, don't say it like that, you make it sound so stupid."

"It *is* stupid," he said loudly, then he apologized. "I'm sorry,
this was just not where I was expecting this conversation to go."

"You shouldn't say things you don't mean."

He didn't have an answer for that, and I was maybe glad that he didn't because the more we talked the more ridiculous and hopeless this all felt. How had I managed to misjudge this situation so badly? I had always been careful with stuff like this, careful asking others for help. Desperation was making me stupid, just like he said. And I was pretty desperate now. I decided to try one more time. "I'm in love with you."

I don't know which of us was more surprised.

"Um." He cleared his throat. "Well, that's one you don't hear every day."

I cringed, watching the frozen drips of wax running down the side of the red glass candle on the table. That was not what I had meant to say. I didn't think it was at least. I knew him better than that. I knew the way we worked. It was like throwing a car into the wrong gear and the terrible grinding noise of wrongness. But now that it was thrown out there, maybe some tiny part of me waited. Just maybe. Maybe. But the silence lengthened, the awkwardness sharp as knives. Fuck. I started to get mad.

What a shitty, shitty world. It wasn't my fault that I was here trying to count on this skeezy bartender with a Smith & Wesson belt buckle. It wasn't my fault that I couldn't call my mom. That I couldn't call Gaby anymore. That I didn't have anyone else. What was I supposed to do? Jonah looked even paler than usual in the flash of lights from the stage, and I felt a revulsion in my stomach. Why had I let this man touch me? What was I looking for? Why weren't these girls wearing any clothes? Why did it smell like empty ashtrays and dead canaries in here?

"Chantal is right, your whole thing's just a stupid hipster fetish. And worse than that, it's boring. You're the bartender version of that guy from *Dazed and Confused* where he gets older, but the girls all stay the same age. Or something." I had never seen the movie, but I didn't think it mattered. I just wanted it to hurt.

To his credit, he didn't argue with any of this. "I just didn't think we were like that," he said, looking at his beer. "Like a 'burying dead pets' kind of relationship."

"Oh shut up."

"I was joking, Rosemary." He glanced up at me, and he was going to say something else, I knew he was, and I held my breath.

Just help me tonight, I thought. *I just need you tonight and then tomorrow you can sink back into the scum of casual encounters. It's cool. I'm cool. We can all be cool tomorrow. And I'll fuck you and listen while you explain the* Sandman *comics and the story of Factory Records and whatever other cold comfort you want to offer me in your cold bed, but be a fucking person tonight. Please.*

But then I saw him bail. I saw the resolve fucking drip out of his eyes. "I mean, I'm still up for the thing we have already, you know, don't fix what's not broken. But maybe on a different, less morbid night, you know."

There was nothing to argue with because there was nothing to gain here. There was a limit to how much you could ask of someone who had only known you in the dark lights of bars and that was fine. I knew that already. Somehow, tonight I had let myself forget.

I got up to leave and he tried to look suitably grave, but then watching the stage and avoiding my eyes, he said, "It's just a lot. I mean, usually a girl offers to buy me dinner before we start burying the bodies." He snuck a look at me. Maybe he smiled. "You've got a style, Rosemary, I'll say that. It's really pretty remarkable. You are, I mean. You're the type of woman to make a man think about the future. I don't know, someday you and I…"

I gave him the finger.

I would panic outside. I needed to go drink. I needed to go drink somewhere familiar. Or anywhere. Actually, a brown paper bag from a corner store would be fine. I needed to get so drunk I wouldn't be able to see. Either that, or I was going to start crying and once I started crying, I was not going to be able to stop. And I wasn't going to do it here in this claustrophobic, disgusting place. If I could get really drunk, falling down drunk, so drunk that I wouldn't remember it in the morning, blackout drunk, maybe I would be able to do it. Maybe I could take care of this myself. I didn't need anyone else. It was time to drink with purpose. I would just drink until I could go home again. Finally, I could sink into something I was fucking good at.

21

Once I realized Gaby was moving toward the door, I hurried to push through the crowd to reach her. Some guy asked if he could buy me a drink and a bachelorette in a wedding veil told me my dance was awesome. I mumbled thanks and excuses and finally caught up with her just as she was passing through to the outside. "Gaby, wait." The door almost hit me, but I caught it, and then we were standing on the sidewalk outside the Sugarlick. "Where are you going? Did you like the show?"

She didn't answer for a minute and kept hitching her purse farther up on her shoulder, something she often did when she was drunk. I was glad to see she was because I was pretty drunk too. I hadn't been expecting how nervous I would be to have her finally come to one of my burlesque shows. I had been asking her for months to come witness this new thing I was a part of. It was strange for me to be back in New Orleans and near Gaby without really seeing her. But she kept putting me off with vague excuses about school and work; it seemed like she never had time for me. I felt like she owed me an explanation for all of that and even more for trying to sneak out like this. "Were you not going to say anything to me? You were just going to leave?"

She was wearing a blazer, which was unusual. I wasn't used to seeing her in one and it perversely hurt my feelings. I felt like she was trying to look extra adult, extra professional, as if she were trying to distinguish herself from me, and I was taking it personally. "And why are you dressed like that?"

She looked down at herself, confused, and brushed something invisible off her chest. "I was at work today. What, you don't like my look?" She sighed. "It's hard enough finding clothes to wear for those clinic hours, I don't need you commenting on it like that. And anyway," she said conclusively, "this is expensive."

"No, it's fine, it's nice. You just look so grown-up, I'm not used to it." I wanted her to yield a little, but she had a coldness, a distance to her that made me bristle like a hurt cat.

"I don't think you need to be commenting on anyone's clothes right now. Look at you." I hadn't bothered to change after my performance, I was so eager to run out and find her that I had only thrown on a robe over my costume. In the dim, boudoir atmosphere of the Sugarlick, it had seemed perfectly normal, but now in the cooler glare of the streetlights, I felt exposed and a little ridiculous.

I crossed my arms over my chest to keep the robe closed. "I didn't want to miss you. Did you like the show? I made the whole costume myself. This bra took me forever to sequin."

"That's impressive. When did you take up sewing?"

I shrugged. "I just kind of figured it out."

"My aunt used to sew all our holiday dresses," she said, not looking at me again. "I always meant to have her teach me but with one thing and another..."

It was getting awkward now, but I couldn't stop myself. I was good at performing and I just needed to hear it from Gaby. She was the only person that really mattered to me, and I wanted her approval. "Did you like my number? I was extra nervous tonight and kept getting ahead of the music, but then I kept reminding myself to slow down so then I almost got behind. It's funny how that works."

"I didn't notice. I don't really think that this is my thing." She waved a hand vaguely indicating the Sugarlick, the street and my appearance. "You know, it just might not be for me." She spoke slowly and carefully.

"What do you mean it's not for you?" I could hear a hint of that voice she would use with our teachers, that careful politeness, and I wasn't having any of it. We weren't like that. "What's not to like? It's just silly, fun, vintage show girls and rhinestones and sparkly things."

"I don't know, those guys in there creep me out. They look like they're going to yell at me for using the wrong water fountain."

"What, the rockabillies?" I asked. "No, they're not like that. It's just a look, you know, like my hair and makeup and stuff."

"I guess I'm not into the '50s." She dug around her purse until she had found a stick of gum and unwrapped it slowly. I thought she was doing it to avoid looking at me. We still hadn't addressed what seemed to me to be the most important part. "Okay, so you aren't into the vintage thing, but what about my dance? Was I good? Did you notice the part where I almost tripped on my skirt? I tried to cover it up, but I was worried people could tell."

She shook her head. "No, I didn't notice anything like that."

"Okay, so what did you notice?"

She sighed and looked me dead in the eyes. I remembered what pretty brown eyes she had, deep and dark like brushed velvet. "I just hate to see you up there like that acting the whore."

For a moment I was absolutely stunned. I mean, yes, in my old kimono and my stage makeup and fishnets, right now on this street corner, I probably quite literally looked like a prostitute. But even that should be okay. I actually knew girls now who chose to be sex workers, who were proud of it; it made the insult feel even more unexpected, more inappropriate. How could she have missed the point so much? "I'm not."

She just gave me an unconvinced look.

"Gaby, come on, you know me," I said. "I wouldn't do this if it wasn't all about being a strong woman. The girls put on the shows and make their own stuff. It's actually really creative and empowering." She was still giving me that skeptical look and I started to get mad. Being drunk probably didn't help. "I don't see why you have to be so judgy," I said finally. "You're my friend. Even if you don't get it, can't you just be supportive?"

She pushed a lock of hair behind her ear, but it kept sliding back into her vision and I could tell it was really annoying her. "Rosemary, all that opportunity you had, and you passed it up to come back here and shake your titties at strange men. Lord knows I have supported you these many years but it's just too much. I can't do it. It just makes me too mad." She shook her head and pushed her hair back again. "Too motherfucking mad. Goddamn this purse." She pulled it off her shoulder where it kept slipping and wedged it under her arm. "Jesus."

I spoke to the dirty sidewalk. "I didn't fuck up at school *to* come here and do this, it's just what happened and performing makes me feel better, that's all. We can't all be perfect, wearing fancy blazers and bragging about professional development programs, you know."

"I never had a choice, I had to be perfect and then some. Jesus, Rosemary. And after all that shit with your mom, this is what you're going to do with your life?"

I could tell I was losing the argument, but its outlines were starting to feel fuzzy and confusing and really everything else shrank before my overwhelming sense of injury. "It was just one dance and you can't even say I did a good job. I worked really hard on this."

"Oh shut up, Rosemary."

"You shut up," I said, almost in tears. Two guys passed by with plastic cups of beers and made yowling cat noises at us. "Fuck you," I yelled at them.

"See, look at this, we're making a spectacle of ourselves." Gaby squared her shoulders and stood up straight as if she were less drunk than she was, but it threw off her balance and she wobbled a little.

"Ooh, Wobble," I said to her, trying to smooth the moment by referring to a song we sometimes sang together, other times when we had gotten stumbling drunk.

"No, you are not talking about Master P at me right now, I swear to God," she said, but she almost laughed and for a minute I thought maybe it was going to be okay. We would fall back into our usual place of easy companionship and unspoken understanding, but then she stopped and closed her eyes and took a deep breath. "I'm going to need a little time. I need a little break from all this." She did that circle wave with her hand again and it felt way too personal.

"All of what?" I asked, worried. "Me?"

She gave me a pat on the arm. "Just don't call me for a little while, okay?"

I was stunned at the request and nodded, not saying anything partly because I didn't want to start crying, but also because I still felt like she was being very unfair to me. If she was going to be mean and judgmental, maybe it was for the best. Surely, I didn't need friends like that in my life. Friends who could misunderstand and think the worst of me for no reason. I had new friends. I didn't need uptight, self-righteous friends like Gaby. I would be fine without her.

22

TWELFTH NIGHT 2004
BOURBON STREET

When I got back outside, I had to close my eyes for a second against all the neon. Too many lights, too much noise, too many bad songs blaring on top of each other, a sonic assault, and under it all, an overwhelming smell of piss from the alley next door. I was trying to get my bearings and whatever resolve I was going to muster for my next move, when a voice startled me.

"Jesus Christ on a cracker, what took you so long?" I opened my eyes and saw Christopher rising from a squat just beyond the door. A pair of mannequin legs dangled from the window above him. I had seen them a million times before, but as I watched the disembodied feet swing back and forth, in and out, advertising the swing that Taylor was riding inside, I thought of her and I envied her, weightless, high above it all.

"What are you still doing here?" I asked, realizing I wasn't actually surprised to see him.

"I figured you'd come out eventually. Although I thought you might be with that scumbag. For the record, any guy you have to go find in a strip club is probably not worth your time." He looked around behind me. "So, where is he?"

"Why?"

"I'm going to fight him for you," he said. "Or try to. I just figured I owed you. One good punch deserves another. It looks like I don't have to. You already figured it out. That dude, he's just not worth it."

I couldn't really argue with that. "Well, that friend of yours probably isn't worth all this trouble either."

He didn't seem to like that and frowned. "It's complicated."

"It always is," I sighed. "Well. Since you're here, do you want to get blind, pissing drunk with me? I'm on my way for a fifth of something clear and deadly."

"Fuck if I do. You might as well ask a sailor if he likes the sea."

"Uh, okay." I started to walk away from Big Papa's. He followed. "That's poetic, I guess, but I'm sure plenty of sailors don't like their job," I said.

"It's possible I don't like drinking if I wake up in a pool of my own vomit, but like the sea, it's a vocation."

I snorted a little, but the laugh made me feel better. I really did kind of like this guy. We turned off of Bourbon Street and both visibly relaxed. I got distracted by a window display full of fancy watches at an antiques store and stopped to look. He waited. "So, now that you're free, how about coming to this party with me?"

"What?" The watches were all motionless in their little velvet boxes. I guess they needed to be wound or something. They were all stopped at ten to two.

"If you're looking to get shit-faced, why not do it for free? And also, like I said, I've heard it's a pretty good party. Like theater people and artists and stuff. I think they really do it up."

I hesitated. Maybe this part of my night was over. Maybe it was time to stop running. I was tired. It was late. My disappointment was hanging on me like weights and maybe I needed to finally accept that I was alone in every way that mattered and just move on with it and go deal with my life.

But when I looked over at Christopher, he looked so damn eager. While I knew he had been waiting for me that whole time because he didn't have anything better to do, it was still kind of touching. He clearly wanted to go to this party. He was also clearly heartbroken about this buddy of his. Would it kill me to put off going home for one more hour or two? I could be his date. Have a few drinks and a slice of king cake to fortify myself for my ordeal. I deserved that much. "How far is it?"

"It's like literally three blocks away, at Bonaparte's Retreat. I've been trying to tell you. We're practically there already."

"Okay, okay." I hitched my bag farther up on my shoulder. "Sure. Why not? I'll come. Just for a second."

"Yes." He punched the air, a quick stab, unembarrassed.

"But I've got to change first." He looked at me, confused. "You said it's a costume party, right?" He nodded, and I patted my duffel bag. "I've got something I can wear right here. I've been carrying this dumb thing around for hours now. At least it will come in handy."

"Really? What's in the bag?" He was following me toward the dark bulk of the Wildlife and Fisheries building. "What an amazing coincidence. I can't believe you even considered saying no. If that's not fate, then I don't know what is."

"Is it?" I asked. "Don't get too excited. It's just because I had a burlesque show tonight. Do you think this is what I usually look like?" I indicated my face.

"I didn't notice. Burlesque, huh? So how long have you

been into that?" We climbed the wide stone steps to where magnolia trees shaded the entrance of the building. The big old light fixtures, white globes on bronze arms that made it look like Atticus Finch was about to walk out onto those marble steps, hadn't worked for years. I set my bag down in this cover of darkness. A police car blipped, turning the corner to the precinct. That ridiculous baby pink precinct building across the street with balconies and palm trees, looking like some kind of banana republic town hall. Which maybe it was.

"For a couple of years. I got kicked out of college and just kind of fell into it."

"Isn't it weird having all those dudes staring at you like that?"

I rummaged around in my bag. I considered trying to explain to him that performing was the only time I actually felt safe from dudes staring at me. Onstage was the only time that I got to set the rules on their desire, that objectifying myself put me in control of a dynamic that otherwise dictated every moment of my life, on the sidewalk, in someone's bed. I didn't think he would understand. "No."

"I'm into pretty girls, don't get me wrong. It's just all that swing-dancing, flaming-dice stuff seems really dorky." He had sunk down, resting his elbows against his knees, his back against the building.

"Oh yeah? You want to talk about dorky? Tell me you don't have a jacket with a Misfits patch on it." I slipped out of my jeans and noticed a dark smudge running down my thigh. I had forgotten I was bleeding. I quickly wiped it away with my sleeve. I needed to go get a tampon or some toilet paper to stuff in my underpants whenever we got where we were going.

He laughed and turned toward me, then noticing what I

was doing, quickly looked away. "Yeah, but the Misfits are awesome."

I decided against my dress. I had patched up the back with Velcro to make it easy to take off and I wasn't sure it would hold up to regular life. Instead I went down a layer. My beaded bra had gotten all twisted and I had to stand there unwrapping the straps from around themselves, feeling the cool night air on my nipples. I snapped the wide belt of the panel skirt to where it hung low on my hips. Out of context I looked like some kind of dour *I Dream of Jeannie* but at least there were lots of rhinestones and fringe. I slid back into my fishnets to hide the blood on my leg and buckled on my heels. Here I was again.

"How do I look?" I felt suddenly shy and needed his reassurance.

He turned around and his expression didn't disappoint. "I can't believe you've just been carrying that around with you. Who are you?" And then he frowned and stood up. "I'm sorry. This was stupid. You're too hot for me. I don't know what I'm doing. I should just go."

Oh thank God. Ever since I had seen him sitting outside of Big Papa's, I had been trying to ignore the rush of gratitude that I felt, terrified that he might be able to tell that our dynamic had changed, that our relationship had undergone a subtle shift in power and that now I was a little dependent on him. I hoped he was too young and blind to recognize that I secretly wanted to cling to his dirty suit jacket and beg him to never leave my side. A few more years, a little more confidence, and he would be able to smell out need in a woman like those land mine–sniffing dogs. But for now, this insecurity confirmed I was still safe.

"I am too hot for you, but I'm not changing back and it's

kind of cold out here, so come on. Let's go to this party." I fished around for my headpiece and adjusted the feathers in a trembling spray to the side. Just for an hour. I would go just long enough to get suitably drunk. I stuffed my street clothes into my duffel bag. "What about you? Where's your costume?"

"Oh yeah." He smiled and buttoned the top button of his dingy white shirt, smoothing down the wrinkled collar and taking a Sharpie out of his pocket. Guys like him always had a Sharpie on them. Sharpies and duct tape, the armature of a generation of punks. Then, biting his lip in concentration, he wrote "LOVE" on the knuckles of one hand and "HATE" on the knuckles of the other. He buttoned his jacket and smoothed his hair back from his forehead and it more or less stayed from the grease.

"Ah." I laughed. "Right, now I get it. *Night of the Hunter.* What was his name?"

"I forget," he admitted. "But it's hard to come up with a costume cheaper than this. I already had the suit."

"Clearly. I feel like together we are looking more Halloween than Mardi Gras."

"In the midst of life, we are in death," he said in a heavy Southern accent. He offered me his arm and we moved on. I had sewn the same beaded fringe as the rest of my costume to the straps of my heels and they beat against my ankles, heavy and satisfying. I walked differently, my stomach exposed to the breeze, the belt hanging over my hips. I felt alert, the way the air sparked around me, a tension in my relationship to passersby, and even to Christopher, who was now trying to pretend like he didn't notice the way my bare skin glowed in the streetlamps. The unsteady ground of my terrible night rehardened for a minute, and I was glad because I wasn't entirely sure I was ready to go back to Bonaparte's Retreat. We arrived, and the bar was old and grimy, but as magical as I remembered.

Sometimes when I was little, I had to hang around the lobby of Mom's hotel, waiting for her to get off work on Saturdays, and we would come here after as a reward. Inside, it was dark, candles in nubby red glass lanterns continuously lit. We would sit in a shadowy alcove, under the old framed prints of Napoleon, where people had scrawled their names and phone numbers in the peeling plaster walls, and she would tell me stories, all totally made up, about the French emperor. There would be the first of many Bloody Marys in front of her. She would fish out the pickled okra for me, the narrow delicate point on my tongue, the soft fuzz and the snap when it burst in my mouth, full of peppery alcohol and slime. I ate muffulettas, the thick greasy sandwiches too big for my small mouth, and with every bite, tangy olive salad would squirt onto my hands and I would have to lick it off, the sharp celery bite of it, my favorite part of the sandwich. We would linger together in the strange hour of three o'clock on a Saturday afternoon, when it was quiet, and opera boomed over the stereo. The door to the courtyard slamming behind the busboys, always black, passing through with their arms full of dishes, the waiters, always white, flirting shamelessly with my mom. My root beer came in a big red plastic cup and it was cold and sweet and sharp, and I'd watch people pass outside through the dirty windows while voices screaming about love and murder made me feel like my heart was swelling painfully in my chest.

History is the story of people that dared to be different, Rosemary, she liked to say. *You've got to go out and make up your destiny. Imagine if Napoleon had wasted his life fishing for sardines on some Italian island. It's the dreamers that really make things happen.* I would drag my finger through puddles of spilled water on the glassy table, unconvinced but loving the dusty, grubby glamor of the room.

"I always get a fascist vibe from this place," Christopher said.

"Fascist?" I looked around, surprised. "This dump? You'd think they would have things running a little better. I used to come here with my mom when I was little. I've always liked it."

"Maybe it's that guy," he said, pointing to an oil painting of a former owner smiling a little sinisterly that hung above the mahogany bar. "Or it's all the pictures of Napoleon and the opera and stuff, the Mussolini vibe. I don't know. It creeps me out. My dad comes here all the time too. He brings clients from out of town and they eat this shit up."

"What does your dad do?" I asked, glad for the excuse to find out a little more what his deal was.

"He's a real estate developer. Fucking scumbag. He makes his living cheating little old black ladies out of their houses. When he's not being a pillar of the community, of course, he's on the tourism board, the chamber of commerce, you name it, and all those dudes love to come here, slumming it, with their steak-fat bellies and get sozzled. Gross."

"Still, it is a pretty bar," I argued.

"You want to sit here and drink their famous gin and tonics like some fucking British imperialist while you look out the window at that?" He pointed to the restaurant across the street.

As I read the sign, I realized I had forgotten that the full name of the restaurant on the opposite corner was Marrero's World Famous Slave Exchange Restaurant. It was one of those things that blended into the background of the bustling, tacky, touristy part of the Quarter that I barely noticed anymore. But yes, now that he was pointing it out, yes, it felt obscene. How could anyone have thought it was a good idea to turn the former site of a slave auction block into a café? And how could I not have noticed all these years? But still, it seemed unfair to condemn this bar just by proximity. "Yeah, but we're not over there. We're here and this place is old and beautiful."

"It's all the fucking same," he spat. "Everything old in this town was built by slaves, it's all the same fucking thing. Nostalgia, a goddamn crime around here."

Just then, a woman pointed at us. "Oh, look honey," she yelled in a delighted Texas drawl. "Just look at that. It must be for the Mardi Gras. Take a picture of me with them."

I could feel Christopher's desperation to tell her it wasn't *the* Mardi Gras yet, but it kind of was, so neither of us contradicted her.

"You don't see that at home," her husband agreed, holding up his camera.

Christopher stuck his tongue out between his first two fingers as he took the shot. "Hail Satan," he said instead of "cheese" as prompted.

The woman just looked at us indulgently, still beaming that she had found the *real* New Orleans she had traveled to see. "Y'all look fantastic, thank you."

"You're welcome," I couldn't help but mutter back.

The waiters were looking especially stern tonight in their black bowties. The guy behind the bar shook his head at us and my outfit, banging the brass buttons of the ancient cash register. "Upstairs," he grunted in the soft accent of Italian New Orleans.

"I didn't know there was an upstairs," I said as we passed through the bar and into the courtyard. "I like secret places."

"Over there." Christopher pointed.

I had never noticed the curved staircase partially hidden in a dark nook before us. French Quarter bars and courtyards often had these extraneous architectural flourishes in the corners. A staircase leading up into shadows, the balcony of an apartment that seemingly had no entrance, these buildings all ran up against each other, soggy wooden Escher drawings, buckling from the leaks of sputtering air conditioners.

A guy was clearing plates from one of the iron tables nearby and it rattled on the uneven bricks every time he leaned on it. He was wearing the loose white jacket and black bowtie that was the uniform of the old-school service industry in the Quarter.

He looked up at us as we passed, and his expression took me by surprise. It was different from the bored contempt of the waiters in the front, and I felt his anger so suddenly that it made me want to apologize but I didn't know what for, exactly, and so I looked away. Then a woman at one of the tables waved for his attention and he passed out of our line of view. But I felt funny. And the feeling lingered as we climbed, and the warped steps groaned under our weight. And I thought about Gaby, how rarely I had seen her angry and I wondered how she had managed it, that smooth, soft exterior from which everything seemed to roll off with a laugh and a wave of her hand. *Oh girl, you know*, and how ambiguous that sounded to my ears hearing it again in my memories now. But I stopped thinking about it. I didn't want to contemplate the possibility that maybe, even after all these years, I barely knew her at all.

23

DECEMBER 2003
BROADMOOR

Chantal had offered to pick me up from the vet and I don't really know why but after, I asked her to drop us off at my mom's house. It was closer to Ida's doctor, for one, and I didn't want to be an inconvenience. "Is this where you grew up?" she asked, taking in the shitty little shotgun and front yard. It looked like my mom had stopped paying someone to come cut her grass and a pile of unread newspapers sat on the porch in clear plastic bags.

"Yeah." It felt way too personal to have her see all this, but this afternoon I didn't have it in me to care.

"It's cute," she said considerately. "Even the little houses are cute in New Orleans."

"Yeah, well…" I lifted Ida gently, placing her on the driveway, but she just looked at me, insulted, so I picked her up again. "Thanks, Chantal, I owe you."

"Not even a thing," she said, waving goodbye. I waited until she had gone before I climbed the steps and rang the bell.

It took forever for my mom to answer, and I thought maybe she was still asleep even though it was the middle of the afternoon. I didn't know where else to go, and I could hear the sound of a TV inside, so I rang again. She finally peeked through the safety latch and then her smile was big with enthusiastic welcome even though I could see creases in her face from where she had clearly been asleep, her face pressed against something. "Come in, what a surprise," she said. "I was just watching the best old movie. I don't know what it's called but it has Judy Garland in it, practically a child, and some terrible leprechaun-looking young man in it with her. They keep singing and dancing, it's delightful." She pointed toward the television as she led the way back toward the kitchen, her long wrinkled caftan trailing behind her. *At least I come by it naturally*, I thought. "Do you want breakfast? What time is it?" She laughed. "What day is it?"

"Saturday," I answered, following her. The house looked even messier than usual. On a good day, it was a charming disarray, sort of like Sally Bowles's room from *Cabaret*. Today it had a sour smell, like it had been a long time since she'd opened a window.

"I know that, sweetie, I was teasing. What do you take me for? Now, what do I have?" She opened the refrigerator and held up a package of English muffins. "I could toast one of these, I'm not sure how old they are." She poked at one doubtfully.

I sat down at my usual place at the table, half a puffy unicorn sticker still welded to the linoleum top. "No thanks, I'm not hungry."

"What brings you here, my dear? To what do I owe the visit? Oh wait, let me get my coffee."

She fluttered back into the living room and I noticed just how skinny she had become lately. She had always been thin but now her robe pressed against her bony frame as she walked and streamed out behind her. Her long black hair was knotted and stringy and she kind óf looked like a ghost or the grim reaper, in spite of the frenzy of tropical birds on her caftan. She looked really bad. She came back smiling and holding a Snoopy coffee mug. "Why don't people still tap-dance in movies? Why didn't I ever learn how to tap-dance? Speaking of, how is your new hobby going?"

"I'm just coming from the vet," I said instead.

"Oh, how is our Ida doing?"

"Not well." I couldn't quite bring myself to repeat the diagnosis: terminal cancer.

"Well, she's a plucky little thing. She will outlive us all." Mom bent down to pat Ida flat on the head but she picked herself up and wobbled a few steps to put herself out of my mom's reach with a squint of disapproval. Then she curled up and fell asleep again immediately.

"I don't think so," I said. Leaning over to pet the dog had brought on a disgusting fit of coughing, my mom hacking and retching like she was about to lose a lung. "Are you okay?"

She nodded, not quite having gotten her breath back yet. "Just a cold that's been lingering." She took a drink from her mug and there was just something in her gesture that made it clear it wasn't coffee.

"Shouldn't you go to the doctor?" I started. "When I brought Ida—"

"I don't want to talk about it," she interrupted me too sharply. "Let's talk about you. Tell me all about your dancing." She smiled dreamily, waving her hand through the air to the rhythm of some song only she could hear. "I'm so proud of you, finally ending up on stage. I always knew you were made for it. Dramatic, like your mom. If only I were young again."

"Mom."

"What?" she asked, offended. "I would have been great at burlesque. Where do you think you get those tits from? I was quite the ripe tomato in my day."

I grunted in annoyance.

"Did I ever tell you I went to the Boom Boom Room, right before it closed? When I first got to town back when Bourbon Street was a gorgeous, mob-run mess of a place. Those strippers were so fantastic, artists really, and it was the '70s, you know, the glory days were over, but they still had the best bands backing them." She started humming that unidentifiable song again. "Are you sure you don't want an English muffin?" she asked again, draining her cup.

"No thanks." It was impossible to talk to my mom. I don't know what had prompted me to come here but whatever it was, I had been mistaken. Now that I was here, all I wanted was to leave. What was I expecting? There had never been anything here for me and certainly nothing now.

I watched Ida sleep and I could see the place in each inhale where her breath caught for a minute in pain, a tremble along her ribs. What was I going to do without her? I couldn't even imagine. A month, the vet had said. One month, maybe less. A whole month of watching her suffer, that catch in her breath, that tremble in her body that I could feel like it was in my own bones. As if my bones were filled with cancer too. Maybe I should just join my mom in whatever she was drinking out of that chipped Snoopy mug, but somehow I didn't want to give her the satisfaction. I could do that at home. At least there I could curl up with Ida in the slight solace of being horizontal. A familiar bed, the safety of my curtains drawn against the bright afternoon. "I should go."

"You just got here, are you sure you don't want to finish watching this movie with me?"

"No thanks."

Mom shrugged, her caftan sliding off one sharp shoulder. "Always so independent. What can I do? It's in your blood."

In my blood, that was what she said about everything. The strange prophecy that I think she intended as consolation but made everything feel so hopeless. "It's your blood too, Mom," I said, getting up.

"Don't I know it," she answered with a chuckle, combing her tangled hair with her fingers.

In the living room, I used her phone to call a cab, those same seven digits of United Cabs that I would remember forever, the little melody of leaving places I no longer wanted to be. On the television Judy Garland and Mickey Rooney were singing "By the Light of the Silvery Moon" in blackface. I turned off the TV, but it still hummed in the silence and I watched a silverfish run quickly across the floor.

24

TWELFTH NIGHT 2004
BONAPARTE'S RETREAT

We came out of the darkness of the stairs and the landing was wallpapered in garlands of pink roses and lit by a crystal chandelier. Christopher paused next to a rolling rack jammed with coats. Party sounds rumbled behind a set of double doors with polished brass doorknobs. "We don't have to go in, if you're not into it," he said suddenly.

"Are you kidding?" I shoved my bag behind a bunch of fur coats. "I had no idea all this was even here."

He looked around. His shoulders sagged, and he looked very small and fearful all of a sudden. "I just, I mean, I feel like you should know, there's a chance Ryan might be here."

"So you said, that's why I'm here, isn't it?"

He fidgeted with the buttons on his jacket. "Just maybe don't punch him again, or anything."

I laughed. Now that we were close to the party, I could hear the sound of inebriation and music and I wanted to be inside. "You don't have to worry about that. I'm here for you. What do you want me to do?"

"I don't know. I just wanted him to see that I didn't need him, you know."

"And you don't. You've got a hot date, or beard, or whatever I'm supposed to be." He was about to interrupt but I shushed him.

He still hung back. "I'm not sure what to say to him."

"Don't say anything. Don't explain, just act natural. Listen, I've had more awkward hookups than I care to admit and the key to getting through the next day is just to bluff it out. Talking will only make things worse." I could hear champagne corks popping. This guy was going to have to buck up. "Look at me." I indicated my outfit. "I promise he will be impressed. Men are like that."

"I thought if you came with me, he would see that it wasn't a thing, that what happened didn't need to change anything…" His voice kind of trailed off. "But what if he's still mad? I really don't want him to be mad at me."

"Sometimes friends get mad for their own mysterious reasons and you don't always have control over it. Come on, Christopher, don't be a wimp. You promised me booze, let's go."

He frowned at me, annoyed, but he opened the door and a cloud of warm air and festive noise burst forth, that distinctive chaos of a party, and it seemed so obvious suddenly. A party. Why had it taken me this long to find a party tonight? In a party, we were all held together, flies in a web of laughter and poor choices and nervous energy. I wasn't alone. And again, I felt damn grateful to belong to my city. I mean, this was an obscure religious holiday on a Tuesday in January, and this room was absolutely full of people dressed in the most beautiful, outrageous outfits I had ever seen. If one was looking for distraction, it would be hard to imagine a room more desirable. Thank you, St. Christopher, patron saint of travelers and the lost.

I stopped on the threshold watching this current of wild humanity in plumes and masks and capes and armor pass by. A buccaneer in a scarlet coat walked hand in hand with a peacock in feathers and purple-pink sequins. A dragonfly fluttered opalescent wings and pushed up his growling dragon mask. Three Elizabethan jesters jangled, bells on their feet and elbows and knees. It didn't look real. Things like this happened in movies or maybe in someone's castle three hundred years ago. I was used to fairly imaginative costumes and a certain amount of flair from the burlesque girls, and Mardi Gras day, of course, always had some impressive efforts, but this was excessive, awesome. Louis XIV walked by and bowed slightly over his gold walking stick and I felt very underdressed. "Holy crap," I said.

"Yeah," Christopher agreed. "I told you."

We started to try to penetrate the elegant scrum, but it was so crowded, it was hard to move. Crystal sconces lit the room in pools of low yellow light and as the figures moved in and out of the brightness, glitter and sequins shattered the reflections, making stars dance across the walls and ceilings. It was hot with the press of drunken bodies and laughter and screams of delight pealing out over the syncopation of a band.

"We should find the bar," I said because Christopher seemed a little dazed by it all.

"Oh look, honey," one burly cancan dancer yelled to another. "Someone came as an Amish." Christopher blushed. "He's on his pot likker! No, what's it called, where they go get drunk for a year?" He put a hand on Christopher's shoulder as he passed. "I love it."

"No, no, he's a Reservoir Dog. What were their names

again? Mr. Purple! He's Mr. Purple. The skinny one." They moved away through the crowd. "Do you remember *Bad Lieutenant*? That Harvey Keitel is something else."

We managed, by following in the wake of someone's papier-mâché shrimp tail, to slide deeper into the room. Julius Caesar roared with laughter and bumped into us, accidentally jabbing Christopher in the eye with a gold laurel wreath. Christopher squinted, and moved aside. The noise in the room was tremendous. A band played old-timey jazz somewhere, but I couldn't see them from where I was.

"Does this party seem…" I hesitated, looking for the right word "…a little flamboyant?" There were a lot of young men here.

"Yeah, I kind of figured," he answered, unconcerned.

"This is really where you were planning on having a manly talk with your buddy about being straight?"

He kind of laughed. "When you put it like that." Then he looked around the room again, and in his strange fragility, pale and sad in his dark suit, he really did look like some kind of religious figure. A mystic or something. "I didn't think it all through very much. I just wanted to find him. This was where he was supposed to be."

A beautiful woman in a slinky black evening gown walked by with wings on her back. They met between her shoulder blades in a glittered skull. "Death's-head hawkmoth," she said, smiling at me as she passed, then pointed at her companion, who was covered in fragile, fluttering gold foil stars and carried an umbrella. "Asteroid shower," she said. "I love your outfit. Memento mori, baby." She reached up to caress one of my ostrich feathers and then turned and drifted away singing "Moonlight Becomes You."

I heard someone yell my name. A man in purple robes and a

three-cornered hat was waving to me. He pushed through the crowd and pulled down a little black domino mask. "Rosie, I didn't know you moved in high society like this, you're far too innocent for this crowd."

I recognized Felix. He was friends with some of the girls and did costumes for the other fancier burlesque shows in town. He hung around the Sugarlick with his boyfriend, and we had formed sort of a friendship out of a shared affinity for Swarovski crystals and historical fashion. He always got my jokes. I let myself be pulled in for a kiss on each cheek. "Someone brought me," I admitted. "What is this?"

"Oh, you know, just the Quarter scene, my little tassel twirler, where high and low bash into each other." He brought his hands together violently, spilling a little of what looked like a screwdriver onto his white gloves. "And get into all sorts of trouble. That guy over there dressed like Genghis Khan? That's going to be the King of Hermes next year, but don't tell anyone I told you. And that Venetian courtesan over there in the outrageous crepe de chine?" He pointed across the room. "They own Domino Sugar and that dress was literally made for her in Italy, it's to die for."

"What about him?" I asked. In the center of the room, a very tall man was wearing mostly silver paint and a crown of towering glow sticks that nearly reached the ceiling.

"Oh, he's a table dancer at Dick's. Don't worry about him. Unless you're looking for poppers. Are you, dear?" I shook my head. "Well, you can always change your mind."

"How did you get invited to this?" I shouted to Christopher over the noise, but he was dumbly watching King Neptune trying to disengage his trident from the long braids of a Valkyrie.

"I'm going to find the bar," Christopher said and disappeared into the crowd.

Just then, someone passed by and handed me a glass of champagne from a tray and I tried to call Christopher back, but he couldn't hear me.

It was in a real flute. I drank it quickly and the champagne tickled my nose and the tulle of someone's skirt tickled my arm and I let my eyelids droop just long enough that everything in the room swam in a sparkling haze. What a paradise. Masked figures swirled around me, following the call of their own pleasures. I was lost among a sea of strangers who were all themselves strangers to each other, and I felt gloriously at home. Everyone was no one, cloaked in anonymity, and everyone was beautiful, and everyone was sliding downhill in the rush of alcohol, and nothing could touch us. A bright envelopment of gauze and satin and feathers and velvet protected everyone in here from tomorrow and I felt so lucky to be a part of it. "Felix, this is amazing."

He accepted this like it was his responsibility. "We throw the best parties, and everyone loves a good party, and these rich folks pay for the drinks. I don't know—" he shrugged and latched on to the tiny red straw in his drink "—somehow it all just works. If only I could have dreamed of coming somewhere like this when I was a young one in Ocean Springs. The most excitement I could manage there was going with my grandmother to the Knights of Columbus Bingo Hall. Although, some of those old coots were pretty fabulous in their own way. If you want to see some impressive hairstyles and can tolerate some light homophobia, the Knights of Columbus Bingo Hall in Ocean Spring, Mississippi, is the place for you." He paused for a minute, lost in reminiscences and then finished his drink in one quick swallow. "Good riddance to bad memories," he said a little brightly and then turned his attention back to me. "And you're what, a slutty vampire?" Christopher popped up again with a drink in each hand and one cradled against his chest. "No wait, you're this Mennonite's moment of temptation? The wet dream of a Holy Roller? Great couple's idea, you two."

"Isn't she amazing?" Christopher handed me a drink, finished his right away and started on the third.

"So," I said. "How did you get invited to this again?"

"I didn't," he answered, still looking around. "Ryan was working at a frame shop on Dauphine and the owner invited him. We meant to come last year but we forgot, you know, who remembers Twelfth Night? And we were so pissed that we've been talking about it all year. It's famous."

"Oh, that would be Richie," Felix said. "He's around here somewhere dressed as the Whore of Babylon."

"I really thought Ryan wouldn't miss it." Christopher put his arm around me in a proprietary way, like we were posing for a photograph.

"I saw another dirty young man milling around somewhere earlier, near the cake. You boys all look so hungry."

"That's cool," Christopher said in a bored tone of voice. Then he apologized to me quickly. "I'm just going to go check." And he pushed back through the crowd.

"Well, what about you, my dear? Your date seems a little distracted. I think I recognize him. He's delivered me cigarettes before."

"He's all over the place. I think he's looking for a friend. Or maybe a lover. I can't tell."

"Who cares? One and the same. He well might be here, it's a small town. I've got about six exes here tonight, but also, my teller from the Whitney bank, which I would not have guessed. She's wearing a lamé fish-tail gown. We all have our hidden depths, I suppose."

A cardinal in velvet robes walked by, leading an altar boy on a leash.

Felix saw me watching. "Not always the best of taste. I'm pretty sure there's at least three blackamoors here." He sighed. "It's the Uptown folks. Some of this old money still doesn't know they lost the war, but when they pay the fiddler sometimes you have to dance to the tune," he said with a shrug.

A unicorn in a doublet ducked his head to avoid the chandelier above us. "You missed Nancy," the unicorn yelled at someone across the room.

"Fuck." A man lifted a black lace mantilla, so they could link arms. "I think she has my keys."

Felix began to steer me toward an adjacent room, and I let myself be led away.

The music was louder here and, as we headed for the dance floor, a friend of Felix's in a dress made of plastic Mardi Gras pearls grabbed us and in a flurry of unspoken signals, pulled us into a corner. He held something concealed in his fist and looked questioningly at me. I nodded and bent over his hands while he cracked something under my nose, and I inhaled deeply. I yelled thank you. A tootling clarinet started playing "If Ever I Cease to Love" and a cheer went up from the crowd. And all my sadness, all the icky feelings, everything exploded in a great wave of effervescence. It was so ridiculous, all these people, all this beauty and ugliness all bouncing to the little bumping rhythm of the jazz band, and I found myself laughing. And laughing. Everyone was singing the nonsense lyrics of the anthem of the royal court of Carnival. "May the fish get legs and the cows lay eggs, if ever I cease to love." And an irrepressible surge of high giggles poured out of me while the world swirled and melted. "Come on, you." Felix pushed me toward the dancers, and some parted to make a place for us and then we were all bobbing together in the fox-trot jostle of silent movies. "Why is Dixieland jazz so funny?" I yelled.

He snorted. "You could watch a funeral and think it was funny right now." But then he giggled too. "I don't know, because they're all dressed like they're on *The Love Boat*?"

I looked at the band. They were all dressed in black and white with nautical-looking caps and Felix was right, it was funny, and still the trumpet kept going *BLAT* in hilarious little bursts, and the tuba kept burping its jaunty bass line. I started a Charleston with a velvet lion, whose nap was wearing off, and we were all elbows and knees and impractical hats and capes and masks. I stepped on a tail and apologized. I was poked by a scepter. We moved aside to make room for the train of a kimono. The dress of pearls rattled and clanked. A kind girl with a marabou fan cooled my hot face. I don't know how long I danced. Everything faded and blurred. I had forgotten the feeling at the pit of my stomach. I had finally achieved it. Here. And it was wonderful. I thought I saw Christopher pass by in the arms of a girl dressed like a swan. Good for him. Good for all of us. I stopped thinking for a while after that.

I'm not sure when exactly I noticed that the party had changed. My feet were starting to hurt and, when I stopped dancing, holding on to the back of a gilt chair to take the weight off for a minute, everything slowed down. People were quieter, pairing off and listening to each other, heads bent in the overattentiveness of deep drunkenness. Spots of bare floor were visible now, elaborate parquet crossed with dirty streamers, lost ribbons, shed feathers, cups, a single shoe. I set off to find Christopher, still humming, a fresh glass of champagne in each hand. I was thinking of him almost proudly. To have brought me, whom he pretty clearly wanted to fuck, to a party to look for his best friend whom he had just put the moves on, and on top of it all to find time to chase some girl dressed like a goose. It was nuts, but it was an escalation of mania that I could relate to.

I passed a man sitting alone in a clump of empty chairs and he had a nasty coughing fit, but he raised one hand and gestured me nearer. I had to stand there and wait until he was done. He was wearing a sort of half-hearted outfit of plush and streamers that maybe looked like a troubadour but mostly looked like dust and thrift stores and reminded me how much I hate hippies. Especially old ones. He had long gray hair and a trilby pushed back on his head and looked like he had been doing smack for forty years. Why had I stopped? He was probably going to hit on me. "Hey, you aren't Natalie's kid are you? Natalie Grossman?"

It felt disorienting to hear someone say my mother's name. Especially here. It sent a weird shiver through me and I had an immediate impulse to run away but I didn't. "I am," I said tentatively.

"Damn, you look just like your momma. I could pick you out of any crowd. Just like her, fuck. Just as beautiful and same devil in her eye." I stood awkwardly while he looked me up and down.

"Do you know my mom?" I finally said, stupidly.

"I sure did. Your mom and I used to paint this town red. She was a wild one, your momma. Damn, I was in love with her." His eyes were watery, and I realized this person was very, very drunk. "Excuse my manners, sweetheart, I'm James

Robineaux. Your mom and I used to run around these parts together. Until she went straight, bless her heart, right about when she had you, I guess." He held out his hand toward me. His skin was a terrible gray color, the nails almost bluish, and I really didn't want to take it. I held out my champagne glasses as an excuse. He read it as an offer and took one from me, but when he tried to drink from the narrow glass, his hands were too unsteady and some of it dripped down his chin. He patted it away with the end of a fuchsia scarf. "She used to love this stuff. 'Only champagne,' she used to say. It was all she would drink. 'Bubbles to raise the spirits.'"

He spoke with a specific tone I was very familiar with, that of alcoholics once they get nostalgic and start lying. My mother was also very often full of shit. "She likes vodka now," I said brusquely.

But he smiled a dumb, satisfied smile that meant he wasn't listening to me and I noticed his teeth were a mess. "I get no kick from champagne," he sang, smiling again at me for approval and I looked at his sunken cheeks and general grayness and it occurred to me this person was dying. Not figuratively. This person was literally drinking or smoking or whatever he was doing, he was doing it to himself to death and I felt a wave of revulsion. It's possible he never even knew my mom. Drunks were such liars. People this far gone would say anything just to keep you there talking to them. He barely knew what he was saying anyway. There was no reason I had to stand here listening to it.

"Excuse me," I said, because even when I was disgusted, I was still Southern, and then I took advantage of another fit of coughing to leave before he could say anything else. He sounded like a punctured bagpipe, and that cough was familiar.

This room was too full of stale heat and gold chairs and people not getting out of my way. I finally found Christopher in a corner on a love seat with the swan girl. Her wings lay on the ground and she had one black Chinese slipper tucked up underneath her. "I'm so sorry," she was saying, a hand patting his back. "You poor boy."

"Hey." I interrupted them, possibly rudely. "Did you find what's his name?"

"No." Christopher seemed unconcerned and very intent on the girl next to him. He was lightly petting a spray of feathers attached to one shoulder of her dress.

"Do you want to leave, then?"

I needed him to make a choice right then, which of us he was pursuing, and to his credit, he raised his head immediately. "Sure."

"Do I know you?" she asked, squinting at me. "Do you dance at Big Papa's?"

I shook my head and she lay down in the space left by Christopher standing up. She crossed her hands behind her head and smiled at me. "You're cute anyway. You both are."

"Thanks." How many strippers was Christopher going to throw himself at tonight? Were we all so boring? So predictable?

I was sick of this place. I wanted my hoodie. It felt ridiculous to still be so naked. "I'll meet you outside," I told Christopher and left. The foyer felt ten degrees colder and strangely, eerily quiet after the noise and heat of the room. It was easy to find my stuff because most of the coats were gone. I was pulling on my hoodie when Christopher came out. "If you want to try and get with that girl in there, don't let me stop you," I said.

"What, Nina? No, she's just one of my regulars. She likes

grilled cheese with tomatoes and a bag of Zapp's in the middle of her shift. Also Diet Dr. Pepper, which, what? How gross is that?"

"Are you sure? I don't know where I'm going."

"I'm sure. I'm going with you." He just stood there looking at me.

I pulled up my zipper with a brusque *thwip*. "What?"

He cleared his throat. "You left me in there." We had to step aside to let a Pierrot pass through. "You disappeared. I was going to find Ryan and when I came back, you had ditched me."

"It was a party, that's how parties work." I considered changing out of my heels but decided it was too much trouble.

"But you were going to be with me when I talked to Ryan."

"Well, did you? He wasn't there so what did it matter?" One of my eyelashes was falling off again. "Hey, will you press this back down for me?" I asked him.

He leaned in close and looked at the corner of my lash I was pointing to. "I didn't want to be alone," he spoke quietly. He wasn't helping me with my eyelash. He was instead staring into my eyes in a way that made me want to look away.

"Okay, fine, whatever. I'm leaving. Are you coming with me?"

"Yes." But he didn't move.

I ran my finger under the strap of my heel to disentangle it and readjusted the feathers in my hair and then stopped because he was still just staring at me in that ridiculously fragile way. I wanted to warn him and tell him not to look at anyone like that because no one was worth it. "I'm sorry," I said instead, but it felt strange and made my voice waver. "I'm sorry I left you."

"It's okay." He shrugged and looked at the ground.

I took his hand and it was cold and clammy. "I want you to come with me now. Stay with me, please."

He smiled, and it turned his face radiant again, radiant and goofy and wonderful all at the same time. "Hold on, I'll be right back." He ducked back into the party for a few minutes and then reappeared with something clearly tucked under his jacket. "Okay, let's go."

25

1990
BROADMOOR

"Oh my God, it's a cockroach," Gaby yelled, jumping up to stand on the kitchen chair she had been sitting on.

"No, it isn't," I said, not entirely sure, since I had seen plenty of roaches in our house, especially in the summer now that we had switched to ceiling fans to cut down on our electricity bill.

"It was. It went under the garbage can, I swear to God, Rosemary, I cannot deal with roaches." She was wearing a T-shirt a cousin had brought back for her from a trip and it said See Canada in wavy rainbow-colored script. I was very jealous of that shirt.

I picked up an old *TV Guide* just in case. "It wasn't." Ida jumped around my feet excitedly, yapping at the commotion and wagging her tail supportively as I slowly approached the garbage can. I knew how Gaby felt about roaches. She had once put on a sneaker and found a roach inside and never recovered from it. She told me the story every summer in gross detail, always ending with a shiver and an emphatic *and that's why I cannot deal with roaches.*

"Just hold on," I said. And then I shoved the garbage aside in one quick motion and I saw it was a roach, a big disgusting palmetto bug swirling its antennas around.

"That's the kind that can fly, get it!" Gaby yelled from the chair.

I screamed and threw the *TV Guide* at it and then stomped on the *TV Guide* for good measure and thought I heard a crunch but it was hard to tell because we were both screaming and Ida was barking, but I figured it was close enough and Gaby and I both ran into the living room and jumped on the couch, still screaming and holding each other's hands. Ida tried to jump up with us but missed and ran around in circles barking under the coffee table instead.

Once our panic had subsided, we sprawled, recovering. "Do you think you got it?" she asked, lifting up a couch cushion and checking underneath.

"Definitely," I lied. I was half listening to see if all the noise had woken my mom up but the door to her bedroom stayed shut. I was pretty sure she and her boyfriend Tommy had broken up last night. There was a shattered wineglass still on the kitchen counter and it smelled kind of like rum in the house. The yelling and shouting had lasted almost until morning. Mom usually took breakups pretty hard. "Will you stop that? There's no bugs in our sofa."

"I'm just checking. You never know. He might have friends around."

"Oh my God, stop it." I gave her a shove.

She squealed and shoved me back. "Don't do that, I'm all jumpy now."

Then we hit each other with the sofa pillows for a while until we were really tired, and I slid onto the floor so Ida could lick my nose. I didn't want her to feel left out. "Come on, let's finish."

"I don't know if I have an appetite after all that."

I stood up and went to retrieve the tube of cinnamon buns she had dropped in the excitement. I wasn't going to give up so easily. I had just had them for the first time at her house the other week and I was still amazed that anything could be so delicious. We had walked all the way to the store to buy them and I was determined we would make them. "Are you sure it has to be a baking sheet?" I asked. "I didn't see one anywhere."

She followed me tentatively, staying near the doorway of the kitchen. "That's what we use and that's what the instructions say. Can't you ask your mom if y'all have one?"

I didn't really want to, but I also really didn't want to go digging around in the dark kitchen cabinets near that roach. "Mom, do we have a baking sheet?" I yelled and we waited for a response. I did this a couple more times until I started to get annoyed. There was no way she couldn't hear me; our house was too small and now she was just being lazy, because she didn't want to get up and help me look.

"Hold on," I told Gaby. "I'll find out." I walked to her room and knocked. There was no answer. Ida came to help by scratching one small paw at the closed door impatiently. There were a whole bunch of little marks on the wood where she had done that before. "Mom?" I asked again. There was still no answer, so I opened the door.

The room was dark, the afternoon barely filtered through the closed purple curtains, but I could see a big lump where she was lying on the floor. The room was filled with a sour smell, bile and pineapple juice. I stood there for a while. I didn't want to go in. I squeezed the canister of dough in my hand. It was comforting the way it yielded, strangely taut under the cardboard like a living creature, and I waited, unsure.

After a minute, Gaby came up behind me and looked over my shoulder. Then she reached over and turned on the hall light. We could now both clearly see the puddle of vomit under my mom's head. "Is she alive?" she whispered.

"Her hair is moving," I said. I pointed at a strand of hair across her mouth that was fluttering with her breath.

"Should we call 911? Should I call my mom?" Gaby asked.

"No." I pushed Ida back. She was desperately trying to get around my legs and into the bedroom. I closed the door. At some point I must have squeezed the cinnamon buns hard enough to unseal the top of the canister because it popped suddenly in my hand, dough leaking out thick and flabby through the diagonal slashes in the unraveling tube of cardboard. "It's okay, it's happened before."

"What did you do?"

"Nothing." I didn't want the cinnamon buns anymore. I wasn't hungry. Gaby followed as I put them back in the kitchen. "Let's go watch TV," I said.

"Okay," she answered, accepting the situation, and I was so glad she didn't ask anything else.

We went into the living room and sat next to each other. "Hey," she said after a minute, "do you want to switch?" She indicated her shirt.

I nodded. I did. I pulled off my ugly white shirt and soon was wearing the coveted See Canada rainbow. It was still warm from her body and it smelled like her. I pulled it over my knees like a tent. "Thanks."

"Sure."

Afternoon turned into night as we watched show after syn-

dicated show—*Amen, 227, The Facts of Life, Three's Company*—
the shows marking time in bursts of recorded laughter. When
we turned on the lights, Gaby called her mom to ask if she
could stay longer. I poured food into Ida's bowl. And we sat
back down on my ugly orange corduroy couch, sharing a box
of Wheat Thins for dinner, both of us careful to avoid looking
in the direction of the hallway or at the closed door behind it.

26

TWELFTH NIGHT 2004
THE FRENCH QUARTER

The bar downstairs was closed, and we had to leave by a side door in an alley, held open by one very tired-looking kitchen employee. "Y'all be safe now," he said half-heartedly.

The street was quiet. Someone's footsteps echoed between the facing buildings. I felt the breeze off the river just a block away and the clouds moved quickly overhead, streaming past slanted roofs and chimneys. There was no moon out. Only thick clouds. A truck rumbled by and the building behind us shook, just barely, almost unnoticeably, the foundations shivering.

Christopher pulled a bottle of champagne from his jacket, where he had been cradling it against his side. "I grabbed this on the way out. I thought we might need it."

I almost said no, I was feeling so gross and exhausted, but then that impulse felt ridiculous at this point in the night and so I took it from him. It was pleasantly heavy, the neck of the bottle cold and smooth against my palm. "Thanks." He looked pleased and it felt nice to have made him happy. "I'm sorry you didn't find your friend in there."

He rocked back on his heels. "Maybe it's better. There will be other times. That was really something, wasn't it? My folks go to Carnival balls but I'm pretty sure they aren't like that."

"They don't go to the Rex Ball, by any chance?" I asked maybe too eagerly. "I watch that on TV every year with my mom."

"You do? How can you stand it? It's so boring. It's like four hours long." He hesitated, clearly weighing something. "I was a page," he admitted finally.

I laughed. "No way. You were one of those poor little boys in ostrich feathers yawning next to the thrones?"

"Yeah, it was maybe the most humiliating moment of my life—the blond wig, the lipstick, the stupid velvet outfit. God. And everyone is talking to you like it's the most glorious moment of your life. I just wanted to fucking kill myself." He shivered a little in the remembering. "I puked all day that day because I was so nervous about it and they still made me do it."

"I wonder if I saw you? Probably. My mom and I never missed a year."

He groaned. "Can we stop talking about it?"

"Sure." But I kept thinking about it. I liked the idea that unknowingly, we had been having the same experience together. Two memories overlaid, from different parts of the city but caught in the low-budget splendor of local broadcasting.

We had instinctively turned left as we started to walk, and I knew where we were going. It was that time, when the night had ended but the day hadn't begun yet. The time to be on the edge of things, the boundary where soggy land gave way to fierce currents. Somewhere quiet. "To the river?" I asked. We were only a few blocks away.

"To the river," he echoed as if it were obvious. Where we

could drink his champagne undisturbed. Where we didn't have to really be anywhere, a place to rest.

"Is that too heavy?" he asked. "I can take it." He indicated the bottle.

Now that I had accepted his gift, I didn't want to relinquish it. "No, I got it."

We crossed up and over the hill of the levee to the narrow strip of boardwalk where the shore of the river was just a big dark space against the lights of the town. Planks and benches and enormous wooden steps leading down into the darkness. I never knew the point of that staircase leading straight into the water, waves lapping up one step or ten, depending on the time of year and height of the river. They were mysterious in the best way, a passage to nowhere, a stately point of egress for drowned pirates and mermaids.

We found a bench. It was strange to stop here, these same benches we had flown past on his bike only a few hours ago. That exhilaration was long gone. Things felt cold now, flat, like an extinguished match. He took the bottle and pressed on the neck of the champagne. The cork rang out like a shot and I started. I tucked the hood of my sweatshirt over my head. We passed the bottle back and forth. Thankfully, Christopher's chattiness had finally worn down and he sat silently plucking at the foil on the neck of the bottle.

The last time I saw my mom, when I stopped by with Ida, she had that same cough as that old guy at the party. I had been telling her to go to the doctor for ages and she always waved me off and we had sat at her kitchen table in irritable silence. Who was I to tell anyone how to take care of themselves? I had enough to deal with, with my poor fucking dog.

But I knew it was coming. I had known forever. The empty bottles, the clanking garbage, the alternating rhythm of cheerful evenings and daytime stupor. Those days pierced by the low voices and odd musical cues of the daytime soaps constantly playing. Those muted voices making an already quiet house feel even emptier, her hangover like a fog around us, a sudden drop of barometric pressure and the same feeling in my stomach.

But there was knowing and there was knowing, and the kind that was rearing up in me now, unavoidable and ugly, was raw in my chest. "Why does everyone in this town drink so much?" I said finally.

"So they can forget." Christopher handed me the champagne.

"Forget what?"

"What have you got?" He smiled. "It's our way. My grandmother is so steeped in port, she's almost pickled. She's trying to forget that she's a racist bitch who hates the maids and nurses that keep her alive. My dad is trying to forget how much he hates his mom even though he's just like her. And so on for my whole family. On the other hand, Ryan drinks to forget he grew up waiting on welfare checks and getting punched by his dad."

"And you?"

He took the bottle back. "You first." He drank. "Or maybe we all drink to forget we're on borrowed time." He pointed at the river. "All that cancer stuff upriver, poison. Just pouring down on us."

"That sounds like a cop-out," I began, but he interrupted me.

"Not to mention the fucking levees. Why not get drunk if you're already doomed?"

"You're taking a very broad view of causality here."

"You've got to. When you think about how fucked we all

are as a community, it makes you feel less bad about the bad shit that's happened to you in particular."

"Does it work?"

"No." He paused and reconsidered. "Maybe. I don't know, we've lasted this long. I'm glad I'm here with you tonight though."

On either side of us, the sparse line of benches spread up and down this old stretch of boardwalk. We were the only people here except for two women in bright pink scrubs, their backs to us, sitting on the wide wooden steps.

Christopher was also looking toward the dark buildings of Bywater and the industrial canal. "Oh, and pandemics, yellow fever and stuff. Don't forget those. They filmed *Panic in the Streets* right down there, you know. The Governor Nicholls Street Wharf."

More movies. "I've never seen it."

He grunted in exasperation. I ignored him because I was straining to overhear the two women. They had big foam daiquiri cups but didn't seem as drunk as one would expect at this hour. One kept glancing back over her shoulder nervously at us.

"It's relaxing here," her friend said assertively. They had clearly been arguing about it. "Just wait. In another half hour, it's going to be worth it."

The first woman shifted. She was wearing a hooded sweatshirt like me, but pink, like her scrubs. She looked back again at us, suspicious. I remembered a cab ride I once took. My driver was off-duty NOPD and told me she lived out by the airport and never came downtown because it was too dangerous. I didn't know what was more outrageous—that the police department paid so badly officers had to moonlight as cab drivers, or that for a whole segment of people, the slice of city where it seemed like I passed my whole life felt too dangerous. Everyone I knew was afraid of black people, and nice black police officers with set curls and quiet, gentle voices who drove cabs in their spare time were afraid of "downtown." That nurse was clearly afraid of two degenerates like Christopher and me. How caught we all were in this intractable web of fear.

Proximity to the water made their voices carry and I realized these women had just gotten off a night shift. They were having an after-work drink. The shift in perspective was dizzying.

Christopher and I were careening to the burnt-out end of a night on the town, while these women were settling in to the easy relaxation of five in the evening, when your efforts of the day were done, and your time, suddenly your own, spun out inviting. "They say she's doing so well, she might get on one of those competition teams. Mathletes or something, they're called," one of the women said, one leg extended and massaging her knee.

"Mathletes," the other woman echoed, amused. "What a name."

"I know." The first one took another sip of her daiquiri and switched legs, massaging the other knee. She chuckled. "But really, I'm so proud of her. I don't know where she gets it from."

I felt my insides curdle up, a special sour milk kind of memory. Gaby was a mathlete. In lower school I used to watch her finishing her quizzes before the rest of us, and the way she would sit back and quietly play cat's cradle with whatever bits of ribbon or string she had at hand. She wasn't a show-off about it. Instead she bowed her head, electric with a rainbow of plastic balls at the end of her braids, and watched her own hands at work. I often rushed through because I wanted to be done next. I wanted to be able to sit with her in shared, silent victory while the sounds of scratching pencils of everyone who wasn't us rustled through the room. Sometimes she would turn around to check on me and in order to be ready to meet her eyes, I sometimes had to leave a question or two blank. It was a small sacrifice for that moment of communion. She was smarter than me. She always had been. I missed her so much.

The fog was rolling in deep and heavy now. Algiers on the opposite shore had completely disappeared. This sweet, steady winter fog that fell hard at twilight and dawn, blanketing those painful transitions in warm, obscuring mist. The lamps above us blurred, melting into the condensation falling around them and I didn't care about my hair anymore. Although I noticed both of the nurses pulled their hoods up and tied the strings tightly around their faces. The sun hadn't risen, but the darkness was different, shading out into an eerie in-between gray, waiting on a change that hadn't happened yet. More of the river sank into the gloom, the bend in the distance, the span of the bridge farther up all vanishing in this visible air. The blurry backs of the women were all that remained. We disappeared together.

Christopher was staring at the bottle of champagne in his lap, still picking at the label.

"Where are you going to go after tonight?" I asked.

"I can probably sleep in my parents' bushes or porch swing or something if I wait for them to leave for work. Although they did call the cops on me the last time I did that. Assholes."

"I'm sorry. It sucks to fight with your friends, to lose the people you depend on."

"Yeah." He was kicking the toe of his sneaker into the cracks of the planks of the boardwalk. "The funny thing is, I'm not the first guy to grab his dick. Some baseball coach was all over him in little league." He got his foot caught for a minute and struggled to get it out. "Catholic school, man. We had that in common." He wasn't looking at me anymore. "So, he should know none of it matters. Grabbing your friend's dick or ending up neck deep in gash, it's all just fucking body parts and what the fuck, you know? But like, we were there for each other."

"Is that what you wanted from me, to be neck deep in gash?"

He winced. "Don't say it back like that, you make it sound so bad. But I don't know, maybe. Maybe I wanted to be around you because you're pretty and it makes everything hurt less when you're being nice to me."

"Am I?" I didn't usually think of myself as nice.

He nodded. "You are."

I let myself enjoy that for a minute. "It almost feels like you're making fun of me to talk about me being pretty at this point in the night," I laughed. "I mean, Jesus."

"Why do girls think that they can just lose their hotness because their hair isn't brushed or whatever? You look the same. Exactly the same as you probably always do."

I looked at a freighter heading toward us from upriver. "Because you can lose anything. Anything you ever have can be lost."

He didn't answer for a while. "Maybe I should just leave," he said. "Get out of town. Go where people aren't full of shit. I don't know. Berkeley or something."

"Berkeley?" I laughed again. He still managed to surprise me in these funny little ways.

He shrugged. "I don't fucking know."

"I tried that. It doesn't work." The freighter sounded its horn. The cry was loud, insistent, and held on to the humid air longer than it seemed possible and my heart cracked. I wanted it to stop. I was furious at all the complicated, intractable, impossible things flooding my nerves, my body, my heart, overtopping the boundaries of what felt possible and leaving me lost, drained. "You go away because you think you're different and special, and then it turns out you're not. Not at all. You belong here, so you just come back."

"I think you're special," he said quietly, and I felt whatever last thing that was holding me together shatter.

It's what she always said. It's what she always said, brushing my hair from my face when she'd come home at dawn, stopping to climb into my bed with me when it wasn't quite light out yet. I could never be sure if she actually came in or if I was just dreaming her, humming that song from *Mister Rogers' Neighborhood*, telling me over and again that I was special. I don't know if it was hope or a prayer, but whatever it was, it hadn't come true. If there was one thing I hadn't turned out to be, it was special. Sorry, Mom. I wasn't going to be an artist or a teacher or a dreamer or have a house and two kids or whatever she thought she was buying me with all those years of private school. Twenty-two years later and all she got was someone exactly like her: a fucking disaster. "I think my mom's dying," I said, before I could even think about it. "She's drinking herself to death." The words sounded so melodramatic.

"I'm sorry." He paused. "You know that shit's genetic," he said, handing me the bottle.

"Yes, I know that shit's genetic," I said, annoyed, taking it. He sounded young again. Young and stupid and strangely it was a comfort. "I tried to stop drinking for a while, in college."

"That sounds fucking grim. Lonely too."

"Yeah, pointless." I took a long drink of champagne and foam bubbled over the top when I brought the bottle down from my lips.

I looked around and could tell it was morning now. The gray was lighter. The boardwalk split into separate planks, a tugboat chugged by, the streetlamps switched off. There was no glorious moment, no streaming dawn, no revelations. The event we had all implicitly been waiting for snuck past and at some point, hidden by the fog, the sun had risen quietly to itself.

The women near us must have realized it too and stood, adjusting their scrubs. "Well, that was disappointing," one said.

"Come on, I've got to go get these kids ready for school."

"We'll come back another time. I've seen it be really special before." She was still arguing with her friend as they strolled away, car keys in hand. "It's this humidity. When it's this wet, sometimes my car won't even start."

I also wanted to leave. There was something embarrassing about having been sitting here, unconsciously hoping for something to happen and being betrayed, caught out. The clammy feeling of confidences hanging between us. He also felt this shift and stood, a little unsteady, and offered me his hand. "Come on. Let's go."

"Where?"

"Take me to your house. You promised."

"I did?" At this point he knew all my secrets—well, almost all—and this same earnest look still hadn't left his eyes. This silent entreaty he had been making all night. I did want to go home. I was tired. I wanted it all to be over. If nothing else, I guess I could always fuck him. That would make him happy. Maybe make him happy enough to forgive what a fucking monster I was. I could sink down into the repletion of men and bodies and mornings after. But he was holding out his hand to me and his wrist looked so pale against the dirty white of his cuff and I was so tired and here he was, offering. "Okay."

He threw away the champagne bottle and it arced gracefully through the air and landed in the trash can with a loud clang. "That's the first time that's ever happened," he said, surprised.

"Congratulations." When I stood up, my bag felt heavier. All at once, exhaustion plowed through me. I didn't know how I was going to make it the few blocks to my house, this enormous bag banging against my knee at every step. "I need a coffee."

"Yes," he agreed. "A fine idea."

When we crossed back into the city, the servers at Café Du Monde were sweeping out the restaurant and everything, tables, chairs, floor, was damp from the fog. A woman in the peaked white paper cap of her uniform looked up from the Vietnamese newspaper she was reading. She had seen so many like me and Christopher, walking the flagstones at dawn and she was clearly profoundly bored of all of us. We stopped at the small window and ordered two café au laits, bitter from chicory and sweet from all the scalded milk. A cook propped open the screen door to the kitchen and lit a cigarette, the air heavy with the warm doughnut smell of hot fat and sugar. I cradled the foam cup and the thin cheap lid jabbed at my lip when I drank. The alley behind Café Du Monde smelled like bleach and piss and wet. The strap of my bag dug into my shoulders. I was so tired. It was time to go home.

27

The burst of flame was more like an explosion, a quick ball of fire that flared high, and I had time to exchange just one look of triumph with Gaby before her features were cast in darkness again. She pointed and I turned my attention back to the lawn to see the final flame withering to blackness. All we had accomplished was a big dark spot on the grass and a few scorched branches of an azalea bush. We paused for a minute in confusion. "What the fuck?" I asked.

Gaby was already laughing. "Girl—" she doubled over to rest her hands on her knees, the laughter making her unsteady in her drunkenness "—what are we thinking? You can't set live plants on fire. Haven't you ever gone camping?"

"No. Of course not, when would I go camping? When have you gone camping?"

"I went with my cousins once a long time ago. In Georgia. They live in Atlanta and—"

"I don't care," I interrupted. "Why didn't you tell me, if you knew so much about starting fires?" The abrupt reversal of all that nervous excitement was making me giggle too.

She had to wait to catch her breath before she could continue. "I forgot." Her voice rose with overwhelming amusement and she sat down on the ground with a thump. "Oh man, I want some Girl Scout cookies about now," she added, wiping her eyes.

I sat down next to her. "What are you even talking about, Girl Scout cookies? We'd be the shittiest Girl Scouts in the whole world. We can't even start a fire with this." I shook the bottle of lighter fluid in front of us and its sloshing seemed even funnier and we started up again.

Just then a light switched on over the front door. "Oh shit." In her efforts to get up, Gaby leaned hard on me and that made me fall over and we flailed together on the street for a second. "We have to get out of here," she said.

The asphalt was hard on my knees and I pulled myself up by the mailbox, still weak from laughing, trying to drag her up too. "Hurry up." I meant to whisper but it came out very loudly. The mailbox fell open and I noticed a Victoria's Secret catalog, which also struck me funny for being in my principal's mailbox. My arms and legs had an unhelpful jelly-like consistency that was making it hard to get stable.

"Wait, where did I put my keys?" Gaby was looking around us at the ground.

"They're hanging out of your pocket," I said, guiding myself along the hood of the car toward the passenger side door.

"Stop right there," a very familiar voice yelled out. I would have ignored this, but Gaby had dropped her keys again and was fumbling for them on the dark ground and our principal, Ms. Mancuso, was halfway down the path toward us already. It was hard not to obey that voice of authority even if we weren't officially on school grounds or anything.

"I've already called the police," she called out, her red flannel robe flapping behind her like the devil herself.

"Wait, what?" I heard Gaby whisper and I froze.

"Come here, who is that? Is that Gabrielle Parker? Then that must be Rosemary Grossman over there with you. What is the meaning of this? How dare you come to my home and destroy my property? I'm pressing charges. A night in jail should teach you, you awful, disrespectful, dangerous girls. What if you had killed someone?"

We heard the blip of a siren, then some flashing lights cut through the trees as a police car turned the corner toward us. Gaby leaned over again and seeing her laughing was about to make my giggles start up again too, but then I realized she was dry heaving. It scared me for a minute; I never saw her lose control like that. Even in fifth grade when I went with her family to a restaurant in Bucktown and her sister had an allergic reaction to some shellfish and almost died and we had to spend the evening in the hospital waiting room. I was terrified, but she had sat calmly eating peanut M&M'S from the vending machine and humming along with the nurses' radio. Right now though, she was definitely freaking out. I wanted to put a hand on her back, but I was scared to move under Ms. Mancuso's furious glare.

When the car finally pulled up, I was relieved to see it wasn't the cops, just the neighborhood watch. When the officer got out, he tried to look serious, but all he really looked was annoyed. I saw he didn't even have a badge and exhaled. This wasn't going to be that bad.

"Whose car is this?" he asked.

Gaby didn't look better though. "Mine, sir," she whispered.

"Gabrielle Parker, I knew you were bad news," Ms. Mancuso cut in. "I knew you had no respect for our school, but

I thought at least you might have some respect for yourself. What you've done is vandalism. I am shocked that an Immaculata girl could ever do such a thing, but then maybe you aren't cut out to be a student at Mary Immaculata."

"Ma'am, it was my idea," I said quietly, but she wasn't paying attention to me.

"Be quiet, Rosemary. Go sit over there." She pointed to the curb. "The officer and I need to decide what to do with you two."

"You come with me," the fake policeman said to Gaby.

"What?" She looked absolutely stricken.

"Are you the driver of this vehicle?" he asked and she nodded. "I'm going to put you in the car while I talk to the property owner here."

She licked her lips. "No, please."

I wanted to communicate to her somehow to not give him what he wanted, to hide it better. Her fear, visible in every part of her body, was making him puff up and act like even more of a dick. He grabbed her roughly by the arm and practically pushed her into the backseat of his car. He and Ms. Mancuso walked a few steps away to speak in quiet consultation and I looked at Gaby inside the car. I wanted to catch her eye, exchange some silent comfort, but she was staring straight ahead and wouldn't meet my gaze. The lights on the roof were still flashing and every time they illuminated her face, she had an expression I had never seen before. I was so used to seeing her cool and collected that now the look on her face was frightening, raw and desperate. Then it faded to darkness for a second before the red light flipped back on again and she looked even worse.

I waited nervously for Ms. Mancuso to stop talking with the cop. It felt like hours before they finally came over. They let Gaby out and Ms. Mancuso assured us there would be con-sequences at school and said she would be telling our parents but that she wasn't going to send us to jail. Then they both lectured us a while longer to make a point, but I could tell they both were tired. Ms. Mancuso yawned at one point and had goose bumps on her arms. Now that we were all calmly standing around, I could see the spot on her grass was really stupidly small, and we had barely caused any actual damage. We promised never to do anything like that again and then they told us to go straight home and expect to hear more about it. We got in the car and drove away quickly.

I waited until they were out of sight behind us before I laughed. "I can't believe Ms. Mancuso was acting like she was going to get us arrested. That wasn't even a real cop. What was he supposed to do with us? That car of his probably didn't even have locks. I bet you could have just opened the door and walked out, fucking doughnut-eating rent-a-cop. We were probably the most exciting thing that's happened to him in weeks."

I stopped because Gaby had pulled the car over and opened her door and was now throwing up for real this time. I reached over to rub her back and she swatted my hand away with-out looking up. When she was finally done, she swished her mouth out with the remains of one of the drinks in her cup holders, spat, and then sat back and stared at the steer-ing wheel. "My dad," she said quietly to herself. "What is my dad going to say when he finds out I almost went to jail? My grandmother?"

I reached behind us into the backseat to grab one of the beers they hadn't bothered to confiscate. I was trying to drink away an uneasy feeling that had blossomed in me the moment they had put Gaby in the car. I had experienced a boundless, almost oppressive sense of relief that I was sitting on the curb, free, in the open air and not beside her in that cop car. And now the shame of the memory made my voice unnaturally cheery. "Oh my God, we were never going to be arrested. Those two were so full of shit."

"Rosemary." She held up a finger warningly and her voice had an edge to it I had never heard before. "Rosemary, I need you not to talk to me while I drive you home."

"Okay, but nothing really happened, it's all going to be fine." She held up that finger at me again and pressed her lips together hard. "Fine. Fine, I won't say anything." I cracked open the beer and sank down in my seat, worried, but grateful for the silence between us. I was terrified that somehow she knew what I had felt and I had no way to explain myself, to answer for it. I drank hard, and quickly.

She reached over and grabbed the beer from me suddenly and threw it out of her open window. I turned to watch it roll out into the street behind us. "Careful," I said, hoping to make her smile. "A girl could get arrested for doing things like that." She didn't laugh and I bit my lip and hated myself because in spite of everything, what I wanted most was to reach around for another beer from her backseat.

28

TWELFTH NIGHT 2004
THE FRENCH QUARTER

Christopher and I turned onto my street in what had become soft early-morning sunshine. I loved this block so much. The lavender house on the corner, sweet olive branches bending over the courtyard gate, three hitching posts, black horse heads on narrow poles, rings dangling from their noses, all tilted at crazy angles. It was all mine, as familiar as breathing. The hydraulics of a garbage truck groaned a few blocks away.

I was careful in my heels to avoid the ridges where the sidewalk buckled around iron plates of the water company, engraved with the moon and stars. I stepped over the wide circular dents where garbage cans used to be sunk into the pavement but were now poorly sealed up with concrete. All the bumps and holes and seams of poor infrastructure that Ida and I had passed over thousands of times, the relentless rhythm of having a dog. Would I stop noticing these things now that I didn't have to keep circling the block, three times a day, every day? Would this familiarity with my block just slip away?

I had a sudden wave of nervousness about going home and

would have stopped, but Christopher was holding my arm in a very self-consciously chivalrous manner and he pulled me along. Maybe I had become a goal for him. I couldn't really hold it against him. So many times, I had found that self-absorption a relief—once you were swept into the riptide of desire, you stopped existing for a minute in men's eyes. I liked becoming invisible, but I felt a funny pang. This morning it made me feel lonely.

We passed the twenty-four-hour deli on the corner, stepping around a small river of soapy water that ran from the kitchen door down to the street. A guy was leaning on a beat-up bike that was chained to the stop sign, smoking and reading a book. He looked up as we passed. "Hey, man." He nodded at Christopher.

"Hey," Christopher said, nodding back, and then the guy looked down again, careful to not address me or even make eye contact. Christopher stood a little taller, and I saw that I was moving through a silent brotherhood of discretion. And it annoyed me.

"What are you reading?" I asked him.

He looked up, surprised, meeting my eyes as if by accident, and then looked away, unwilling to be drawn into anything that might in some way compromise Christopher's ability to seal the deal, or whatever he thought. "*Snow Crash*," he mumbled.

"Oh man, that book is so good." I could hear Christopher's swell of talk about to burst forth again.

But then, this guy thinking he saw Christopher's chances hanging in the balance, cut him short instead. "See you around, man." He extended his hand which Christopher met in a strange upside-down three-fingered grasp. And then he looked down again at his book, ending the exchange.

We crossed the street. "What was that about?" I asked.

A tired mule walked by pulling an empty carriage. "It's a thing the delivery guys came up with," he said, shrugging. "Just like this club we all belong to. But it's supposed to be a secret."

We reached my gate, the narrow brick alley that ran under my landlady's building back toward my apartment. Even in this bright morning, it was dark, one gas lamp flickering against the bricks. I hesitated. Something about this felt like a betrayal. I thought he didn't have any other friends. I thought he was here because he was heartbroken and alone with nowhere to go. I looked at him carefully and wondered, how well can you know someone in a night? Maybe this guy didn't need me at all. Had I mistaken his fragility, his desperation? Maybe we had nothing in common. I waited with my key, deciding.

He put his hands in his pockets, hyperextending his elbows in a gesture of submission. "It's a shitty job and it rains a lot and delivery guys get mugged, I don't know, so it helps."

"And Ryan?"

"Ryan's the one who got me in, we got the tattoos together."

He pulled up his sleeve and showed me what I had thought was a really terrible tattoo of a star was actually something else, an old-fashioned straight razor crossed over a set of handlebars. An insignia.

"You dumbass."

He smiled. "Yeah."

Matching tattoos. That was love. I couldn't help but laugh. I wasn't sure why, I mean, I was still wearing ostrich feathers in my hair. We were all ridiculous. I ran my finger over his ink, feeling the hot skin pulse under my touch.

"I could make you a member," he offered eagerly. "Any of us can, it's part of the charter."

"I'm not a delivery boy."

"No, but you're one of us." He spoke with conviction, and I let my fingers close around his forearm, sliding down until I held his hand, grateful.

"I would never join a fraternity under false pretenses," I said and meant it, but I held on as I turned to let us into my gate. "Careful." The bricks were slick in this passage where the sun never penetrated, heavy with the cool smell of moss, and I shivered. The ceiling arched above, and we walked into the first courtyard, green with plants and algae, a round fountain gurgling in its center.

"It's nice back here," he said, admiring. "Ryan and I were living in such a shithole."

"My landlady likes to rent to girls in the business. It's the only way I could afford it. There are some issues." I pointed to a row of ceramic Aunt Jemima planters, cracked and untended, ceramic faces rolling their eyes toward the tangled herbs spilling over their sides. I thought I saw the lace curtains of the second story move and wondered if she was awake. Miss Couteau didn't really leave the building and I never knew when she was at the window, watching, an uncomfortable presence that alternated between aggressive Southern friendliness and suspicion. "It's more private in the back. My place is in the slave quarters."

"Don't call it that."

I was confused. It was what everyone said about the small back buildings behind French Quarter houses. "But they were."

"Maybe, but it makes you sound like my dad. It's a good rule of thumb to never sound like my dad."

"Okay, whatever." I shrugged as we passed through another, shorter passage that opened into a second, smaller courtyard—a square of bricks surrounded by banana trees, grown wild with neglect. Here the stairs led up to my small place, three rooms that ran the length of the tiny building, with a skinny covered balcony where I liked to sit out long days, just me and Ida watching the wind rustle the banana leaves of the quiet courtyard.

As we reached the bottom step, I looked up, startled, and saw someone was sitting at the top. It was Gaby, smoking a cigarette and picking at the crease of her gray slacks. She watched me climb, turning her head to exhale a plume of smoke that was carried on the breeze over the low wall next to us and into the next courtyard. "Rosemary Grossman, girl," she sighed. "You look a mess."

Her hair was in a neat set around her face, the loose bob that I always thought, a little enviously, made her look like one of the Supremes. She was wearing a thin V-neck sweater and strung the gold cross on her neck back and forth along its chain with her free hand. I first felt a wave of elation that she was sitting there, and then fear. I held my breath.

She looked me over for a long minute, from the hairpiece hanging off the back of my skull, to the dirty sweatshirt and fishnets. Then she leaned over to look around me. "And who is this?"

"This is Christopher," I said, knowing what she would think of him, as well.

"I see. Hello, Christopher." When she spoke to him, she smiled with that sudden bright graciousness that she could snap into so easily. "It's very nice to meet you." Her politeness told me everything I needed to know about what she thought of Christopher. I waited, terrified that when she spoke to me again, she would use that same tone. She didn't. Not quite. "Rosemary," she said, taking another drag from her cigarette, "why is there a dead dog in your apartment?"

"Wait, what?" Christopher asked behind me.

I climbed the stairs and sat down next to Gaby and took the cigarette from her. The end was damp, and I tipped ash onto the green-painted floor beside me. "I didn't know you started smoking again."

She snorted and opened the purse next to her to rifle for another cigarette. "My supervisor smokes like a goddamn chimney, and I just couldn't take watching her slip out all the time." She flicked a lighter and inhaled. "I'm a social worker," she explained politely to Christopher. "Well, I'm still working on my certification, but I still have to spend more time than I would like in the office. I'm starting to shadow client visits."

He just nodded, looking a little dumbfounded. "About this dog…"

Gaby ignored him. "Rosemary, bad enough that I get a message from you sobbing so hard on my mom's answering machine that I can't even tell what you are saying. Girl, you know I don't check that machine. I have a cell phone."

"I couldn't remember the number."

"Lucky for you, I only noticed this morning. Last night I was damn tired from work and my mother was giving me such a hard time about not putting in my share of the Entergy bill, I went to bed and when I got up this morning and heard that thing, I almost had a heart attack. You really need to speak more clearly if you're going to be dropping words like *dead* and *murder*. And here I am. I dragged my ass all the way down here to the goddamn French Quarter on my way to work." She paused and spoke to Christopher, politely including him in the conversation. "It's actually not that far from my office if you just head up Tulane. The parking is a lot better around here at this time of day than I would have expected, thank God." She addressed herself to me again. "And I get all the way here, worried sick about you, and then I have to see that. You know how I felt about that dog."

"How did you get in?" I watched my cigarette glow.

"I asked that crazy bitch in front, and you know—" she stopped meaningfully and when I glanced at her she almost smiled "—and you know what that took. 'Yes, ma'am, I'm here in my Ann Taylor work clothes to rob your house. And I'm so well brought up that I ring the fucking doorbell to ask permission first.'"

"I'm surprised she let you in."

"Girl," she said again and let it just hang there. She was the only person I knew who used that expression that much and it always felt natural. And sometimes I said it back to her, but only when I got too excited, caught up in some excess of shared feeling and then I worried about it after. It didn't sound right in my voice. But she never mentioned it.

"Um, so there's really a dead dog somewhere?" Christopher asked, picking nervously at the peeling paint of the banister.

I watched the flecks of paint scatter onto the stairs. There was a moment of silence. "I didn't know what to do," I said, my voice catching a little. "I was looking for someone to help."

"You take her to the vet," Gaby said softly.

"She hated the vet." The stupidity of this hung in the air between us. "I couldn't pick her up," I admitted.

"When did it happen?"

"Yesterday." Gaby put an arm around me, and I didn't know what to do. Her touch was instantly familiar, her smell made me think of Smurf pajamas and the peppermint face masks we used in middle school. Hers was the only shoulder I had ever cried on. The only one. My friend. How could she be so mad at me when I needed her like this?

"I remember when you got her," she said. "That summer all we did was watch *The Little Mermaid* all day, and we kept having to pause the video to run Ida outside if she looked like she was going to pee."

"Do you remember how all we ate that summer was Lean Cuisine fettucine Alfredo? And I didn't have a microwave, so we were always boiling those little pouches?"

Gaby laughed. "Oh Jesus, yes. I can still taste them. Why did we think we needed to be on a diet when we were ten years old?"

"I think it was the only food that was at my house."

"Yeah, your mom was like that. But at least your house wasn't full of sisters getting in the way of our TV time—our *Little Mermaid* and our *Pretty Woman*." I breathed in deeply, thinking about me and Gaby lying on my faded carpet on our stomachs watching the same two movies over and over again while Ida skittered back and forth on the linoleum chasing a little rubber ball that was still too big to fit in her mouth. I wanted to rest for a minute in this safety of childhood, before everything got so complicated. Gaby and I spending whole afternoons trying to braid friendship bracelets like the other girls in our class. We were so bad at it. "You know you can't just leave her there," she said finally.

"I can't see her like that."

"How did she pass?" Gaby asked, biting on the edge of one of her cuticles, another gesture so familiar it just shoved back all those years and made me feel thirteen years old.

I hesitated. "She was really old."

"You remember when I had that little black kitten? We

might not have been friends yet, I can't remember. She was hit by a car and I took it so hard."

I didn't want to hear about her life before we had been friends. It pushed her further from me and she was here now, and I was so glad. And I couldn't keep what I did in my chest any longer, the raw, sharp edges of it lacerating my insides. "I killed her."

"What?" She took her thumb out of her mouth in shock. "You didn't."

Christopher made some unquantifiable noise and I didn't look at him.

"I had to. She was suffering, and I couldn't stand it. I couldn't leave her like that."

"How did you..." She stopped.

"Pillow." I flinched, remembering the shudder and then the stillness. How devastatingly easy it had been.

"Rosemary," she said and then stopped.

I had started sweating a little. My armpits felt damp, remembering. "She was suffering," I whispered again.

Gaby took a deep breath. "That is when you take her to the doctor." She was enunciating a little too clearly and I could feel a sharp prickle come off her. "How do you know whether or not she was ready to go? You can't know that. That's God's decision."

"She hated the vet. Why would I take her somewhere that terrified her just because I was too much of a coward to end it for her? I owed it to her. She was my baby. I couldn't give my baby over to a bunch of strangers because I was afraid. It was my responsibility, my burden. I had to give that to her."

"Hmm." She sounded unconvinced and I was hurt by her tone.

"It's true. I was trying to do something right by her."

She made another disapproving noise and pressed her lips together.

"I was. What?" She looked away and took a drag of her cigarette. "What is it? What are you so mad about?" I said finally. "Why don't you like me anymore?"

"You should have taken that dog to the doctor."

"I was helping her."

"Always helping," she said in a way that made me bristle.

"I can help," Christopher said suddenly. "I'll do it. I'll bury her for you."

"What?" We both looked at him.

"I can do it right back here." He pointed to the banana trees below, the dirt plantings that lined the stone courtyard. "There's room for a dog. Is it a big dog?"

"Chihuahua mix," I said, shaking my head.

Gaby looked skeptical. "Is that legal?"

"Who cares?" Christopher practically beamed. I could see the mission reignite the last sparks of drugs in his body, the sudden relief of purpose against the dying of the night.

On some level I knew that this was what I had been hoping for since I had decided to bring Christopher home, but now that he was here, offering, I couldn't meet his eyes.

"Where is it?" he asked.

"She."

"Where is she?" he asked more gently.

I tilted my head toward the apartment.

"Let me go see."

"Door's unlocked," I said, as he stepped carefully between us.

A tightness lingered in the air between Gaby and me. "Are you still mad at me? About that dumb fight? About me doing burlesque?" I had to ask, to highlight the unfairness of it. She couldn't possibly hold anything against me right now. My dog was dead.

"Here we go," she sighed. "It wasn't about that. I mean, I still think it's messed up. You should not be disrespecting yourself and your body like that."

"I'm not. I told you."

She raised her hand to silence me. "Please don't start going on about how it's some empowering thing. Save it for your other friends."

"I don't have any other friends," I said angrily. She still wasn't understanding how desperate I was.

"Rosemary, it's been hard seeing you come home and throw your life away. I don't like watching it," she answered just as angrily.

"It's not very nice to be judgmental when a friend is having such a hard time."

"And drinking too much."

"Oh come on. You've always drunk just as much as me." She didn't say anything, and I felt uncomfortable. I wasn't sure that was totally correct.

We smoked in silence for a minute. The strap of my shoe had made a tear in my fishnets and I plucked at it, scratching my ankle bone in the process. Gaby watched me until she pushed my hand away. "You're ruining those."

"Remember how you used to get holes in your knee socks right there, always in the same spot?"

"Yeah," she agreed. "I must have sharp ankles."

"I miss you."

She didn't answer. Instead she said, "Do you remember that time you talked me into setting Ms. Mancuso's dirt on fire?"

My stomach seized up, but maybe it wouldn't be so bad. Maybe we were just talking about old times. "Of course.

I was just telling that guy about it." I pointed back toward Christopher. "He was very impressed with our badassness."

"You were helping me then too, right?"

"Of course I was. I would do it again. I would do anything for you. That woman was such a bitch." I took her arm and squeezed it.

She pulled away. "The fucking police came. Do you remember? The police. Do you know what that meant to me?"

That old wave of shame came back to me and I wanted to say something about it, let her know that I felt it and I was sorry about it all, but I couldn't. It was too dark and sticky. "I remember, you were so freaked out," I said. "You've always been too much of a good girl, Gaby. That's what you never figured out. At some point you just have to say fuck everybody and then you can finally be free of all the bullshit."

She looked at me with a kind of disbelief and I thought for a brief minute she was going to hit me and I wouldn't really have blamed her at that point. "You know she refused to write me recommendation letters after that. For my college applications. For scholarships. Did you know that?"

"I didn't." I spoke quietly. "She was such an asshole. Is that what happened? Is that why you stayed home?" She nodded, not looking at me. "Why didn't you tell me? You acted so strange that whole last year and then when I left. I knew something was wrong, why didn't you just say what happened?"

She didn't answer, carefully rolling the ash off the point of her cigarette. "When you saw me in the back of that cop car, you knew what that would mean for me and you never apologized for it. I kept waiting, thinking you would at some point, but you never did."

The dark, sticky feeling ignited into remorse so powerful,

I couldn't even look at her. "It wasn't my fault it happened like that. I just thought it was a dumb thing we did together."

"No. It's not your fault." She spoke evenly in a way that scared me. "She wrote you a recommendation letter though."

I unexpectedly started crying at the anger in her tone. I didn't mean to but once I started, I was having trouble stopping. "Yeah, but that's not my fault. I didn't know. You didn't tell me. And it didn't matter anyway. I still fucked up and ended up back here. We're together now. I didn't even want to go."

"I did. I worked my whole life for it." She stubbed out her cigarette hard against the floor. "Jesus, Rosemary, what do you want from me? To congratulate you for being a stripper? To tell you it's okay that you killed your dog?"

"I want you to still be my friend," I said, tears and snot running down my face in a big soggy mess.

Just then, Christopher came out of my apartment with a towel bundled in his arms. "Can you give us a minute?" Gaby said. He looked confused but he backed away into my apartment again.

The horror of it all made me laugh in spite of myself, nervous half-hysterical giggles. "We can't leave him in there like that."

"You need a tissue," she said.

"I know," I said, rubbing my face with the dirty cuffs of my sweatshirt.

She opened her bag. "All I've got—" she looked at the piece of paper in her hand "—is a receipt from Winn-Dixie. You want it?" But she smiled.

"No thank you," I said, grateful for the break in tension. "You think I'm a shitty friend."

She sighed, leaning back against the railing of the stairs.

"I've been learning a lot this year about family trauma and—" she glanced quickly at me "—substance abuse and family structures and childhood development."

I wanted her to stop talking and my words came out in a rush. "The thing is, you never needed me. Even when we were little, you had your mom and your sisters and your cousins and your neighbors. You only were just barely putting up with me and I knew it then and even now, since I've come back. You just don't need me at all."

She thought about this. "We spent a lot of years together, Rosemary."

"Our whole life, and now you're walking away from me."

"You've never been good at seeing the full picture. At times it's something I've admired about you, the sureness you always brought to whatever was going on with you. I never knew how a person could be like that, so wrapped up in their own feelings. As my mom would say, 'can't see the forest for the trees.'"

"But trees are beautiful."

She smiled. "There you go again."

Christopher called from the apartment, "Uh, can I come out now?"

I was almost glad for the interruption. "Yeah."

"Sorry, excuse me." He passed between us with his bundle and I looked away.

Gaby kissed her little cross. "Goodbye, Ida."

He carried the towel to the back of the courtyard where he was blocked by the big green leaves that draped around him. "Is here okay?" he called.

"I guess," I answered.

He came back and disappeared under the stairs. I could hear him rummaging in the gardening tools and the clatter of metal as he moved stuff around. He walked back through our line of vision with a rusty shovel.

I stood. I couldn't watch. I couldn't bear the sounds of shovel hitting dirt. "Do you want some coffee?"

Gaby also stood and brushed off the back of her pants. "Sure."

I opened the French doors that led from the balcony to the tiny galley kitchen and reached for my coffeepot. It had been a couple of days and when I scooped out the tightly packed grounds, they smelled bitter, like tin and dirt. I caught Gaby watching me through the dusty window. "I'm going to wash it," I assured her. I did and refilled the pot and set it on the stove. When I smelled my milk, it didn't seem too bad yet and I poured some into a small saucepan and set it to heat, as well. I went back to the balcony and stood in the open doorway. In spite of my efforts, I could hear the soft *chunk chunk* of steel striking dirt down below. Gaby leaned on the railing, looking out at the maze of connecting walls and roofs of all the buildings and courtyards of the block. "Is that big building the school over there?" She pointed.

"Yeah."

"Pretty tree." She meant the huge magnolia in the school playground that you could see all the way from here, three blocks away.

"Yeah." It was. I was glad at least that we were Southern. We could relapse into civility so easily.

"Poor Ida," she said. "She was a sweet dog. Except when she would lick all the lotion off my legs. That dog had a taste for cocoa butter like nothing I've seen."

"It's true. She thought you were delicious."

"That poodle of my grandmother's used to do the same thing."

I was thankful we had retreated to safer territory and didn't want to risk anything by saying much more. "How's work?" I asked.

She waved me off. "Fine. Hard. Work. It turns out I'm pretty good at this stuff."

"I bet you are."

"But it's a lot. You see some things. Some families. Some people should not have become parents."

"Like mine, probably."

"No, girl, listen to yourself." She shook her head. "You have no idea."

The coffeepot behind me began to burble and I went inside to turn off the stove. I waited a minute and then poured two cups, filling the mugs with hot milk and chasing the scalded part off the top with a spoon. "You still take sugar?"

"Do you have any other sweeteners?"

"You know that I don't."

"Fine, two scoops, please."

I brought out the cups and stood next to her against the banister. The coffee was sweet and milky and soothing.

"Do you hate me?" I asked.

She sighed and blew on her mug even though I knew she liked to drink it hot enough to burn. "Rosie, same old Rose-mary." She tilted her chin to indicate the thumping down below us. "That kid looks like he's going to steal your credit cards."

I smiled. "He does, kind of. He won't though. His family are some kind of Uptown millionaires."

She made an irritated grunt. "That's just ridiculous."

"Maybe," I agreed. "But he's sad."

"We're all sad." She drank from her cup, muttering into the rim. "But you don't see me looking like a vagrant."

The day was going to be even warmer than yesterday. The morning's fog was burning off and the sun shone bright, the false January spring, gentle and clear. "How's your mom?" I asked, wanting to prolong this soft conversational moment hanging between us. "I think about her a lot. And that shrimp she used to cook." I could still see Gaby's mom in the yellow-and-brown kitchen, standing at the stove, her body thick and soft. She moved slowly, and was always cooking the wonderful things that I never saw in our house: shrimp and rice and crabs and stews.

"She's good, had some health things lately so she hasn't been cooking as much. She says hello." Gaby didn't ask about my mom which felt like a mercy.

"Tell her hey from me." I wondered what Gaby had told her mom about me, at that kitchen table under the colored glass of the light shade, the vinyl chairs that exhaled when you sat on them. I didn't want to think of her mom's face. The disapproval. The way she talked with Gaby when I wasn't there, the shift in intonation I sometimes overheard when they spoke to each other, different somehow than when either of them spoke to me. I missed that house. More than I had ever missed my own.

I put my coffee down and wrapped my arms around her neck, desperately, hoping she wouldn't push me off. "I love you."

She let me. "I know. I love you too. But this is all kinds of fucked up, all of it."

"Is it because I'm white? Is that what fucked us up from the beginning?" I asked suddenly and then froze, horrified at myself. I kept my face against her neck so I wouldn't have to look at her while I waited, barely breathing. I wasn't supposed to say things like that. I never had and it was only this fear that maybe I was losing her forever that made me act so foolishly. I had broken some silent contract and now that I had asked, I was terrified of what she might answer.

"Don't be stupid," she said finally but I still didn't know. I knew I would never say anything like that again. I wondered if she would ever forgive me.

"I'm so sorry," I whispered. "Everything is so fucked up."

"Yeah," she sighed. "I'm sorry about Ida."

And then I knew I had to release her, and I did, and she fiddled with the chain of her cross again and looked disturbed and I didn't know what to say.

Finally, she squeezed my hand and put down her cup and picked up her purse. "I've got to get to work." There was a pause when she would normally have said *let's get together soon*, or *let's not let so much time pass*, but she didn't, and we both felt that empty space, its raw edges. "Bye now," she said finally, and it pierced my stomach.

"If I did anything wrong, I'm sorry," I said quickly. "I am."

She stopped like she was going to say something, and I felt my heart surge toward her. All our years, all our scrunchies and sleepovers and midnight laughter, I wanted it to all add up and make her realize that we could get through whatever this was, because we loved each other, we did.

And then I saw her decide to let go. She just looked at me, calm and kind of sad, the strap of her purse digging into her shoulder in a way that looked like it must have hurt. "I've got to go, I'm going to be late for work."

As she turned to leave, she met Christopher on the stairs wiping his dirty hands against his pants. "It was nice to meet you," she said, squeezing past. I saw her trying to keep from brushing up against any part of him, but he didn't seem to notice.

"Oh hey, nice to meet you too, maybe I'll see you around sometime." He cheerfully stumbled over the words that she and I hadn't been able to say, and I almost thought Gaby would glance back at me in recognition of his foolishness, but she didn't. Then she turned, dragging her hand over the post at the foot of the stairs, a casual, regretful pat, and then she was gone.

29

1999
BROADMOOR

The military band on TV played some thumping waltz and my mom passed me her big foam daiquiri cup. Daiquiris weren't her usual style but on Mardi Gras anything went. Especially by nine o' clock in the evening when a full twelve hours or more had passed since we had woken up and headed out into the streets.

"Here come the dukes, or knights, what are they supposed to be again?" Mom picked up a cold biscuit from the Popeyes box on the couch between us. "My favorite part is when they're still wearing their ugly glasses over those masks. They're all dressed up like sultans or whatever, but then those glasses just give it away. That's still some Uptown urologist under all those capes and feathers and things. Like, these guys are rich enough, can't they get contacts for one day? They owe it to us to maintain the pageantry."

Gaby and I had been on St. Charles Avenue all day and had discovered vodka and Red Bull that year. I was only half following my mom's commentary. This was our tradition, watching the meeting of the Rex and Comus courts together, the presentation of the debutantes, the whole boring thing that was broadcast on local TV every Carnival evening. Mom's daiquiri was White Russian, a flavor I had only recently gotten a taste for and it made me feel mature and sophisticated. Bahama mama was the choice for middle school kids. I was a senior now, soon to be leaving for college and was glad Mom knew to share this grown-up concoction with me.

Thinking about college was exciting but scary. "Take good care of her for me next year," I said. Ida was lying upside down on my lap, stretched full length, her belly exposed like the frogs we had to dissect in biology last year.

"What, Ida B. Smells? She and I will be fine. Two old gals like us." She reached over and tapped Ida on the chest and Ida woke up just long enough to snarl at her fingers before going back to sleep. Mom turned back to the television. "Look at that nose, you think that deb is Jewish?"

"No," I said, poking the straw around to stir the daiquiri and flinching at the squeak of the plastic straw against the plastic lid. "But seriously, I'm going to miss her so much, she's my baby. You have to not forget her arthritis pills, and don't get the bacon-flavored nibblets. She hates those." Mom wasn't listening. I was starting to feel a little mopey and wiped away a tear. "I can't imagine being without her." It was true I had been drinking for many, many hours, but still the sadness felt urgent.

"Oh my God, look at the pages." Mom grabbed my arm, laughing. "If only I could have found an outfit like that for you when you were little. Look at those things. The plumes on his hat. Those boys look so miserable." She shed biscuit crumbs around us on the couch.

I looked up at the TV. A little boy in a very fake blond wig was surreptitiously trying to pick his nose, while on the screen his illustrious-sounding five names were written in big scrolling font. "I feel bad for them."

"Don't. Those boys are going to grow up to own this place, they'll be fine."

"I don't know, that one looks like he's about to cry."

"You can't have that whole thing, you have to share." Mom took the daiquiri back and in doing so jostled Ida again, who woke up and sleepily began to sniff toward the box of fried chicken. "Can I give her a chicken bone?"

"No," I yelled. "Oh my God, Mom, you're going to kill her."

"I'm kidding, I'm kidding. Here." She opened the cup and poured half of the thick liquid into an empty water glass. I took it and rested my head against the back of the old couch. On TV the band was playing "If Ever I Cease to Love" on a long loop and to my heavy brain, it sounded like a lullaby and I let my eyes droop a little. It was nice in here, the three of us together, Ida snoring again, my mom drunkenly blowing her nose, while the city around our house sank down into fitful rest, the civic-wide surrender to intoxication. Tomorrow we would all suffer our hangovers but for now it was peaceful. Soothing. "Ooh, here comes Comus himself. I still can't believe they quit their whole parade rather than let black people in. These guys have no shame."

"We're still watching him swirl around on TV, so maybe we should be the ones ashamed."

"We're just their subjects, we have nothing to do with it." She waved me off. "And anyway, I forgive them anything as long as I get to end my Mardi Gras watching the meeting of the courts. It's like getting to be the queen of England for a night. Or at least watch her. Here's to Rex and Comus and

all the other assholes that make this thing possible." She tip-
sily lifted her cup. "Here's to all of it, it's fucking magic."

"You only think so 'cause you're not from here," I mumbled, even sleepier now. "You chose it. I'm cursed with it."

"Oh, you're so dramatic, sweetie. You think it's magic too."
She slurped the daiquiri. "I know you do."

"You'll see when I end up moving to Syracuse or something. I'm never coming back here. I promise you that much.
Just don't kill my dog while I'm at college."

"You think I can't tell it's me you're running away from?"
she said, looking at the TV. "Anyway, I managed to raise a
child, I think I can take care of a dog," I heard her mutter,
but then I must have passed out because at some point I felt
her take the glass of White Russian out of my hand and set it
down somewhere. Ida was curled up in the crook of my elbow
and I slept, the face paint of another Mardi Gras still on and
smearing itself all over the sofa cushions, but I knew Mom
wouldn't mind. She was probably already too drunk to notice.

30

I felt Gaby's fresh absence as acutely as if I had stood up suddenly and found both legs asleep, a stabbing, painful space where my limbs had been just moments before. For a moment, I let the feeling wash over me, helpless, while I bent in half and rested my chest on my legs. I could feel my heart beat against my almost bare thighs. Everything felt final and hopeless and I closed my eyes against it all. I hoped I hadn't made her late for work.

Christopher was standing on the stairs watching me. "I think I did a pretty good job. Do you want to see?" he said finally. I shook my head. "You should maybe put a headstone or marker or something. Just so you know. I stuck a bunch of sticks there, but they will probably scatter as soon as it rains."

"I'll do it later." I straightened back up. In the sharp morning sun, I could see the circles under his eyes, dark smudges, like thumbprints on either side of his youthful face. He looked so tired. I was glad he was here. "Thank you."

He smiled and ducked his head a little. "So that's why you

didn't want to come home, huh? I would have never guessed that one. People sure will surprise you."

"Do you think I'm a terrible person?"

He pointed behind him. "For that? Nah." He considered. "Maybe? Who cares? I can think of many people who have done a lot worse things, some to me personally, so...fuck it."

"What happened to you, Christopher?" I asked, looking into his big dark eyes.

He paled and swallowed nervously. "We've all got our bullshit," he said, rather unconvincingly shy after all this time. He held out his hands. "I should probably wash these."

His hands were black with dirt and I decided not to press him anymore. Let him and Ryan carry their secrets together. We all grabbed on to whomever or whatever we could in this fucked-up world, and he had found someone, so he must be doing something right. Maybe. "Come inside." I stood up. "Do you want some coffee?"

"No thanks," he said, following me through the next set of French doors that led to my living room. "You're not very neat, are you?"

I had been finishing my costume the last few days and the table was covered in piles of fabric, bowls of sequins, hot glue, fabric tack, an explosion of dark beads and satin. A box of expensive dog treats I hoped might tempt Ida back into eating. A little plate of raw hamburger turning brown. So many pill bottles. Alcohol swabs and Nature's Miracle for all the times she'd peed on herself, the floor, my rug. The clutter of a small life drawing to a close.

The rest of my house was a disaster too. One of my chairs had been duct-taped back together after Ida discovered years ago that it was stuffed with horsehair and tried to eat its insides. Stacks of books about to topple over and many empty bottles of mineral water. It was my one extravagance. Just the thought made me thirsty and I got a bottle from the fridge while Christopher went to the bathroom to wash his hands. It hissed as I unscrewed the cap and I knew why I wouldn't be able to give it up. It was like everything was suddenly washed clean in the bursting of millions of tiny bubbles in my mouth. I was rock and mineral and the purity of European springs I had never seen, and everything sparkled for as long as I held the dark green bottle in my hand.

Then Christopher came back and took the bottle from me and drank most of it in a long gurgling sip. He came up gasping, wiping his mouth with his sleeve. "Holy crap, that is delicious. Why do I feel like I've never drunk water in my life?" He finished the bottle and then looked at it wonderingly in his hand.

"You're probably a little dehydrated after last night."

"I'm probably a little dehydrated after my last year."

"I know the feeling."

"You should maybe stop drinking," he said, and I looked at him, surprised. "I mean, because of your mom and whatever."

"Were you eavesdropping?"

He looked hurt. "No, you told me just a little while ago. Sorry, it's none of my business."

That's right, I had told him. I really had lost control over it all.

He set the bottle of water down and looked at me with a change of attitude, a seriousness that I knew all too well. "Where's your bedroom?" he asked.

With a sense of the inevitable and because I felt I really owed him now, I took his hand and led him to my room. My mattress was on the floor and I dropped my feathery head-band onto it and tried not to look at the little fleecy pouf in the corner where Ida used to sleep. All of a sudden I couldn't bear to look at his filthy clothes anymore and he let me strip them off of him with a kind of dumb passivity. He was almost holding his breath, as if he were scared I might stop at any minute. In his wrinkled navy boxer shorts, he was all skin and bones, like a foal who hadn't yet grown into his joints. Without the authority of a suit, he was a little kid in a bad haircut, and he blinked at me, hopeful, sad. I could see his heart pounding in the hollow of his pale chest, and I pressed my fingers against the vein in his throat where his neck met his collarbone and it bumped against my fingertips, urgent and fragile. I shed my clothes too and lay down in my underwear, feeling the cool air across my breasts, my nipples still tacky with spirit gum. One rhinestone that had come loose from something was stuck just below my sternum. In a moment, he was on top of me, unexpectedly light and kissing me hard and messily, like he had done so many hours ago in the park. He still smelled like a laundry hamper, the sour tang of dried sweat, and his breath was thick from booze and drugs and nervousness. I could feel his dick pushing against my thigh through the thin cotton of his boxers and he nudged my head aside trying to kiss my neck, leaving a trail of wet marks. "Wait." I pressed gently against his shoulders and he rested back on his elbows, looking into my eyes, fearfully, guiltily, waiting for a reprimand.

"Just wait," I said. I scooted up the bed to the pillow and rested his head down on my chest. He collapsed against me, still breathing hard, and I felt the bony bumps along his spine and the slope of his ribs, evenly spaced ridges that expanded with his shallow panting. I ran my fingers through his greasy hair, and against the shorter prickling fuzz behind his ears.

"I'm sorry," he said, tentatively reaching for my breast and then just cupping his hand to it, surprisingly gently.

"For what?" I felt the delicate curve of his earlobe.

"I'm not twenty," he whispered. "I'm seventeen."

I laughed. "Yeah. No shit, you dummy."

"I just didn't want..."

"Yeah, I know." I brushed my fingernails softly down the back of his neck.

"I didn't have anywhere else to go."

I didn't answer. I wasn't the one he was looking for, but I was the one he had found. It was enough. The ceiling fan hovered motionless above us and I could see the thick layer of dust that had settled on one side of each blade. Outside a bird called a recurring, rising question. I stroked his neck and the hollow between his shoulder blades. All at once, his body twitched and became heavy, and I felt his breath, deep and steady now across my skin. He had fallen asleep, as sudden and profound as a baby animal. I lay, enjoying the soft weight of him, holding me in place, trapped by the selfish fatigue of his slender body. The bird thrummed his request again, breaking the morning sounds into delicate shards and I let myself drift into sleep, finally falling down that ragged slope in his silent company.

When I woke up, Christopher was gone, and I was in a puddle of my own blood that had spread far over the sheets. I smiled thinking of his probable horrified confusion. A patch of sun on my wall had the gold light of afternoon in it and I felt as slow and disoriented as a patient coming out of anesthesia. I took a shower, throwing my sheets into the tub with me, standing in the pile of wet cloth as the water ran pink and fell over my head like an absolving rain. The afternoon was warm, like summer almost, as I stepped onto the balcony, tying the sash of my kimono tight around my waist and drinking from a flat bottle of mineral water I picked up on my way out. The stairs held some of the warmth of the afternoon and the wood groaned as I walked down. I dragged a flimsy iron chair scraping over the bricks of the courtyard and set it down in front of the pile of fresh dirt. The bottle made a clink as I set it down at my feet. He had set a pile of sticks like a little tepee at one end of the mound and laid a banana leaf lengthwise across the grave like a green blanket, its ends already curling up as it dried. I had cried all my tears that morning and I watched a worm curl around, tossing in the freshly turned dirt. I leaned back against the twisted iron support of the chair and closed my eyes against the sun. The breeze ruffled my robe and fluttered it open against my thigh. One tear caught me by surprise, sliding out of the corner of my eye and down toward my ear. Then the calliope started up, booming the hideous "Way Down Yonder in New Orleans" from the top of the *Natchez*, out over roofs of the neighborhood, summoning more tourists, more idiots, to the Quarter, to the river. But even that didn't bother me now. I crushed a big leaf hanging just below my shoulder, creasing its flesh with my nails, and inhaled the deep, sweet, irrepressible scent of life. It was all a fucking mess. But my courtyard bloomed, thick and insistent, the shadows deep against the mossy stones and I sat waiting, I wasn't sure for what, resigned, quiet, glad if for nothing else than to be here, finally at home again.

★ ★ ★ ★ ★

Acknowledgments

To JaNét Peters for thirty years of friendship and for letting me pillage and borrow and steal parts of our shared past for this book, thank you for being the most loyal, generous, funniest, smartest, best-hearted woman I know.

To my editor Laura Brown, who inherited this orphaned manuscript and turned it into a real book, thank you for your faith in this project and your brilliant advice. To my agent Dana Murphy who is a wonder and a champ, to Laura Gianino and Kathy Daneman who worked so hard to help this book find its audience, and to everyone at Park Row who has made publishing these first two books such a pleasure, thank you, I am so grateful.

To my parents for choosing to live in the French Quarter and giving me an upbringing so unique, I will be mining it for dozens of books to come, and to their friends for showing me the magic of what Twelfth Night could be, thank you.

To everyone that was around, drinking and performing and making the New Orleans I knew of twenty years ago into such a magical place: some of you were close friends, some I only knew by name, some by only sight, thank you for your style and creativity and all around moxie. A very personal and therefore incomplete list: Alison Fensterstock, Robert Starnes, Kris Alexanderson, Chris Cummings, Dave Clary, Gabe Soria, Deborah and Gary Parky, Lefty Parker, Dan Cooper, DC Harbold, Mimi Kersting, Cindy Romero, Rakia Faber, Ruth Caffery, Lorelei Fuller, Nina Bozak, Taylor Strong, Jessica Melain, Vanessa Neiman, Maureen Johnson, Allyson Garro, Sandy Moorman, Trixie Minx, Suzy Black, Patti Meagher, Matt Vaugn, Will Trufant, Matt Uhlman, Michael Hurt, Blake Thompson, Barry Goobler, Dave Rhoden, J. Lloyd Miller, Ron Rona, Clint Maegden, Helen Gillet , Savannah Strachan, Jaime Szczepanski, Jude Matthews, Stephen Rhodes, Susanna Welbourne, Ryan and Marcy Hessling, Candice Gwinn and Robyn Lewis, Henry Rhodes, Morgan Higby, Edith Leblanc and Patty, Alexandra Scott, Davis Rogan, Christian Trosclair, Marigny Lee, Paul McCord, Henry Griffin, Veronica Russell, Chris Lane, Jeffrey Dammit, Mike Lenore, Luke Spur Allen, Alex MacMurray, Ronnie Magri, DJ Kristin, DJ Pasta, Quintron and Miss Pussy Cat, Juvenile, Dr. Ira, Ingrid Lucia, Mystikal, The Ponderosa Stomp, The Shim Shamettes The Southern Jezebelles, The Sophisticats and the Sophistikittens, Doctor A Gogo, Mod Night, The New Orleans Bingo Show, Morning 40 Federation, Happy Talk Band, The Royal Pendletons, Noisician Coalition, Q93,The Deliverators, Trashy Diva, The Matador, The Shim Sham, The Hideout, The Whirling Dervish, The Saturn Bar, The Hi-Ho, The Dragon's Den, The R Bar, The Circle Bar, The Saint, Fifi Mahoney's, Heart and Soul, Kaldi's, Zotz on Royal, The House of Lounge, and finally the big red house at the corner of Elysian Fields and Dauphine Street.

To Madeline Stevens, Yardenne Greenspan, Karen Havelin, Hala Aylan, and Matthew DiPentima, thank you for all the brilliance and support. I would definitely have quit this whole thing by now without you guys.

And finally to Matthew, Oliver, and Violet, thank you for being my heart, my family, and making everything worth it.